Books by Nancy King

FICTION

Opening Gates

Changing Spaces

The Stones Speak

Morning Light

A Woman Walking

NONFICTION

Breaking the Silence: A Memoir

Dancing with Wonder: Self-Discovery through Stories

Playing Their Part: Language and Learning in the Classroom

Storymaking and Drama

Storymaking in Education and Therapy (co-written with Alida Gersie)

A Movement Approach to Acting

Giving Form to Feeling

Theatre Movement

Beyond This Crossing Place

The Cracked Pot's Gift

Editor: Judyth Hill
Book Design: Mary Meade
www.wildrisingpress.com

First Edition
ISBN 978-1-957468-51-8

The Cracked Pot's Gift

Stories to Challenge & Comfort

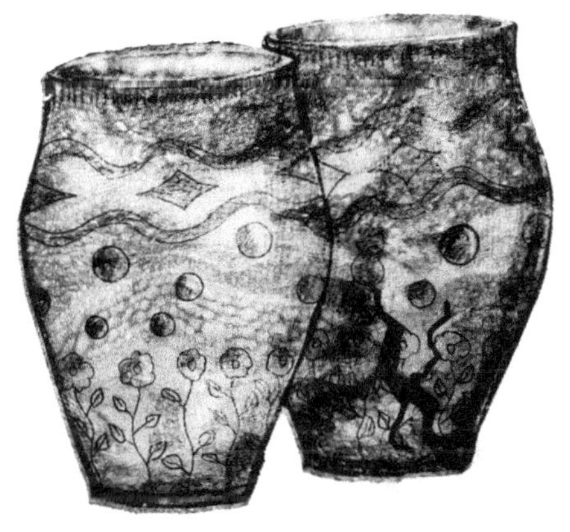

Nancy King

Evergreen, Colorado

For

Sydney Taylor King

&

Eliora and Hadara Ancowitz

"I will tell you something about stories

(he said)

They aren't just entertainment.

Don't be fooled.

They are all we have to fight off

Illness and death.

You don't have anything

If you don't have the stories."

CEREMONY
-LESLIE MARMON SILKO

Foreword

I MET NANCY KING years ago through a literary association. We connected immediately—like two magnets which swoosh together—unstoppable. Our professional collaboration and friendship have developed and deepened continuously ever since. I live in the UK but we communicate online. When we speak on Zoom, we usually take a few moments to exchange a poem or story.

Building on this history, it is a delight for me to write this foreword. Nancy is an extraordinary person of huge integrity and huge energy, regularly hiking many miles three times a week although she is 88 (at the time of writing). Professionally she was a progressive professor with a doctorate in creative writing and literature, teaching for many years at the University of Delaware (UD).

Nancy is a renowned storyteller, essayist, playwright, and novelist, with a range of beautiful books to her name, as well as being a well-known teacher of creative approaches to education in both the US and across the world. She has taught in UD's international studies program, working with people, often women, from Kazakhstan, Ukraine, Uzbekistan, Germany, Russia, Hungary, and other countries.

Her workshops and sessions focus on storymaking through an innovative hands-on method of exploring new ways of learning and knowing. Nancy's teaching often makes use of finger painting and sculpting to lead into the creation of stories. This method of teaching honours the people concerned, enabling participants to learn about self as well as subject, reaching into the deeper places within us all.

Her bookshelves are packed with thousands of stories from all over the world. She draws on this comprehensive knowledge and wisdom in *The Cracked Pot's Gift: Stories to Challenge and Comfort,* which, as far as I am aware, is like no other book. The structure is very unusual, possibly unique, and has given rise to a volume which is wise, personal, insightful, and far-reaching in scope.

Nancy has selected a wide range of world stories from mainly indigenous cultures and regions. She then illustrates each one of these tales with specially written stories of her own, building on and reflecting the wisdom within the original. The result is a charming volume, a treasure of a book that one can dip into for insights and sustenance, a book for browsing. Each "set" of stories opens new vistas of thoughts, feelings, and insights.

The world tales Nancy has selected have their origins in a dizzying array of countries, including Thailand, India, Brazil, Asia, Korea, various African countries, Russia, Eastern Europe, China, Venezuela, South Sea Islands, Canada, and the US. Some originate in a variety of Native American traditions; some have Buddhist and Sufi roots.

Each world tale is followed by two or three new stories often derived from Nancy's life experience and learning. Together, each set of stories gives rise to specific questions that Nancy puts forward so readers can make use of them in their own lives, if they wish. The collection ends with a world story and a final question for the reader.

In one set of stories, Nancy tells the beautiful Brazilian tale of Hummingbird and Panther where Hummingbird helps Panther regain his sight after he has been temporarily blinded. Rather than eating her, he reciprocates by helping her develop her brilliantly coloured plumage. The first follow-up story, in response, has Nancy, aged 3 years, being asked to entertain an older relative who is seriously ill with polio. Nancy is initially frightened of her cousin's difficulty breathing, but, through the experience, she learns to read and amuse the six-year-old girl who lies in bed, comforted.

The second story describes Nancy's rejection for a teaching job in dance, which leads to what she really wants, a long-term university position teaching drama, creativity, and world literature. The question asked at the end of the set is: "Have you experienced a rejection that led to something new and unimagined?" This exercise cannot fail, I suggest, to be an invigorating one.

I would be spoiling the unique beauty of the book for the reader by summarizing any more of these imaginative sets of stories, but the above example gives a little window into the power of the world tales, and the intriguing stories and questions that follow.

In my view, this is truly bountiful storytelling. The book is a revelation, told by a consummate author of stories and an authority on world tales. It has been my honour to have been involved with it, and I highly commend it to you.

Professor Emerita Gill Hague CBE
Poet and author
Professor of Violence Against Women Studies
Co-founder, Centre for Gender and Violence Research
University of Bristol, UK

Preface

ONCE UPON A TIME, *long ago, in a place far away . . .*

For centuries, these ancient words have drawn people into the magical world of story. A marvelous world capable of affecting how we feel about ourselves, the issues we face, the situations in which we live. An awe-inspiring world able to create community out of disparate individuals. A world that saved my life.

I'm a reader of world tales, as well as a teller. World tales reflect universal life concerns—being born, growing up, becoming an adult, dealing with obstacles, developing relationships, growing older, dying. Many people associate folk and fairy tales with happy-ever-after endings, causing them to dismiss these stories out of hand, as nothing more than facile wishes of make believe. But these endings reflect a deep psychological truth, as Shakespeare knew only too well; relentless misery deadens us. Happy endings, or silly scenes like the night watchman's in Macbeth, allow us to take a breath, rest, relax, recoup, restore—giving us energy to deal with the next problem, which inevitably arises.

Stories matter. I was born to parents mired in darkness. There was no safety. No security. What enabled me to survive were the stories I told myself. I don't know how they started, but from an early age I would find a place to "disappear"—under a bed, behind a couch, outside when possible—hiding as best I could. Then, in my mind's eye, I created worlds and situations where I was the hero. Strong. Brave. Powerful. Safe.

My first attempt at telling stories to others began when I was three, as the designated entertainer for my six-year-old cousin recovering from polio, then for my younger sister. When I started babysitting as a ten-year-old, I told stories as a distraction, as well as to make myself feel better, later realizing how stories relaxed kids and eased them into sleep.

The interest and need to tell stories intensified when I became a teacher. I discovered students liked hearing stories from around the world; they listened with rapt attention. Next, I discovered the stories I told evoked stories in those who heard them and dissolved tension, creating a sense of community and connection among listeners and me.

A third discovery: stories are alive. From my experience telling stories, ending a story with a moral, or explaining what a story means (which is always from my point of view) kills the story. We may read or hear the same story, but our response is personal, evolving and growing out of our uniqueness as human beings—in how we live our lives. From one day to the next, a story can mean something different, evoke a newly remembered incident, or help us deepen our sense of who we are.

While reading or hearing stories, we may be comforted or challenged—even encouraged to think in new ways as we take in the characters' situations and struggles, and are, perhaps, reminded of our own. When I am feeling down, I tell myself world tales that comfort me. One of them, "Little Parrot," describes how Parrot is trying to save a forest on fire. The words she says to a sarcastic Eagle, "I don't need advice, I need help," resonate. I think about all the ways we need help in difficult times, which is often not forthcoming.

Since there have been times in my life when I have wandered in and out of a kind of spiritual loneliness, the stories I wrote were a source of comfort. During the pandemic, when so many of us were isolated, I thought about sharing monthly stories on my website so there would be new material for people to read each month. This, I hoped, might be a way to create community and connection.

The first entry I posted on my website surprised me by being a poem about the comfort of walking in the mountains. It restored my center, lifted my spirits, and calmed the PTSD with which I live. Quite a few people responded, telling me they found the poem moving, how even though they weren't in the forest, my words helped them feel better. Since I am a storyteller, not a poet, I chose to tell stories, hoping they might similarly comfort readers in the difficult times in which we live.

Responses to the monthly stories were strong and supportive. Readers shared stories of their lives after reading mine and urged me to continue writing. Many suggested I collect the stories I wrote and the world tales that inspired them and put them into a book. Thus, *The Cracked Pot's Gift: Stories to Challenge and Comfort* was born.

The tales in this book, which come from all over the world, have little or no violence and a balance of gender and age. Each world tale selection begins with an introduction, to focus the reader on a theme. This is followed by the world tale and then by the stories that have emerged from how that world tale resonates within me. The stories end with a question designed to encourage readers to think about how the world tale lives within them. My intention in writing this book, a book of stories, is to inspire readers to uncover, discover, or recover their stories, and to share them, to create community.

Readers, I thank you for your continuing enthusiasm and support. May the stories in this book provide you with ideas to think about, experiences to share, and ways to reflect on how you see yourself and your life.

Contents

1

WORLD TALE

A Choice

BUDDHIST

A young man's decision has unintended consequences. The stories, Anger vs Anger and Conned by a Cat, end unpredictably.

• • •

THERE WAS ONCE a king who attacked a neighboring country, killing the king and queen and many of their people, but could not bring himself to kill the baby prince. He took him home to raise as his son. The child grew up feeling loved by the parents he thought were his birth parents.

As he grew older, the prince heard whispers and murmurs about a long-ago battle, about a baby boy rescued. In time, he confronted an old courtier and asked about the long-ago battle. At first the old man refused to speak, but the prince persisted. "Tell me what you know," he pleaded. In time, the old man told him how the king had attacked the neighboring country. The man he knew as his father was the king who murdered his parents.

The prince, filled with rage, decided it was his duty to kill his adopted father. He made and discarded many plans until he created one he knew would work. Every afternoon his adopted father sent his guards away and took a rest. The prince sharpened his sword and prepared to act. The next afternoon, when he saw the king sleeping soundly in his royal chair, the prince moved behind the chair, lifted his sword and . . . Try as he might, he could not bring himself to lower the sword.

The king awoke and saw his son with the sword raised. "Why do you have a sword in your hand?"

"I know you are the man who murdered my parents. It is my duty to avenge their deaths. But, to my great shame, I am unable to bring down my sword."

The king told his son to put the sword by his chair and sit beside him. "You have chosen wisely. Had you killed me, my other sons would have felt it was their duty to kill you. If you had sons, they would feel it their duty to kill those who killed you. By choosing to lower your arm, you have saved many lives."

❧ ❧ ❧

ANGER VS ANGER

I'd been hired to lead a workshop in stage combat and had asked my partner if he would join me as the antagonist in the scenes I planned to stage, to show students what each technique looked like when playing different characters. He eagerly agreed. Since he was more than a foot taller and almost a hundred pounds heavier, my ability to make the combat look realistic, given the height/weight difference, would add to the power of my presentation.

The night before the workshop, we got into a heated argument, continuing into the morning of the workshop. I was so angry I almost asked him not to come. He was too angry to speak to me. I drove us to the workshop seething, my inner dialogue so complex I almost missed the turnoff to the university. I parked. Walked to the building. He followed. An ocean of emotional space between us.

Silently, we changed into our clothes for the workshop. Silently, we walked into the faculty lounge where coffee and pastries had been set up. I was still so angry I had to work at being pleasant, smiling and conversing with various theatre faculty who'd hired me.

I began the presentation by explaining the framework for stage combat: cooperation, connection, clearly planned moves, no improvisation. I laid out the moves I would teach—slaps, punches, kicks, and tripping.

Since my partner and I were so different in size and weight, I decided that when he started to attack me, I would respond, showing my anger, beginning with a kick to his crotch. But just before we were to begin, I felt weird in ways I can't put into words. I felt emotionally paralyzed, as if I couldn't *role play* anger and *be* angry with any degree of realism. I would have to let go of my anger if I wanted the demonstration to be emotionally rich and realistic. There was no time to talk or explain. I whispered to my partner, as if giving him staging information. "I'm sorry," and gave him a kiss on his cheek.

Visibly surprised, he hugged me. "I'm sorry too."

With the energy cleared, we staged our fight; students cheering me, the obvious underdog, as I kicked and tripped my "attacker."

Have you ever changed the way you were feeling in order to do what you needed to do?

CONNED BY A CAT

When I saw the photo of Lira on the website, just looking at her eyes, I felt a strange connection, but it wasn't enough to make me act, despite being pressured by people to get another cat. Finally, a friend offered to drive me to the shelter, "just to visit." Hah! The moment I saw Lira's paws reaching out under the door to touch my feet as I walked by, I was hooked.

The friend took photos of me picking up Lira and of her licking my nose. I was told she was a difficult cat. She'd been booted out of foster care for biting and scratching and had bitten everyone who saw her at the shelter. There was even a description of her, which I didn't read until after I adopted her. *Lira is a beautiful cat, patiently waiting for her forever home. She loves to sit and chat with people about all things, aliens, snacks, and new movies coming to theatres soon.* Hah! Nothing about liking to cuddle, sit on a lap, or purr, which would have given me even more specific warnings had I looked at it.

Lira walked into the carry case and settled herself in it. I signed the papers. We drove to my house. Once she was "home," she responded to my hugs with claws, bites, and growls. She'd been spayed, but had gone into heat twice before the shelter vet had done the surgery. More months passed before her hormones settled down. Friends, even the shelter vet, urged me to give her back. She was too difficult. I was too tense. I had scratches and bite marks on my hands, face, and legs.

Still, something about her made her my cat. I turned down all opportunities to give her back. Eventually she slept by my feet at night. There were fewer bouts of biting and scratching. Then, January 1, 2024, fifteen months after I adopted her, I woke up to watch her saunter from my feet to my chest and snuggle against it, even allowing me to gently stroke her for a short time. What a wonderful way my cat chose to help me greet the New Year.

What helps you keep going when it seems you've made the wrong choice?

2

WORLD TALE

Hummingbird & Panther

BRAZIL

Hummingbird and Panther have an unexpected interaction. The stories, Reading—Ready or Not and A Rejection That Changed My Life, reve–al how a difficult situation can lead to a new beginning.

• • •

HUMMINGBIRD HATED HOW SHE looked—utterly colorless, unlike the beautiful flowers, the brilliant sky, and the glorious shades of grasses and leaves. Nothing she did changed the color of her feathers. One morning, while feeling glum and miserable, she heard a loud groaning, a horrible noise. Much to her horror, it was Panther, an animal who terrified her. His sharp teeth were almost as big as she was. As he moved closer, his moans grew more unbearable until Hummingbird blurted out, "Why are you making so much noise?"

Panther told her, "Last night, I accidentally stepped on Mouse Mother's children as I was running through the forest. To punish me, when I was asleep, she put mud on my closed eyes. Now the mud has hardened, and I cannot open my eyes. I'm blind. How will I find enough food to eat?" He began to wail louder than ever.

"You're not the only one with a problem," snapped Hummingbird. "I'm so dull no one notices me."

"That's not a problem. I know how to help you become more colorful."

"You do?" asked Hummingbird, not sure she believed him.

Panther said, "I'll make a bargain with you. If you peck the mud from my eyes so I can see, I will help you become as colorful as you like."

Although Hummingbird wanted to be colorful, getting close enough to Panther to peck the mud from his eyes was almost too frightening to think about. But, her yearning was so strong, despite her fear, she gathered her courage and flew to Panther, making him promise to keep his mouth closed. She carefully removed the mud from his eyes, hoping he wouldn't open his mouth and eat her when she was finished. When Panther could open his eyes, he danced gleefully. "I can see. I can see."

Hummingbird grumbled, "What about your promise? What about our bargain?"

Panther stopped dancing and looked at Hummingbird. Shaking his head, he said, "You really are drab. No wonder you're unhappy." Hummingbird started to tell him he didn't need to make her feel bad, she already felt awful, when he said, "Follow me."

He led her to a clearing in the forest near a bubbling stream and told her to gather as many different colored plants as she could find. He put a pot of water over a fire and heated up the water. Hummingbird filled the pot with flowers and grasses and seeds and leaves. Following his instructions, she stirred and stirred. When the mixture was cool, Panther told her to jump into the pot and wet herself all over. Then he told her to fly out and shake herself off. Panther looked at Hummingbird and said, "Better do it once more."

After the third time of jumping into the pot and shaking herself dry, Panther said, "There, that's more like it. Fly to the river and look at yourself."

Filled with dread Panther's plan had not worked, Hummingbird made herself fly to the water, afraid of what she would see. "Look!" commanded Panther.

Hummingbird took a deep breath and did as she was told. "Oh," she gasped, hardly believing her eyes, amazed to see such a brilliantly hued bird reflected in the water. "I'm colorful," she said, stunned.

"Yes, you are, and I'm hungry," said Panther, and he walked into the forest.

~ ~ ~

READING—READY OR NOT

When I was three years old, I became one of the designated entertainers for my six-year-old cousin Rose who'd been stricken with polio. I heard my mother and others talk about how lucky it was that Rose didn't die. I didn't know what *die* meant, but the way they talked about Rose, dying didn't sound good.

She lay in bed, motionless. I sat in a chair next to her bed, trying to think of things to say that would interest her or make her laugh. I wasn't good at telling jokes and often couldn't remember the punchline. This made her mad. She told me I needed to learn to tell jokes. Since I was tired of sitting, I left the bedroom and went into the kitchen where my mother and aunt were drinking coffee. My aunt told me to go back because Rose needed company. When I stood there, unwilling to leave the kitchen, my mother scolded me: "Nancy, you're always telling stories; go back and tell Rose a story."

I walked to the bedroom as slowly as I could, hoping she'd be asleep, but she was awake, waiting for me. I told a few stories as best I could, but Rose soon let me know she was bored with my stories. "Read to me," she said in a voice that scared me.

"I don't know how to read," I admitted, petrified.

She looked angry and made a terrifying chest noise. It sounded like what people described when they talked about her dying. When she caught her breath, she said, "Reading is easy. I'll teach you." She showed me words and how to sound them out. When I made a mistake, she made the terrifying sounds that scared me. I was desperate to learn as quickly as possible. I didn't want to be the one who made her die.

I learned fast enough and well enough to suit her, but sometimes I didn't know a word and stumbled. Disapproving of my mistake, she'd make the horrible chest noises that petrified me. I'd panic. What would they do to me if my cousin died while I was reading to her? The sounds she made when I mispronounced a word made me so anxious, the next time I didn't know a word, I made one up. Since she couldn't see the book, she didn't know the difference. I began to enjoy reading to her, making up half of what I read. No mistakes. No terrible chest sounds. No die. Big relief.

How did you learn to read?

A REJECTION THAT CHANGED MY LIFE

I was a single mother with an irregular income teaching dance, no health insurance, no child support. I needed a full-time job, but I couldn't bear teaching physical education or science, both of which I was credentialed to teach. When I saw an advertisement for a position teaching dance at

Swarthmore College, I immediately applied, despite memories of being a graduate student at the University of Wisconsin where the two dance professors continually criticized my dance and choreographic ability.

Elated to be invited to teach a master class as part of the interview process, I paid no attention to the nausea I felt as I walked to the studio. What mattered was the secure position, doing creative work, a good salary, and benefits.

Students walked into the dance studio and began warming up. One young woman asked if I was the new dance teacher. "I'd like to be," I said, hoping my grin was not a grimace. She wished me good luck and joined her friends. Time to begin.

I told the class to move as they felt inspired by the story I would tell them. The students looked surprised, but began moving in their own ways as I related "Hummingbird and Panther," about Panther who is blinded by mud in his eyes and Hummingbird who hates the way she looks.

I then asked students to take an intriguing aspect of the story and create a movement sequence using found sound or any of the musical instruments in the studio. They quickly began to create, intensely focusing on the assignment. When I asked them to share their work, one woman asked, "You going to judge it?"

"No. I'm not interested in judging, but if you want help in deepening your work, let me know." She looked suspicious but volunteered to be first.

After the last group finished, one student said, "We never did anything like this before. It was fun. I hope you get the job." I blushed, thanking them for their wonderful participation. This time my smile was real, and my stomach felt fine as I watched them leave.

The retiring dance teacher walked me to my meeting with the dean. Before parting she said she'd heard good comments about the class and was sure I'd get the job because the other interviewees had not been interesting or innovative.

The dean, a woman in her fifties, with twinkling blue eyes, welcomed me into her office. She told me she'd heard I'd taught a challenging and imaginative master class. While we sipped coffee, she asked about my work, how I came to teach as I did—always responding to my answers with encouraging nods and smiles. When it was clear the interview was over, when I thought she was going to offer me the teaching position, she looked at me. I felt seen. "You don't really want to teach dance, do you?"

I was too stunned to lie. "No, I don't."

She spoke kindly. "I'm going to do you a favor. I'm not going to recommend you, even though you did a fine job teaching the class and have wonderful recommendations." My distress was too spontaneous to hide. "It's not what you think," she said.

"Then what?" I managed to blurt out.

"I've listened to you talk about your interests, your previous work, how you create. I don't think you want to teach dance. I think you want to teach movement to actors and create theatre pieces. If I recommend you for this position, you'll be teaching something you don't love. I can't do that to you. You're a wonderful teacher, a woman with marvelous creativity and ingenuity. You need to follow your heart as well as your mind. It may not feel like this right now, but I'm doing what's right for you professionally and personally. I'm sure you'll find a way to teach what you love."

The dean's refusal to hire me was an unexpected, albeit painful gift. I found a way to teach what I loved during a thirty-four-year university career during which I created almost all the courses I taught, using all the arts.

Have you experienced a rejection that led to something new and unimagined? What was that like?

3

WORLD TALE

The Old Man and the Villagers

AFRICAN

The Old Man is besieged by villagers' pleas for his help. The stories, Fulbright Fellowship and A Time of Healing, explore the power of no.

• • •

THERE WAS ONCE A village where people enjoyed many years of prosperity. The rains came regularly, and their crops flourished. In time, the grain bins were so full, one of them collapsed and the grains scattered. However, people had so much stored they left the grain where it was.

In a short time, birds found the grain and decided the village was a good place to live. When the people finished working in the fields, the birds flew down and began eating. The next morning, when people saw how much grain the birds had eaten, they began to worry the birds would find a way to eat the stored grain. So, when the birds flew down to eat, people tried to shoo them away with noise. When this didn't work, they shot arrows into the air, but this too failed to deter the birds.

The villagers called a meeting to discuss how to get rid of the birds. Although no one wanted to be the first to mention the Old Man, he was on everyone's mind. They looked at the Headman who said, "We shall soon starve if we do not rid our village of these birds. We have tried but nothing works. Perhaps the Old Man will help us once again." Everyone was silent. "It is true. We chased him away because we were afraid of his magic, but he is our only hope. I will go to him. Perhaps he will take pity on us and agree to return to help us."

The next morning the Headman went in search of the Old Man. Although the Old Man was dressed in worn clothes and had little in the way of goods, he was not pleased to see the Headman, nor did he want to return to the village. But when the Headman told him children would starve if he didn't help them, the Old Man agreed to return.

Before going to the village, the Old Man collected roots and plants to make a powder. That evening, after the village thanked him for coming, he showed them how to dip their arrows into the powder and the way to use them.

The leader of the birds saw the people with their bows and arrows but was not afraid and continued to eat. When the Old Man quietly said, "Now," the villagers shot their arrows into the leader of the birds. Seeing this, the other birds flew away in fear.

The villagers held a great feast to honor the Old Man, and, for a time, all was well. Then, whispers began. People said, "If he has magic to kill birds, he can kill us. We must tell him to go." The whispers grew into a loud chorus, and soon the villagers forced the Old Man to leave.

In time, the birds returned. The villagers watched helplessly as their grain disappeared. Once again, they tried to deter the birds, but nothing stopped them from eating their grain. The villagers decided there was nothing left to do but ask the Old Man to come back to help them.

The Headman told the Old Man of the village's troubles and how sorry they were they'd asked him to leave. The Old Man listened carefully. Then he said, "No."

FULBRIGHT SCHOLARSHIP

In 1992, I was teaching in Hungary at Janus Pannonius University for a month. Many of the faculty suggested I apply for a Fulbright Scholarship to teach with them for a full year.

Given their encouragement, I talked with the Chair of the Department of English and Linguistics, who was enthusiastic and urged me to apply. He had a big concern he thought I could address. After the Russians left Hungary in 1990, Hungarian students were no longer required to study Russian, so very few students elected to study it. The Russian teachers were told to teach English, a language in high demand, which was absurd given that many of them spoke English poorly, if at all.

As part of my conversations with the Chair, I suggested techniques to help teachers of Russian transition to teaching English using innovative methods that relied on creativity and imagination rather than rote learning, which was still widely practiced. He was receptive and supportive. Given the Chair's interest, and the warm welcome by potential colleagues, I decided to apply.

I spent the better part of a year gathering recommendations from faculty in Hungary and the US, filling out forms, only to have to fill out more forms. I wrote an essay describing why I wanted to teach in Hungary, passing each hurdle with ease. While I was applying, I continued teaching in the Department of English and Linguistics in Hungary and had long talks with the Chair about what I would teach during my Fulbright year.

Finally, after what had been a long and tedious process, I passed all the requirements and needed only the Chair's signature to receive the Fulbright. Despite all our conversations, and his high praise for my teaching, he refused to sign the final paper. He gave the position to his girlfriend.

What is your experience of being told, "No."

A DAY OF HEALING

It was early morning in December 2013. Snowing. Cold. I had to be at the hospital clinic for another round of chemotherapy at noon. The treatments, which had been going on since early October, were long. My arms were sore. I had no interest in food and was exhausted. The holiday season of cheer left me feeling depressed, hopeless, and helpless. I knew being in the mountains would help me feel better. Despite the weather, I called a friend. "Would you drive me up to Big Tesuque so we can hike up to Aspen Vista Road?"

"No!" he said. "It's cold. It's snowing!" His incredulity was palpable. "Besides, if I remember correctly, your treatment starts at noon. No!" It was like couch potato talking to ultramarathoner. What I needed was beyond his imagination, out of his comfort zone.

All I knew was what I badly wanted. Trying to use my most persuasive tone of voice, I begged. I pleaded. "I need to be in the mountains. The hike's only a mile each way. We can easily do it if you'll drive me to the hospital afterward."

He offered reasons why it wasn't a good idea. I countered each of them with, "I know, but . . ."

After a while there was a silence. A sigh. "Okay, if it's so important to you, I'll pick you up in half an hour." I started to thank him, but he'd already hung up. I got dressed—long underwear, sweater, insulated pants and jacket, wool hat, neck gaiter, mittens, and handwarmers.

I greeted him with a grin. He shook his head. "Nancy, I hope you know this is totally crazy. I don't know why I let you talk me into it. I should have said no and hung up."

"You're doing it because you're my friend and you want to make me happy." He swatted my mitten as we drove up a snowy, slippery Hyde Park Road.

When we got to the trailhead, the snow was coming down fast, thick flakes sticking to my hat. I stuck out my tongue to taste the cold ice. "It's not too late to turn back," he said. I ignored him and started up the narrow side of the Big Tesuque creek trail. I could feel my hopeless, helpless depression dissolve into awe and joy.

I kept telling him how happy I was being in the mountains, in the snow, in the majestic silence, how grateful I was for his help. He wanted none of it. "Pay attention to where you're stepping. The wet stones are slippery. This is a terrible idea. I should have said no."

When we got to Aspen Vista Road, he said, "Let's go back on the other side of the creek. It's easier going down. Not so many rocks. You don't want to miss your appointment." I was too happy to argue. We hiked down the trail in silence. He drove me to the hospital. I thanked him again and again. He blushed, shook his head, wished me well, and drove off.

What does it take to listen to yourself rather than others?

4

WORLD TALE

How Light Came to the World

CHEROKEE/NATIVE AMERICAN

Aging still gets a bad rap in media. The stories, Not Too Old and Vision Quest, reveal ways in which aging can be a time of discovery.

• • •

In the beginning, when the world was new, there was no light. People huddled together in the cold and dark to keep warm, bumping into each other because they couldn't see. It was a hard time. Feeling hopeless, they held a meeting. One of the animals said, "I have heard there are People of the Light on the other side of the world. We should go and ask if they will give us some."

"Don't be foolish," responded another. "If they have all the light, why would they give us any? We will have to take it."

The animals agreed someone should go, but who? It would be a long, hard journey. "I'll go," said Buzzard. "I'm big and strong. They will have to give it to me." The animals cheered as he left.

Soon he returned with nothing to show for his effort but a burned place on the back of his head where the light had scorched him. Other big, strong animals agreed to go, but each came back empty-handed, all singed on part of their body.

The animals were in despair. No one knew what to do. None of their warriors returned with light. In the silence, Grandmother Spider spoke up. "I will go."

Everyone laughed. "You're old. You're tiny. What makes you think you can do what those who are bigger and stronger and younger than you could not?"

"Yes, I am old and small, but those who are bigger and stronger and younger did not succeed. I have a plan. I will bring back light." The people laughed even harder at her foolishness, but they agreed to let her go.

Grandmother Spider molded a tiny bowl out of damp clay and waited for it to dry. Then she spun a fine web as she moved toward the People of the Light so she could find her way back. She was so little and so quiet, none of the People of the Light noticed her. They were looking for the warriors coming to steal the light. Carefully working so that no one could see her, Grandmother Spider put a small piece of light into her clay bowl and spun her way back to her people.

When she arrived with the light, the people were stunned and astonished, then joyful. "Now we will have light and warmth." They gathered around Grandmother Spider. "We will always honor you," they promised. And they have.

❧ ❧ ❧

NOT TOO OLD

Soon after my chemotherapy treatments ended in 2006, I celebrated my seventieth birthday by joining a Sierra Club hiking group. My first hike with them was supposed to be eight miles, at least a mile more than I had done to get into shape hiking local mountain trails. I worried about it being a loop hike; once I started there'd be no turning back.

When the group gathered, I realized I was the oldest hiker. Although no one said anything, I saw their questioning looks. I felt my confidence ebbing, but my determination to do the hike gave me energy.

I was managing to keep up with the group when we came to a wide stream. I didn't know there'd be a water crossing and was dismayed as I watched younger hikers navigate the slippery stones. I had no water shoes. The hike leader kindly offered me his flip-flops, which helped me get across without falling in. As I was drying my feet, I asked a hiker how far we'd gone. "About four miles," he said.

"Oh!" I said, pleased and relieved. "That means we've gone halfway." He told me the hike was actually ten miles, more than I'd ever hiked at one time. I had no choice—nothing to be done but to do it. I ate an energy bar.

We hiked through a variety of ecosystems—forests, wetlands, steep inclines, and long stretches of high grass. I was beginning to feel the hike would never end when we encountered boulders. Big ones. I needed my hands as I clambered up and down, but my poles got in my way. The hike leader put them in my backpack. Suddenly I felt like a little kid, with more energy than I could have imagined, scrambling up and down the rocks.

At the end of the hike, I was filled with joy, more than a little surprised at how well I'd hiked, even more amazed at how much better I felt at the end of the hike than at the beginning. If I had known the hike would be ten miles, I might not have gone. Doing the hike made it possible to discover I could do more than I thought—a valuable lesson when it comes to aging.

How does being the oldest one in a group affect you?

❧ ❧ ❧

VISION QUEST

As part of my eightieth birthday celebration, I chose to do a vision quest—four days and four nights alone in the wilderness with no phone, books, watch, or digital devices. I hoped being alone, without distractions, would enable me to shed emotional and psychological burdens I'd carried all my life. I knew I was the oldest participant the leaders had ever taken on a vision quest, and that I'd be the oldest by more than fifteen years. When friends asked why I was doing this at my age, I told them, "Because I need to."

There were nine months of preparation—making a string of one hundred forty-four prayer ties knotted onto a red thread filled with cornmeal and tobacco to encircle our vision quest spot. We visited with the vision-quest leader each month during which we talked about being alone, how we wanted to spend the four days and nights, and our preparation for the twelve-hour mini vision quest in a local forest.

Once we were at the retreat center in Southeastern Canada, we met, as a group and individually, with our retreat leaders—we discussed our intentions, participated in sweat lodges, and performed ceremonies for two days. The day before we began the vision quest, each of us brought a sleeping bag, mat, four gallons of water, tarp, bag with personal items, and a journal to our space in the forest. Nothing we did prepared me for what happened.

We entered our separate, designated locations the first morning at five o'clock. I lay down on my sleeping bag and immediately slept for hours, lulled by the sounds of the forest. I was woken by an inner voice telling me it was time to get started.

What I did during the four days and nights is considered medicine, not to be shared. What I can say is that each time an inner voice told me to do something, like stamp on dead branches, memories of my early childhood surfaced. At times, I viscerally remembered events I'd been told never happened. Other times, experiences surfaced for which I was blamed and shamed. I began to understand the pernicious effect of the childhood abuse I had experienced. Although I'd blamed myself, the abuse was not my fault. No child asks to have her bones broken, her joints dislocated, her body violated, her will shattered.

As I thought about relationship choices I'd made during my adult life, I realized I'd had a metaphorical sign on my chest saying, "Abuse me." I worked hard to allow memories and feelings and thoughts to arise without judgment, to remove the metaphorical sign. Being in the forest, feeling the warmth of the sun, the chirps of the birds—all helped to soothe and comfort, and give me hope that I had done my best to leave the wilderness, knowing more, feeling more, less burdened by the past.

On the morning of the fifth day, we were awakened by drumming, calling us back to the retreat center where we processed our experiences. I had no desire to share and never raised my hand to offer. I was the only one who had not spoken. It was my turn. I cried for the first time since I was sixteen, when I'd been refused entry into a school club because I was Jewish. The other retreat participants waited calmly until I was ready to speak. They listened with no judgment, many quietly crying. When I finished there was a perceptible silence. No one moved. Had I said too much? Had I said the wrong thing?

Then they came, offering hugs, encouragement, kindness, caring. For the first time I felt part of a group. For the first time I felt good enough. I understood my age didn't matter to them. Although the issues we dealt with during the vision quest were different, we were all questers, all seeking inner knowledge.

How might you celebrate your eightieth birthday?

5

WORLD TALE

Ant and Elephant

INDIA

Ant finds a unique solution to a challenging problem. The stories, My Friend the Forest and Inner Darkness/Outer Light, reveal imaginative ways to counter difficult situations.

• • •

THE ANIMAL COMMUNITY DECIDED they needed a king and voted to make Elephant King of the Animals because he was the biggest and strongest, yet very gentle. But after a short time, he changed drastically, and not for the better. When he saw animal mothers carrying food to their children, Elephant grabbed and ate it without listening to their cries. He stopped caring where he walked and trampled on nests without apologizing or repairing the damage.

The animals were upset and terrified. They called a meeting when Elephant was sleeping, but no one knew how to stop Elephant from his rampaging. When Ant said she had a plan to make Elephant stop behaving badly and apologize for the misery he'd caused, the animals sniggered in spite of their despair. If none of the bigger animals could think of a solution, what could a tiny creature like Ant possibly do to end their misery? Ant persisted until the community agreed.

Ant observed Elephant's behavior for a few days, noticing he took a long nap after lunch. One afternoon, when Elephant was snoring, she climbed up into his brain and started to dance. Elephant woke up with a terrible headache and roared in pain. Ant told him her dancing might be causing his headache, but she would only stop if he promised to behave.

Elephant roared his displeasure. "I am Elephant, king of the animals. I do what I want, when I want, as I want." Ant said nothing. She just kept dancing. Elephant's headache grew so unbearable, desperate to stop the pain, he finally agreed to all of Ant's demands—anything to make her stop dancing. Anything to ease the agony in his head.

Just to make sure Elephant didn't change his mind once she stopped dancing, Ant reminded him, "I have lots of relatives, and we all love to dance."

INNER DARKNESS/OUTER LIGHT

As was my custom, I started class by telling "Ant and Elephant," about a tiny animal who figures out how to respond to a big problem. Everyone in class had a minute to finger paint an image of ingenuity. When a student showed his image, the class and I gasped. Normally, I never comment on students' images, but time and again his images were so brilliant, this time I couldn't help myself. Neither could the rest of the class. "How did you do it in one minute?" asked a student. He shrugged. "You're an artist," exclaimed another. The class murmured their agreement. He deflected all compliments. It felt as if the more they praised him, the smaller he got.

I had noticed his images becoming darker and his words bleaker as the semester progressed. Now I worried about his inability to take in the class's feedback. I asked to speak with him in my office after class. "I can't," he said. "I'm busy."

"Whatever you have to do can wait. We need to talk." When he told me he had to go, I said we could talk outside. The more he resisted, the more certain I was we needed to talk. As a professor I have a certain amount of authority, and I used every bit of it. "Let's sit on that bench. Now!"

I didn't mince words. "Why did you get so upset when the class called you an artist?" He stared at the grass, watching an ant carry a crumb twice its size. "If ant could make elephant be kind, why can't you be an artist?" One thing didn't have anything to do with the other, but it was all I could think of.

Reluctantly he said, "I used to draw a lot when I was little. My father always made fun of me. It got so bad I stopped showing him what I painted. When I came to the university, I wanted to study art, but he told me the only major he'd support was engineering. He says he won't pay for my *doodling*, as he calls it. I just can't do it anymore. Life isn't worth living." He refused to look at me.

"Your father is wrong. You are an artist. You have the right to do what you love." He shrugged. "If your father is worried about you not being able to support yourself, tell him you'll sign a contract promising not to ask for money after you graduate." He laughed bitterly. "Take back your life. If your father won't pay for your studies, apply for a scholarship. You have talent. You're smart. Let me help you. Please!"

He looked at me. "Why do you care? What's one student more or less?"

"Every student matters to me. Why don't you matter to you?" I made him look at me. "If you feel the life you're living isn't worth living, why not do what you want? Change your major to art. Take control of your life. I'll help in any way I can. So will other faculty. What your father told you is wrong. He has money, but you have power. Use it!"

I pushed him to contact the art department to ask for help. With continuing support from me and other professors, he changed his major. His father disowned him. He qualified for financial aid, work/study, and scholarships. He graduated summa cum laude, majoring in art.

When you notice someone is in trouble, what might you do?

❧ ❧ ❧

MY FRIEND, THE FOREST

I didn't want to go to sleepaway camp. It didn't sound good, despite my father telling me I would love it. When I asked what I would love, he said he wished he'd been able to go to camp. I knew this wasn't an answer, but there was no point in asking again. I didn't want to leave my baby sister. I didn't want to be sent away from home again. I had no choice. My mother spent nights sewing labels with my name on my clothes. One morning she packed my suitcase, made a picnic lunch, and told me to get into the car. "Right now!" I got in the car.

I was seven, but I'd been put in a bunk with nine-year-olds. The counselor told me to take off my dress and put on shorts and a T-shirt. I didn't want to. She said I had to; those were the rules. "Who made the rules?" I asked. She ignored me. When the counselor wasn't looking, the kids in the bunk called me Titsucker and Babysnot, refusing to call me by my name. They kept telling me I didn't belong. I silently agreed, but where was I supposed to go?

When it was time for supper, the smell of food made me sick. I ran out of the dining room, gasping for air, hoping I wouldn't throw up before I got out. A counselor followed me, told me to go back and sit at the table like the others. She made me sit, but she couldn't make me eat. After supper we gathered around a fire to roast marshmallows. There were too many kids huddled around the fire. No one made space for me, so I sat on a log and watched, slapping mosquitos, wishing I could leave.

The next morning my dress was gone. I put on the shorts and T-shirt and went to the infirmary. I told the nurse I didn't feel good. She checked me out and said there was nothing wrong, I was just homesick. I didn't tell her I was campsick. Since she was no help, I decided to run away.

When no one was looking, I ran as fast as I could, into the forest at the edge of the camp. The cool air, smelling of earth and wildflowers and grasses comforted me. I felt better. Then I saw a boy who smiled at me and said, "I'm Peter. What are you doing here?"

I told Peter I hated camp and my counselor and the girls in my bunk. He told me he loved the forest; did I want him to tell me the names of trees and flowers and birds? I nodded. He took my hand, and we walked into the woods, stopping when he showed me a wildflower hidden near a fallen log, a baby oak tree, a bird's nest. I forgot about camp. I wanted to stay in the forest with Peter until it was time to go home at the end of the summer.

Peter looked at his watch. "We need to go back now; otherwise, they'll start looking for us." He said, "Don't worry. I'll meet you here tomorrow, same time. Okay?" I nodded. "Just make sure no one sees you leaving the forest." I promised to be careful.

One morning, as we were leaving the forest, our counselors caught us. Furious. "We've been looking all over for you. We were worried something happened to you. Don't you care about anyone besides yourselves?" Peter said he was sorry and walked off with his counselor. I wasn't sorry about being in the forest. I was sorry I was caught. My counselor tried to take my hand, but I wouldn't let her. I didn't believe she cared about me. I didn't care about her. She was mean.

The next morning, after breakfast, when no one was looking, I ran into the forest. The forest was my friend. I missed Peter, but I felt free and happy. I found a path and walked on it. Maybe it would lead to a little house in the forest where I could live until the end of the summer.

After walking for a long time, I felt tired and leaned against a huge oak tree and closed my eyes. I imagined kind people who lived in the house and how they would make food I liked to eat. Suddenly there was a lot of noise. Someone yelled, "There she is! We found her!" A lot of people rushed toward me. I tried to run, but a woman knelt beside me and put her arm around me. I tried to pull away, but she held me tight.

"I'm Marty, the nature counselor." I didn't know what that was. She told me she liked to study trees and wildflowers and birds. That sounded nice. "Would you like to be my assistant?" she asked. "You can come to the nature shack and help me out, but you have to promise you won't run away anymore."

I nodded, but she said she had to hear the words. The best I could say was, "I'll try." She took my hand and wrapped hers around mine. I let her.

How do you react when you feel powerless?

6

WORLD TALE

Tortoise and Leopard

AFRICAN

Tortoise marks where a struggle for justice took place. The stories, Haircut Day and Friday Afternoon Class, explore various struggles for justice.

• • •

ONCE UPON A TIME, Leopard, who was very hungry, saw Tortoise and chased after him, ready for a fine dinner, but no matter how hard Leopard tried, Tortoise managed to escape. Then, one day, Leopard came upon Tortoise walking slowly on a road. Leopard pounced on Tortoise, ready to kill. "Tortoise, prepare to die."

Tortoise, realizing there was no escape, asked Leopard to grant a favor. Surprised, Leopard asked what Tortoise wanted. "It is not right for you to kill me, but since this will happen, I would like a bit of time to prepare myself, to prepare my mind." Leopard agreed, thinking Tortoise would stay still and be quiet. Instead, much to Leopard's astonishment, Tortoise scratched the road, digging up stones and dirt and plants, throwing them every which way, creating a huge mess.

"Why are you doing this?" asked Leopard.

"So after I am dead," Tortoise replied, "people passing by will know that here is where a great struggle for justice took place."

❧ ❧ ❧

HAIRCUT DAY

In 1956, I was working as a summer recreational therapist at Creedmoor, a huge mental hospital in New York City. One morning, when I arrived to take out my patients, I was told I had to wait; it was haircutting day. All patients had to have their hair cut before they could go out, which made no sense as most of the women already had short hair. I watched the haircutter set up her chair, and her assistant get ready to sweep up hair before the first woman sat down. Then, one by one, each woman got the same haircut, as if a bowl had been placed on her head and the haircutter had cut around the edges. The patients looked awful afterward, but there were no mirrors for them to look in and no way to complain about the way they looked. They had quickly learned to do as they were told to avoid punishing consequences.

The haircutting was going smoothly, despite the results, as each woman sat down with a blank look on her face. Next up was Carol, a woman in her thirties with freshly washed and curled hair. Instead of sitting, she told the haircutter she didn't need a haircut. She was being released the next day, and her husband liked the way she did her hair. She looked happy and had obviously taken pains to make sure her hair looked good—clean and well-shaped.

The haircutter ignored her words, told her to sit down immediately; she had to have her hair cut just like all the other women. Carol repeated what she'd said, but the haircutter ignored her words. "Sit right now. There's a long line behind you."

"But I don't need a haircut," she pleaded. "My husband likes the way my hair looks. I'll be with him tomorrow. Please. Please!"

Unable to bear it any longer, I stepped between Carol and the haircutter and said, "She doesn't need a haircut, but if you need to cut her hair, couldn't you just snip a little piece?"

"I don't do snips. I cut hair. And you have no business interfering with my patients. Stop right now or I'll have you fired." She pushed me out of the way and said to Carol, "Either you sit down right now, or I'll make you sit down." Carol panicked, yelled she didn't need a haircut, and started to run, but there was no place to hide. Much to my horror, two attendants caught her, and when she struggled to get away, put her in a straitjacket and carried her out of the room. I later learned they took her to the building housing violent patients.

"Next," yelled the haircutter. Except for the tense silence in the room, it was as if nothing untoward had happened. The next woman in line sat down in the chair.

I froze, unable to believe that a woman who looked so lovely and was so rational could end up minutes later in a straitjacket. I don't know how long I would have stood there had the Head Attendant not come to me to tell me I was wanted in the main office. My supervisor opened the door, looked at me with disgust, and said, "Miss Rubin, you are not to interfere with patients' treatment. If I could, I would fire you immediately. Now leave and do what you were hired to do."

I went back to the ward. I offered to take out any woman who wanted to go. About ten women followed me. Silently we walked down the steps. Silently we walked to a tree in the inner courtyard. Silently we sat down. Some cried. Some muttered so I couldn't hear them. When I had given out all my tissues, I said, "I tried to help," feeling as hopeless as they looked.

"At least you tried," said one of the women. It was no comfort. Not to me. Not to them.

Why couldn't they fire me? About two weeks after I'd started work, one of the summer recreational therapists, whose father was the chief pathologist, had seen an administrator threaten to fire me for "insubordination," i.e., sticking up for a patient. He told his father that if I was fired, he would go to the newspapers and tell them what he knew. I don't know what he knew, but it kept me from being fired.

Have you ever tried to right a wrong? If so, what was that like?

FRIDAY AFTERNOON CLASS

A friend who taught at a high school two hours south of my home called me on a Friday morning, in a panic, asking me to please do her a huge favor and lead a storymaking class that afternoon. The desperation in her voice as she explained the situation made it hard for me to say no. The session would be the last class of the day. For the last two weeks, the eleventh graders had had a substitute teacher, who'd suddenly quit because she couldn't control the class. None of the other teachers wanted to face these students—a group notorious for discipline problems. No one was willing to risk getting a black mark on their record. I agreed after more urging, not looking forward to teaching the class.

A few minutes before class was scheduled to begin, I began rearranging the desks into a circle. The space was limited, and I wasn't sure all the desks would fit. As I struggled to move one, a Black student entered, told me his name was Thomas, and asked politely, "What are you doing?".

"I'm leading a storymaking session for your class, and I'd like us to be in a circle if possible."

"What for?"

"So we can see each other rather than looking at the back of people's necks."

He shook his head as if this was weird, then, taking his time, checked out the space in the room. "It's possible. I'll do it." In an unbelievably short time, all the desks were in a circle. As students walked in, noticed the new arrangement, and asked what to do, he smiled as I told them to take any seat they liked. At the same time, a few teachers took seats in the back, apparently there to watch what I was going to do, without asking if this was okay with me. I thought, ungenerously, it wasn't fine for them to teach this class, but it was fine for them to watch me teach. I decided to ignore them.

After introducing myself, I welcomed the students to our storymaking class, asked their names, and gave out finger paints and clay. I began the session by telling them "Ant and Elephant," a story about Ant, the littlest animal, who figures out how to get Elephant to stop being a tyrant and be kind, as he was before becoming king.

The students listened respectfully. At the end of the story, I told them they had a minute to make an image and write a few words that came to mind when they thought about the story. After they finished, I said we'd go around the circle and share briefly what had been painted and written. The first few students, obviously uncomfortable, shared, but the next student, looking terrified, shook his head and said, "I can't."

Thomas went to him, put his hand gently on his shoulder, and said, "Sure you can. Just show us what you did. It's okay." The student, whose fear was palpable, showed his image and read the words he'd written. He looked up at Thomas, then breathed a sigh of relief when the student to his left continued. Thomas returned to his seat.

The next task was for students to sculpt an image of an animal who was or could be in the community of animals, and to write a brief statement about how the animal felt and what the animal wished he/she could do to help make Elephant behave as he did before he was elected King. When it was Thomas's turn, he showed the group his image. "I'm Jerry the Giraffe. I want to help but I don't have a voice. My words stick in my throat and die. No one knows what I'd like to do if I could."

I didn't know anything about Thomas, but I appreciated his presence in the class. During each activity, he encouraged hesitant students, and when we began the period of reflection, he thanked me for teaching such an interesting class. Other students talked about how unusual it was, and most said they enjoyed not having to worry about how good their work was. As they were leaving, Thomas asked if I'd like him to move the desks back. I said yes and thanked him for his kindness and help. He grinned, restored the desks to their original configuration, and left.

I looked at the teachers, who had expressions of disbelief on their faces. When I asked why, a few of them spoke simultaneously. "Do you know who Thomas is?" *How was I supposed to know a student I'd just met?* I shook my head. One of them said, "He's the school bully."

Shocked, I told them, "He's a student who feels he has no voice. I hope you'll help Thomas find his voice. He needs support."

How comfortable are you expressing what you genuinely think and feel?

7

WORLD TALE

The Story Spirits

KOREA

A young man refuses to tell stories, with unforeseen consequences. Don't Tell and Breaking the Pattern, Breaking the Silence reveal why telling stories matters.

• • •

THERE WAS ONCE A boy who loved to hear stories. Although he asked everyone he met to tell him a story, no matter how people pleaded, he refused to tell any. Since he was the child of wealthy parents, no one dared complain. After his parents died, people felt sorry for him, and his faithful servant saw to it, whenever the boy asked, there was someone to tell him a story.

In the corner of the boy's bedroom hung an old bag, tightly tied with string, forgotten by everyone. But every time the boy was told a story, the spirit of the story went into the bag. In time, there were so many stories the spirits could hardly breathe.

Time passed. When the boy came of age, his uncle arranged for him to marry. The night before the ceremony, the old servant stopped outside the young man's bedroom and heard angry voices. He crept into the room and listened.

"He's going to be married tomorrow."

"We must do something. It's our only chance."

"Let him feel what it's like to suffer as we have all these years."

"What can we do?"

"I know," said a deep old voice. "Tomorrow, he will ride to the bride's house. It's a long ride and he will soon be thirsty. When he stops to drink water from the well at the side of the road, I will put poison in the cup, and he will die."

There were murmurs of approval until a tiny voice asked, "But what if he doesn't drink? A little further down the road is a field of strawberries. The young man loves strawberries. I will offer him a strawberry that guarantees him eternal sleep."

"Good idea," said a husky voice, "but just in case he isn't hungry, I will be a red-hot poker in the sack of rice husks he will use to dismount from his horse. When he steps down, he will be engulfed in flames."

"But he is very rich," argued a high-pitched voice. "Suppose someone carries him off his horse."

"I will be a poisonous snake under the rug that lies under the bridal bed. I will bite him when he sleeps, and he will never wake." The voices uttered their approval, relieved there would be an end to their suffering.

The old servant was horrified, knowing if he told anyone what he had heard, they would think he was crazy. They would keep him from accompanying the young man to the wedding ceremony. He had promised the boy's parents he would take good care of him, but how could he protect him now? All night he worried. When morning came, he had devised a plan.

As the procession was preparing to leave, the old servant begged the uncle of the young man, "Please sir, let me lead my young master to his new home. This would be a fitting end to my years of service." The young man raised no objections; the uncle agreed.

They had barely gone a quarter of the way when the young man said to the old servant, "Look, there is a well just ahead. Let us stop. I am thirsty." Instead of stopping, the old man increased the pace, and before the young man knew it, they had passed the well. "Did you not hear me say I am thirsty? Why did you not stop?"

"Oh, sir, I was thinking about your beloved, and we passed the well before I knew it."

"Well, just ahead is a field of strawberries. They will quench my thirst and my hunger. Arrange to stop the procession and pick me strawberries." Once again, the old servant urged the horses to move so fast they passed the strawberry field before the young man could yell, "Stop."

The young man yelled at his old servant. "Why did you not stop? Do you want me to die of thirst and hunger?"

"I am so sorry, sir, but just think, the sooner we arrive, the sooner you will see your beloved."

The uncle spoke with barely contained fury. "This is no way to treat a young man on the way to his wedding. I will take care of you later."

All too soon they arrived at the home of the young man's beloved. Just as he was about to dismount from the horse, the old servant slapped the horse's behind, and the young man fell off the horse into the dust. As the uncle helped clean his nephew's clothes, he whispered to the old servant, "Just you wait. There is no punishment too harsh for you."

After the ceremony and the dinner and the celebration, the newly wedded couple retired to their bedroom. They had just fallen asleep when the old servant ran into the bedroom with a sword, pulled back the rug and slew the snake. The bride screamed. The young man called for the guards. There was so much noise and commotion, the uncle awoke and rushed into the bedroom where he saw the old man, sword in hand, a dead snake at his feet.

"Take this old servant away. Tie him up and …"

"Please, sir," pleaded the old servant, "I beg of you. Do with me as you wish, but first let me explain." He told them of the bag in the young man's bedroom, the voices he had heard, and about the poisoned water and strawberries. "If you don't believe me, look in the sack he would have stepped down on and you will find a burned poker with charred straw. If all else failed, the snake under his bed was prepared to bite him."

"Why?" asked the young man. "What have I done to deserve such enmity?"

"All your life you have asked for stories. Each time you asked, someone told you a story. Yet whenever someone asked you for a story, you refused to tell one. All the spirits of all the stories you would not tell were whisked into the bag on the wall where they were imprisoned, cramped and uncomfortable with no way out until you agreed to tell stories."

"Oh," said the young man, seeing the pain on the old man's face. "You have served me better than I knew. I promise you, from now on, I will tell a story to anyone who asks."

And he did.

❧ ❧ ❧

DON'T TELL

When I was four, I lived in New Jersey for almost a year with my cousins, aunt, and uncle, a pedophile. Since my bed was in an alcove off their bedroom, and my aunt often woke when my uncle forced me out of my bed during the night, she knew something was wrong but never tried to stop his abuse.

My uncle warned me. "Don't tell, or else . . ." I didn't know what "or else" meant, but I didn't tell. He didn't say, "Don't write." I told myself stories, and when I learned to write, I wrote stories like the one about an unhappy bunny who runs away from home, where she's treated badly, and finds a place to live in the forest, where she feels safe. I wrote another story about a turtle who leaves her home because the family says she's a bad turtle. She moves very slowly, and it takes her a long time to find a new home. My first-grade teacher asked why I always wrote about animals. "I like animals," I told her. I somehow knew not to write about what my life was actually like. Sometimes, at recess, I told stories, always about animals, always about them finding new lives. Children liked the stories, and I was often asked, "Tell us a story about . . ."

Writing or telling stories about animals allowed me to express my feelings, yet kept me safe from further harm for telling the truth about my life. My world was dangerous—at home there was constant violence and emotional abuse. Outside, there was virulent anti-Semitism. Writing "safe" stories made it possible to release feelings too dangerous to express at home, and unwanted at school.

How did you express your feelings when you were younger? And now?

BREAKING THE PATTERN, BREAKING THE SILENCE

I've always been a storyteller, yet there were stories I could not tell; others I tried to tell, but no one wanted to hear them. Editors rejected the memoir I wrote, part of my PhD thesis, as "too bleak and troublingly personal." Agents rejected my novel *Morning Light*, a fictional account of my life, as being too dark. I felt ashamed of who I was and what I'd experienced. To keep going, I created a cheerful, independent, strong persona. Although it helped me disconnect from the inner darkness with which I lived, I felt emotionally isolated.

After returning from a vision quest in 2016, I started writing what I thought would be my sixth novel—only what came out was nonfiction, stories of my life. No matter how I tried, I couldn't create a character whose life was not mine. It was a struggle similar to the one years ago when every story I wrote involved sexual abuse and violence despite my efforts to write differently.

I gave up and gave in, grudgingly allowing what wanted to come out to emerge. To distance myself from the emotional content, I tried writing third person, past tense, naming no names, but this became impossible. There are only so many words for she, woman, her … Even worse, the writing was impassive, unemotional, more like journalism, which was how a therapist described the way I talked about my life.

I felt desperate. I wanted to write fiction, about someone who was not me, leading a life that was not mine, with problems I had never experienced. Yet something inside was pushing me to tell the truth of my life just as strongly as something was pulling me back into inner darkness. To stop the struggle, which was uncomfortably intense, I gave in. There was nothing left to do but write first person, present tense. This opened a floodgate of memories, painful, dark, emotionally upsetting. I wrote associatively, not caring about chronology, not caring about age or place. It was hard going because writing first person/present tense brought me back to the time and place of the actual experience. I could smell and taste and feel my four-year-old terror when I wrote about what happened with my uncle—experiences I could never talk about, never even let myself acknowledge, until the vision quest when I was eighty years old.

I kept writing, but I worried. Was it too much me me me? Would my writing interest anyone else? I sent a few chapters to a former student, asking her if any of it mattered. She wrote back saying she was going through a difficult time emotionally and that the chapters I'd sent were helping her feel she wasn't alone. Would I please keep writing and sending her what I'd written. This kept me going.

When I'd written about three hundred pages, I sent the material to my editor. "Nancy," she said, "the writing is fine, but it has to be chronological. I need to read how your voice changes as you grow, how you develop as a woman. Right now, I can't tell how old you are, where you are, with whom you're living. It's all a jumble and vitiates the power of your writing."

Oy! I'm not good with computer stuff. The prospect of rearranging so many chapters was daunting. I printed out the book, manually reorganized the chapters so they were chronological, then, with the real pages in hand, I slowly rearranged what I'd written to make the chapters chronological. This allowed me to see what was missing, what needed to be tossed. I also realized the arc of the book was about healing from childhood trauma and subsequent abuse as an adult. The bad choices I'd made as an adult—which I'd known were bad at the time, yet had been unable not to make—had always puzzled me, but now made sense. At the time, I didn't know about the psychological forces acting on me, shaping my choices. After writing the memoir, I was finally able to fit together disparate pieces of the puzzle of my life to make a rational narrative.

Writing *Breaking the Silence*, finding the wherewithal to tell the stories of my life without censoring, enabled me to break through my families' silence, lies, denial, blame, and shame.

Telling the story of our lives is the first step toward becoming our authentic selves.

What is your story?

8

WORLD TALE

The Coming of Fog

NATIVE AMERICAN

A family is torn between love and community customs. The stories, Not Only a Mother and A Proposal, reveal how choices may have far-reaching consequences.

• • •

When Sila was very young, the boat she was on with her family capsized. Her parents drowned, and she was left in the care of her five older brothers.

Sila loved the sea and swam far and well—better than anyone else in the village. At first her brothers were proud of her, but when villagers complained the brothers were not teaching her properly, they told her it was time to stop swimming and learn the ways of village girls. Sila loved her brothers and did as she was told, but away from the sea she grew thin and pale. Her brothers were so worried they asked Raven for help. He told them, "Your sister is not like other young girls. She must be allowed to be who she is if you want her to be healthy and happy." Reluctantly the brothers agreed for they loved their sister.

As Sila grew up, the villagers ridiculed Sila and her brothers. The brothers grew ashamed and forced Sila to do the tasks of young village women. Sila tried, but she became quiet and sad. She never talked or laughed as she had when she was allowed to swim. Once again, her brothers called on Raven. He reminded them, "Your sister is not like other young women. She must be allowed to be who she is if you want her to be healthy and happy." Fearing for her life, the brothers allowed Sila to return to the sea.

They began to follow Sila and noticed she swam with a strange creature. The brothers were afraid the creature would harm their sister, so they tried to kill it, but the creature escaped. The brothers made new, sharper arrows. Sila pleaded with her brothers, "Let the creature be. He is no danger to anyone." But her brothers refused to listen. In time, the arrow found its mark. The creature died.

Sila was beside herself with grief. Her brothers assured her they had killed the creature for her sake, but Sila was not comforted. They kept Sila under their watch in a tepee, and when Sila gave birth to a child, the brothers noticed the child did not look like other children. They were afraid and asked Raven for advice. He said, "Your sister is not like other young mothers. She must be allowed to be who she is if you want her to be healthy and happy." The brothers listened reluctantly, not happy with Raven's advice. They took to watching Sila and the child closely.

Although Sila swam with her child, she feared for his life. She knew she could not keep him safe for very long. One day, she swam with her son to a place he had never been. She told him what he needed to know and bid him leave her even though her heart was breaking.

For a second time Sila was consumed with grief. Her brothers tried to keep her busy helping their wives and children, but Sila yearned for her child. She knew her brothers would kill him if they saw him, so she called on Raven. "Help me safely see my son. I cannot live this way."

Raven took pity on Sila and created a thick white cloud, separating Sila from her brothers. They could not see her as she ran from the village and, once again, swam in her beloved sea, joyfully greeting her son.

When Sila did not return, the brothers called on Raven to help them find her. He refused. "You would not let her be who she is; therefore, you do not deserve to live with her. She has gone to be with those who love her as she is. There will always be a thick cloud of fog between you."

This time it was the brothers who grieved.

❧ ❧ ❧

NOT ONLY A MOTHER

In 1966, I was a single mother, with no child support, working part-time teaching dance and preschool movement classes. Although I had some savings secreted away, money was tight. Despite this, I managed to pay for a university course in children's theatre, which affirmed the work for children I'd done for years. Desperate to change my life, I decided to get an MA in theatre offered by the University of Delaware.

Friends and family were equally horrified. How could I be so irresponsible? How would I find work with just a master's degree in theatre? Not even an MFA. I had a child to support. I had a mortgage to pay. The roof needed replacing. How would I pay for it all? Why wasn't I using the teaching credentials I had to make life easier for my son, if not me?

I tried to explain. For more than six years I'd taken care of my family, focusing on their needs, finding work to fit their schedules, losing a job interview because of their illnesses. I felt emotionally dead and needed something to do that was mine, that nourished me. Nothing I said to friends or family made a difference.

Ten years before, in 1957, I had a technical scholarship to Connecticut School of Dance. Now, in 1967, that technical director was the new Chair of the Theatre Department. He remembered how hard I'd worked. When a student with a university technical fellowship had to leave because of mental illness, the Chair phoned, "Would you like to take over his fellowship for the spring semester?"

I wanted it more than anything, but I told him, "I can't do what he did."

"That's true, but you could teach movement for actors." I had no idea what this involved, but I said yes. I had to develop whatever I was going to teach—a daunting process. I knew about the body. I knew about acting. I just had to find a way to put my knowledge into a coherent whole.

Fortunately, it was the late sixties. Even at conservative University of Delaware, students, with my encouragement, asked challenging questions. What I didn't know I figured out. I relished the challenge. I felt invigorated because it was a wonderful semester, depressed because I had no money to continue.

I spent the summer directing and teaching a Title One Grant: creating theatre with street kids, culminating in a performance attended by their friends and family. I earned just enough money to pay bills and living expenses.

Toward the end of August, days before the new term was starting, the Chair called. "How would you like to finish your degree?" I told him I didn't have the money. "You won't believe this," he said, "but the woman we hired to do costumes decided to teach in Vietnam. Want the fellowship? You'll be able to graduate by the end of the school year."

I was excited by the offer, then saddened by my reality. "I can't make costumes, and I have a kid to take care of. I can't be out nights and weekends."

"I know," he said, "but you can keep teaching movement for actors and do a theatre program for children as part of your performance thesis. Create whatever schedule and courses that work for you."

His words changed my life. I developed a program using movement as part of actor education and wrote and directed a play for kids. My MA thesis became my first book: *Theatre Movement*. Not only did I create a career that nourished my soul and spirit, I was able to support my son, pay the mortgage, fix the roof, and look all my disparagers in the eye. I never had a plan. It all unfolded—each choice opening up a new opportunity.

Was there a time when you made a difficult choice? How do you feel about the choice you made?

❧ ❧ ❧

A PROPOSAL

He was a great dancer, popular with all the single women who attended the Wednesday night folk dance sessions. There were always more women than men, and they flocked around him, some waiting to be asked, others asking him. His dance prowess spoke louder than his looks.

The first time he asked me to dance, a particularly complicated Swedish dance, I was thrilled and nervous. The woman and man do different steps in a complex rhythm that only works if the woman allows the man full control, swinging and swirling her in time to the music. While dancing with this man, I felt women's eyes on me. My discomfort increased. His arm around my waist, almost to my breast, felt supportive and dangerous as he led me around the hall. After the dance ended, he said, "You're a good dancer. I like dancing with you." I nodded, mumbled thanks, and walked away, knowing he danced with a different woman each time.

I began to look forward to dancing with him, easily the best male dancer who regularly came to folk dance. The only time we ever saw each other was when we danced, so I was surprised when he phoned to ask if we could meet for dinner. I had a seven-year-old son. I told him he'd have to wait until I found a babysitter who could also give him dinner. "Okay," he said, "let me know when you're available—the sooner the better." Weird. Our only time together had been while dancing. We'd never even talked between dances.

I was on a tight budget; eating out was a treat no matter the occasion. It wasn't until coffee was poured that he came to the point—forthright and clear. "I'd like to have sex with you once a week for a year. I'll pay you four thousand dollars."

I was stunned. At the time, I was earning about that amount. This would more than double my income, and yet, could I have sex with a man with whom I had no chemistry except while dancing? How would he claim his *right*? Tattoo my toe? I'm not a prude, but the idea of a man owning my body, even for a few hours once a week, even for badly needed money, filled me with revulsion.

When I regained my composure, I said, "I appreciate your thinking of me, but I can't do it."

"Why not?" he asked. "We like each other. We dance well together. It's no big deal. I'm a good lover and we can have a great time."

"No."

"Okay, forget I asked." He paid the bill and left.

He never invited me to dance again.

What would you have done?

9

WORLD TALE

Speaking Truth

THAILAND

A created reality obscures the truth. In the stories, Peekskill 1949 and If He Dies, truth depends on who is doing the telling.

• • •

A LONG TIME AGO people discovered that the lorikeet, a small, intelligent bird, could speak with little teaching. Not only was she able to repeat what she heard, she could also give voice to her own thoughts.

One day, a farmer working in his rice fields saw his neighbor's buffalo. The hungry farmer killed the buffalo, cut up the animal, made a fine meal for himself, and hid what he could not eat.

His neighbor came by and asked, "Have you seen my buffalo?"

The man said, "No."

The farmer's lorikeet flew to the neighbor and said, "He killed and ate part of your buffalo. The rest he hid in his fields and rice house." The neighbor searched and found the meat, just where the bird had said. He asked the farmer whose meat it was.

The farmer said, "This is not your buffalo meat. This is my meat."

The lorikeet repeated her words: "He killed and ate part of your buffalo. The rest he hid in his fields and rice house." The neighbor was puzzled, wondering which one spoke truthfully. He asked the magistrate to hear the case the following day.

The farmer was clever. He covered the lorikeet's cage with a huge pot. All night he beat on the pot to make the sounds of thunder. He poured water over the pot to create rain. He shook the pot to make it feel very windy.

In the morning, the farmer took the bird and appeared in court. The bird told her story. The judge was impressed by the bird's intelligence and clarity.

The farmer spoke: "The bird speaks well, but she speaks nonsense. Ask her to describe last night's weather."

The judge agreed. The lorikeet replied, "Last night we had a ferocious storm with much thunder, heavy rains, and a strong wind."

"You see," said the farmer. "She speaks well, but she speaks nonsense."

The judge spoke: "It is true. Last night was calm and clear. Case dismissed."

The lorikeet was exiled to the forest where she lived as she had before she knew people.

One day she saw a new, brilliantly colored bird. She asked, "Who are you? Why are you here?"

The bird preened its feathers and spoke: "I have come from another country, but I will live here. I speak the language of people."

The lorikeet said, "I welcome you with some advice. If you would speak to people, let them teach you what to say. People are not interested in truth or wisdom. They wish to hear only their own words."

And so it is. Parrots repeat what they are taught. People are content.

PEEKSKILL 1949

In 1947, my mother and I attended a concert in Peekskill, NY, where Paul Robeson sang in an outdoor setting. We were seated in the back on grass. I couldn't see, so I stood up. Suddenly there was a deep voice saying, "Folks, there's a little girl with blonde pigtails standing up in the back. Would you mind if she came up front so she can see better?" The next thing I knew, waves of people were lifting me up and over until I was in the front, face to face with Paul Robeson, a tall handsome Black singer with a broad chest sitting on a high stool. He beckoned me to come up, sat me on his lap, and asked what song I'd like him to sing. The audience yelled, "Old Man River." He asked if I'd like to hear it. I was too dumbstruck to do more than nod. He sang as I rested against his chest, lulled by the power of his voice and the safety of his presence.

Two years later, in 1949, we went again to hear Paul Robeson sing. Although I was now thirteen, I wasn't much taller and still had blonde pigtails. Secretly, I hoped Mr. Robeson would invite me to sit on his lap and sing a song for me. As we approached the concert area, there were police everywhere, blocking the entrance. My mother showed a policeman our tickets. He said, "The concert is cancelled. Go home before there's trouble." With his body movement, he made it impossible for us to do anything but turn around and go home. At the time, we didn't know there had been so many threats of violence, the promoters had decided to cancel the concert. I was disappointed and shocked. Why would someone want to hurt such a marvelous singer as Paul Robeson?

About two weeks later, my parents heard that performers, among them Paul Robeson and Pete Seeger, would be singing at a concert in a picnic ground about seven miles from our place in the country, near Peekskill. Many members of the community decided to go, even those who didn't care about politics—they just loved to listen to Paul Robeson. Since there had been so much talk of violence, World War II vets and union members were recruited to guard the area. I got dressed to go, but my parents said I had to stay and babysit my sister. I was furious. Before leaving they told me they expected to be home around seven at the latest.

Seven came and went. Even though it was still early, I had a funny feeling in my stomach, like something was terribly wrong. My sister said she was hungry, so I made her favorite supper, but I was too worried to eat. Eight and nine o'clock came and went. I told her our parents probably went out for dinner and put her to bed. I knew something bad had happened. Around midnight our parents arrived, unscathed and upset, too tired to talk. I learned what had happened the next morning.

There were seven entryways to the picnic grounds. People drove in and parked. The concert was held with vets and union members surrounding the concert area in a protective circle. But after the concert ended, all but one of the entryways was blocked off. Drivers were forced to use this one exit. Photos show hoodlums throwing rocks and bottles at drivers, overturning cars, tossing fireballs, screaming at passengers—all while police stood by, some with smiles on their faces, doing nothing. Stopping nothing. No local hospitals would accept the injured who had to drive about twenty miles to Ardsley-on-Hudson before they could get medical help. My piano teacher's wife lost an eye. My parents avoided the violence because my father heard the commotion. When he saw entryways blocked off, he drove into an area hidden by trees and waited until he thought it was safe to drive home.

The newspapers reported that communist agitators had rioted, causing all the casualties and property damage. Despite the photos showing police standing by, watching the violence, no one was held accountable. I was outraged. I knew very well the concertgoers had not incited violence. The violence was done to them, not by them. How could newspapers call people like my parents and me, if I'd been allowed to go, perpetrators, agitators, commies, troublemakers? I asked my father, "How can newspapers lie?"

"Welcome to the world, Nancy."

Paul Robeson later said, "The only time I feared for my life was not in Nazi Germany, in 1939, but in Peekskill, NY, in 1949."

Have you had occasion to question media reporting? What was that like for you?

❧ ❧ ❧

IF HE DIES

It started with a sniffle. Since my husband was working twenty miles north, in Providence, and had our car, I walked to the office of a doctor who agreed to see my eighteen-month-old son. "It's nothing," he said, dismissing my concerns. "Just a little cold. Give him lots to drink, keep him warm, and he'll be fine tomorrow. Don't be a nervous mother." I wheeled the carriage home, feeling embarrassed for making a fuss, for worrying about nothing.

My embarrassment turned to bewilderment a few hours later when my son and I were playing with blocks. Suddenly he began to gasp for air, making horrible sounds as if each breath were his last. Then it stopped. And started. And stopped. And started. I ran to a neighbor and begged to use her phone. I called my mother-in-law who'd been a pediatric nurse and asked her to come as quickly as she could.

As soon as she and my father-in-law arrived, they watched in astonishment as one minute my son could hardly breathe, the next moment he was playing with toys. "Nancy," said my mother-in-law, "I've never seen this before. I think we should take him to the hospital." Stunned, thinking about the doctor saying it was nothing, just a little cold, I wrapped him up warmly and held him to my body, begging all the powers that be that he be well and this would pass.

When we arrived at the hospital, the admitting clerk began asking a lit any of questions. I answered automatically until she asked what religion he was. "Why do you need to know?" I asked.

"In case he dies," she responded.

"Oh, for goodness sakes," blurted my mother-in-law. "I used to work here. I'm taking him up to the ward." Still holding my son, I followed her to the elevator. "You can't come with me, Nancy—they won't let you up there."

"But I'm his mother. He needs me." My mother-in-law took him from me and disappeared as the doors to the elevator closed. Despair overwhelmed me as I waited for her to return. Hoping she'd be carrying my son. I lost track of time. Waiting. When she stepped out of the elevator looking grim, without my son, I knew something was terribly wrong. "They've put him in an oxygen tent and started IV antibiotics." How was this possible? The doctor said it was sniffles. Nothing to worry about.

I had to be with my son. To comfort him as best I could. I stepped into the elevator, but my mother-in-law stopped me. "You can't go up. They don't allow parents to see their children."

"But he needs me. We've never been separated."

She shook her head. "It doesn't matter. It's the rules. No parents allowed. If you try to see him they'll call security." I couldn't stop shaking. Although my mother-in-law was never comfortable with physical affection, she put her arm around me and said, "Let's go to my house. The doctor has the phone number. He'll call as soon as they have a diagnosis."

I sat by the phone, waiting. My in-laws did their best to distract me, but I was in a world of darkness. When the phone rang, I picked it up. The doctor's voice was hard and cold. "I'd like to speak to Mrs. King."

"Speaking," I said.

"Your son is extremely ill. If he dies it will be your fault."

The next thing I remember is sitting on the couch. My father-in-law was handing me a shot of whiskey.

He was in the hospital for over a week. I tried to sneak up to see him, and a policeman said if I did this again, I'd be arrested. For seeing my ill child? When he came home, I had explicit directions for his care, which I followed as if my life depended on it, not only my son's, yet he failed to recover and was soon hospitalized for a second time. Once again, the doctor blamed me even though I explained I'd done everything he told me to do, just as he'd told me to do it. When my son came home after the second hospitalization, he was not the same child he'd been before being hospitalized. He didn't cry. He hardly slept. He hardly ate. I spent most of my days holding him, crooning songs off-key, trying to soothe him.

It took six months before he was well. I never recovered from the doctor's accusation.

Have you been in a life/death situation? If so, what difference did this make in your life?

10

WORLD TALE

The Poor Tailor

EASTERN EUROPE

The tailor finds a way to use what he has. In the stories, From Chaos to Community and When Memory Fails, creativity turns desperation into possibility.

• • •

THERE WAS ONCE A poor tailor who made coats for many people but never made one for himself even though he wanted one.

One day he decided to save whatever money he earned so he could buy himself material for a coat. Little by little, and bit by bit, he finally had enough to buy what he needed to make his coat. He brought the material back to his shop and carefully cut it out so as not to waste any of it. The thought of having a new coat was so pleasurable he worked on it all through the night. When morning came, he had a new coat. Satisfied with his effort, he wore the coat until it was in tatters.

One day he looked at the worn-out coat and thought, if he was careful, he could cut a jacket from the less worn bits of the coat. And so he did. He wore the jacket until it too was in tatters.

One day he looked at it and thought, if he was very careful, he could cut a vest from the jacket. And so he did.

From the vest came a cap.

From the cap came two pockets.
From the pockets came some buttons.
From the buttons there was just enough material to make a story.

❧ ❧ ❧

FROM CHAOS TO COMMUNITY

Between my junior and senior years of college, I was hired to be a recreational therapist in a large mental hospital, in charge of a building of three hundred women. When my supervisor told me I had to meet with a psychiatrist, my first thought was to wonder what I'd done, if somehow I'd be transformed from staff to patient. In our meeting, the doctor told me he had requested my supervisor to shift my schedule so I could tell stories to mentally ill children three times a week. No one asked if I wanted to do it, or even if I could. The decision was simply assumed, based on the stories I'd told my women patients.

The first time I'd worked with the kids, I'd entered the room, scared by the violence, and had sat on the steps leading into the room, waiting for them to notice me while they fought, attacking each other with venom. When they finally stopped, looking at me with curiosity, I managed to get their attention, and their fighting stopped. I even managed a weird kind of storytelling session, but here I was, once again, sitting on the steps, watching kids fighting. Kicking. Screaming. Shouting. Yelling. Crying. Wondering what to do. It was as if the first visit had never happened.

I couldn't leave. There was no place to hide. Once again I sat, my head in my hands, hoping they wouldn't turn their wrath on me. It seemed forever, but was probably only a few minutes when the chaos waned. One by one the kids stopped and looked at me. "Why are you here?" asked a boy. It had been only a few days, but no one remembered me.

"I'm here to tell you a story."

"We don't want your story," sneered a girl.

"Okay," I said, not about to impose my task on them. "Maybe we could sit in a circle and make a group story."

"What's that?" asked the smallest boy.

"Come sit in a circle with me and I'll tell you about it." I got up and walked a few steps then sat down on the floor. One by one they slowly sat down, leaving a lot of space between them and me. The fragile quiet seemed like the lull in a storm, so I quickly said, "I'll start with: Once upon a time, in a place far away, there lived . . ." I looked at the girl sitting closest to me and said, "You can say a few words, and when you're finished, the boy sitting next to you can add what he wants to say. We'll keep going until everyone who wants to be part of the story has told their bit. Okay?"

The girl picked up from what I'd said, spoke briefly, then poked the boy on her right. Despite a lot of giggling and some yelling, one by one they created a story from what had previously been said. The last boy to participate added a little, then said, "But the story isn't finished. You finish it." I asked the group if this was okay with them. They nodded. I wove the strands they'd created into a whole and ended with what I hoped was a satisfying ending.

"That was good," said a girl with a contented look. Judging by the peaceful silence and their relaxed faces, I guessed they agreed.

The boy who asked why I was here, now asked, "You coming back?"

"If you want me to."

"We do," they said, almost in a chorus.

"Okay, I will."

Just then, the door opened. The grim-faced woman who'd locked me in, opened the door, visibly shocked by what she saw. "Time to leave," she said, hurling her words.

"Thank you for the great story," I told them. Maybe next time they would remember me.

"Time to leave," she snarled. I could see the kids tense up, so I smiled and left as quickly as I could.

What would you have done?

❧ ❧ ❧

WHEN MEMORY FAILS

In the fall of 1984, I had a grant from the University of Delaware to do story-making projects with faculty, returning adult students, undergraduates, graduates, and administrative units. Each group was formed by volunteers.

The faculty who chose to participate came from a variety of fields. Most did not know each other. All went well until the fifth, and next to last, meeting.

With the ten of us sitting in a circle, I began telling a story about how the first storyteller came to be. Suddenly, I had nothing. I couldn't remember what came next. Not a word. I was stunned. The group looked at me, waiting. Embarrassed, ashamed, feeling terrible about myself as a storyteller and group leader, I had to admit I could no longer remember the story.

I expected at least some of them to react unsympathetically. There'd been a lot of initial skepticism about the value and power of stories, and it had taken time for the group to trust they could talk about their feelings and personal reactions to the stories we'd shared without being judged.

After what felt like a too-long silence, while I was still trying to remember the story and judging myself harshly, Marion, a business professor, spoke up. "Maybe your forgetting the story is a gift to us. We can tell how we've become storytellers. I'll begin." She talked about how she'd always read stories to her children, but when they asked her to make up a story, she could never think of anything to say. "Since I've been taking this workshop, I've learned to trust my imagination. I couldn't make up stories for my kids, but I can make them up for my grandkids."

I barely heard her. I thought Marion was being kind and waited for the judgment to begin, steeling myself for their disapproval.

Instead, one by one, participants talked about becoming storytellers, each in their own way. I still felt they were being compassionate rather than honest until the last person spoke. George, a chemistry professor who'd found it difficult to talk about his feelings, said, "Maybe this is the wrong thing to say, but I'm glad you couldn't remember the rest of the story. I even wonder if you did it on purpose, just to make us feel better." *How could anyone think I'd say I'd forgotten a story as a strategy*? He continued, "You're a terrific storyteller and you have an amazing ability to help us tell stories. Me, for instance. I only signed up for this group because Marty [a math professor] dared me to do it. I never thought for one moment it would be anything but misery." We all laughed. "Boy! Was I wrong. I come in tired, feeling depleted, and I leave full of energy. You might not believe this, but last night I told my daughter to name three things, and I made a story from them. Imagine! Me, a storyteller … Who would have thought it possible?"

Marty guffawed. "George, I didn't think you had it in you. Miracles still happen." George rolled his eyes.

Out of my failed memory came their stories and a new sense of themselves as storytellers.

What stories might you tell if you knew someone wanted to hear them?

11

WORLD TALE

Anniko

AFRICAN

Anniko, who has a short neck, finds herself in a village of long-necked people. The stories, Cooking for 100, The Only Woman in the Room, and Meeting His Mother, describe ways of responding to unexpected challenges.

• • •

It was far away, her small village. So far she could not find the way back in a day. This is where Anniko found herself.

Anniko leaned her tired body against a tree. Though she knew her village was a great distance from where she was, yet she did not know where to find another village. In her loneliness, she looked up at the bird whose song she had followed. It was a lovely song, so beautiful she had forgotten to look where she was going. Now, watching the sun leave, she shivered, knowing night would soon come. To keep herself safe from wild animals roaming at night, she climbed up into a tree. When she heard the roar of a lion circling the trunk of the tree, she wished more than ever she had never left her village.

The return of the sun's warmth woke her, welcoming her to the new day. When she looked around, she knew she was lost. Afraid of walking in circles, she decided to follow the path of the sun. Just before dusk, she came to an unknown village.

Anniko and the villagers stared at each other, amazed. She had never seen people with long necks. They had never seen a person with a short neck. They might have stared at each other until the sun went down, but Anniko was hungry and thirsty and tired. "Please," she asked, "might I have something to eat and drink?" Overcoming their astonishment, the villagers gave her food, water, and a mat on which to sleep.

The next morning, Anniko rose with the sun. As she had done every morning in her village, she sang a song to welcome the day. Once again the People of the Long Necks were filled with wonder. They had never heard such beautiful sounds. Anniko was happy they liked her music and offered to help with the day's chores. As she worked, she sang, easing their effort.

Although the villagers and Anniko grew fond of each other, there was one man who did not like her. He especially did not like to hear Anniko sing and waited for an opportunity to get rid of her. One day, when Anniko was alone, sitting in the sun, combing her hair, he quietly crept up behind her. After looking around to make sure no one was nearby, he confronted her. "You are ruining our village with your short neck and constant singing. You need to leave our village, now!"

Anniko was too upset to say anything. Perhaps the others think as he does but are too kind to tell me, she thought. With the man's words ringing in her ears, Anniko quickly left the village.

That night, the villagers gathered to hear the song Anniko sang to greet the evening, but they heard no song. "Where is Anniko?" they asked. No one knew. The man said nothing, pleased with the quiet. When the villagers began to leave, there was one who said, "I think I know the person we should ask. Follow me!" They went to the house of the man and asked, "Where is Anniko?"

At first he denied knowing anything, but the villagers kept asking. "All right," he said, "I will tell you. Anniko does not belong in our village. We are the People of the Long Necks. She has a short neck. If she lives with us, we can no longer say we are the People of the Long Necks. Listen to me. Let her be wherever she is. We don't need her to spoil our ways, and we don't need her songs. We did well enough before she came."

But the villagers missed Anniko. They had grown fond of her singing and helpful ways. They decided to go into the forest to look for her even though they had no idea where she might have gone. After they had been looking for a long time, one of the villagers suggested, "Perhaps we could sing to her as she sang to us. Perhaps she will hear our singing, and we will find each other." Although everyone thought this was a good idea, no one knew how to sing. But they wanted to find Anniko so badly, they decided to try.

Their first sounds were noises, more like screeches and squawks than song. They put their hands over their ears and kept trying. Finally, they decided it was too hard to learn to sing, and to sing a song, so they simply chanted, "Anniko. Anniko. We are here. Anniko." There was no response, but they kept chanting. "Anniko. Anniko. We are here. Anniko." Although they heard nothing, they kept shouting the words. Then, in the distance, they thought they heard a sweet sound. A song. Listening intently, they followed the sound, walking toward what they heard. The song got louder and louder until the villagers and Anniko were face to face.

They greeted her joyfully, but she remembered the words of the man and remained quiet. The villagers understood. "Never mind what that man said. We want you to stay in our village. We are the People of the Long Necks. Your presence does not change this. Your songs lift our spirits and fill our hearts with happiness. Please, come back with us. Please, stay with us."

Anniko looked at the villagers and saw they spoke the truth. Holding her head high, she sang to them as they left the forest and made their way home.

COOKING FOR ONE HUNDRED

As a junior counselor, part of my job was to oversee a table of campers at mealtime. Most of them hated breakfast, especially the lumpy oatmeal. One morning, I was doing my best to encourage them to eat when I heard a loud, unpleasant argument coming from the kitchen. Soon the cook stormed out of the dining room, followed by the director who stood, dismayed, watching the cook leave. I heard her say to some of the senior counselors, "I don't know what I'm going to do. I'll be lucky if I can get another cook by tomorrow." No one suggested any action.

What possessed me, I don't know, but without thinking whether I could do it, I went up to the director and said, "I can make the meals until the new cook arrives."

She stared at me, incredulous. "Nancy, you're only sixteen. What makes you think you can cook for one hundred people? Don't be ridiculous."

Her words infuriated me. How did she know what I could do? Just because I was sixteen? So what? "I helped my mother cook for twenty-five—how hard could it be to multiply it by four?"

She shook her head, dismissing me as if I were an annoying gnat. "There's a huge difference. Besides, some of the pots are almost as tall as you are. How will you lift them even when they're empty?"

Once I offered, it became a matter of my self-esteem. I needed to prove to her she was wrong about me. "I know I can do it. The kitchen guys will help me."

Caught between desperation and disbelief, she said, "Okay. Let's see how you do making lunch." She had no other choice, and we both knew it. I followed her into the kitchen, feeling a crazy kind of confidence and a profound need to prove my capability, to do what she said I couldn't do. She showed me where the meal plans were, the recipe files, told the kitchen guys to help me, and rushed out.

The two guys hooted with disbelief after the director left, which I did not appreciate, and told them so. "Look, I know it seems weird, me offering to do the cooking, but I'm not like the cook who left. I don't yell. I can't give orders. You know more about this kitchen than I do. We can do what we want. I think it'll be fun."

Felipe grinned. Damon shrugged. They showed me where the day's lunch menu was posted. Grilled cheese sandwiches, carrots and celery, chocolate chip cookies. I suggested I start baking the cookies, Damon preparing the carrots and celery, Felipe getting the sandwiches ready to grill. "Is this okay?" They nodded. We got to work. I remember my mother telling me that recipes could be doubled but not tripled. The industrial mixer made it easy to make the batter a few times. Damon helped put the cookies in the oven. Felipe took the baked ones off to cool. I was feeling pretty confident, but the director checked in on us so many times I wished I had the nerve to say: "Could you please just do it once. You're making me nervous." Lunch went off without a hitch.

Supper was a bit more complicated, but Cook's recipe helped. Stew. Rolls. Fruit for dessert. Lots of chopping, cutting, dicing, spicing, putting everything into big vats that were at least half my size. The two guys, enjoying our camaraderie, were quick to offer suggestions that I readily accepted. When they told me how badly Cook had treated them, I said, "No one deserves to be yelled at and cursed. He was stupid. You know a lot. He should have been grateful for your good work." I enjoyed making the dough for the rolls, and we had fun pinching bits, putting them on a large baking tray, and tasting our first efforts hot out of the oven, slathered with cold butter. Scrumptious.

Except for the director, no one seemed to notice the change in cooks until breakfast. I was determined to make oatmeal without lumps. I asked the guys how Cook made it. Hah! I knew what was wrong. He put cold water into the oats. Wrong! I heated the water until it was almost boiling, put in some salt, and a bit of cinnamon just because I liked the smell, then added the oats as I continued to stir. When the oatmeal was served, I heard campers voicing their astonishment. "Wow! NO lumps. Smells funny. Tastes good."

At the end of breakfast, as the two guys were washing pots, and I was cleaning up the wooden tables, the director came in. "I didn't think you could do this," she told me.

"It wasn't just me. We worked together," I said, needing to give the guys all the credit they deserved.

"Nancy, I hired another cook, but he can't come until tonight. Can you handle another lunch and dinner?"

"Sure. The three of us, we can do it for as long as you need," I said, grinning. "We're a team."

Have you done something others thought you couldn't do? What prompted you to do it? What was the experience like for you?

THE ONLY WOMAN IN THE ROOM

As the newly elected executive vice president, I was not responsible for chairing the meeting, but the president had been called home to deal with an emergency, letting me know about fifteen minutes before it was scheduled to begin. I wasn't worried. I had the agenda. As a professor, I was used to chairing committee meetings.

I watched the members of the board file in. All men. All wearing dark pants and white shirts, some with ties and jackets, similar enough to have been bought as a group. My long blonde hair, purple outfit, and long earrings looked as out of place as I suddenly felt—the only woman in the room. No one knew I was taking the president's place.

As he came in, one of the men said to me, "While we're waiting for the meeting to start, get us some coffee and donuts from the kiosk downstairs." He pulled out his wallet, preparing to give me money.

I stared at him. Astonished. None of the other men seemed to notice my reaction. They acted as if his request was perfectly normal. They were men. I was a woman; therefore, I was meant to serve. Not me. "Get the coffee and donuts yourself if you want them. I'm here to chair the meeting. We start in ten minutes." I busied myself looking at notes for the meeting and the posted agenda.

Now he was stunned. None of the men said anything. Suddenly they were busy looking at folders. He sat down. No coffee. No donuts. I chaired the meeting with an efficiency the president lacked. The meeting was short, to the point, and effective.

At the end, a few men complimented me on how well I'd run the meeting. The rest walked out with only a wave of their hands. Mr. Coffee-and-Donuts was the first to leave.

Have you experienced a situation where you are singled out and treated with condescension and contempt? How did you feel? How did you act?

❧ ❧ ❧

MEETING HIS MOTHER

He was Black. I was white. He was tall. I was short. He was a southern Baptist. I was a northern Jew. He was a scientist. I taught world literature. He dressed with elegance. I favored loose-fitting ethnic clothing. He lived in the city. I lived in a small rural community. He grew up in the south in a time of overt segregation. I grew up in the north in a time of mostly covert segregation. He was married. I was divorced. Outwardly we were totally different.

We met while sitting at a table under trees, drinking cold water to cool off after playing tennis with other people, and somehow began talking about education. For two hours we discussed my role as educator, his role as tutor to inner-city kids. The more we talked, the more we discovered how much we had in common. Not what was visible, but ideas and feelings. What began as a friendship turned to love and then to loving after his divorce.

My parents were dead. His mother, with whom he was close, lived in Georgia. After hearing so many stories about her, I asked if I could go with him the next time he visited her. At first, he refused, but, during a phone conversation, she asked when he was going to bring me to meet her. With both of us asking, he reluctantly agreed to a visit.

We flew down to Atlanta and walked to the car rental kiosk. The white woman in charge tried to ignore us. Then, when we were the only customers in front of her, she coldly asked for the rental agreement, reading it as if it were a matter of life or death. I could feel his anger. With no way to deny our rental, she threw the keys across the counter and left. We walked to the rental car in silence. Fortunately, it was the car he'd requested—large, clean, with no smell of cigarettes. His rage simmered.

Not wanting to talk about the racism, we drove in silence to his hometown, where he stopped to buy flowers. There, the Black woman behind the counter gave us a big smile, created a special bouquet for us, and wished us well. We drove to his mother's place feeling lighter in spirit, with me wondering how his mother would react when she met me.

He stopped the car in front of the senior housing unit where his mother lived. As we walked toward her door, she came out to greet us. A neighbor, seeing our arrival, also came out and said to his mother, "Babe"—that's what everyone called her—"you have company."

"No," Babe told her, "my children have come home." With the bouquet in one arm, she hugged me with the other, her tears wetting our faces. "Nancy," she said, "thank you for putting the smile in my son's eyes."

Before we met, I had no idea how his mother felt about me, being a woman of another race, religion, and culture. At best, I hoped for cordiality, maybe even friendliness. I never imagined she would welcome me, as she did, continuing to love me for the rest of her life.

Have you had experiences with people of other races or cultures? What was that like for you?

12

WORLD TALE

What We Carry

BUDDHIST

Two men respond differently to the same situation. The stories, Unexpected Compassion and The Bolt of Lightning, explore the healing power of letting go.

• • •

TWO MONKS BEGAN CROSSING a torrential river. At the midpoint they encountered a young woman struggling to stay above the water. One of the monks lifted her up, put her on his back, and carried her to safety on the far bank. They bowed to each other in thanks. She left and the two monks went on their way.

Shortly after they began walking, the monk who hadn't carried the girl berated his fellow monk. "You carried a woman on your back. You've broken your vows. How can you live with yourself? How can you keep being a monk?"

He replied, "I carried a woman to safety. I put her down and began walking. You're still carrying her."

UNEXPECTED COMPASSION

My husband, son, and I lived in the same community as his ex-wife and two daughters. Since the girls' mother and I were friends, the girls felt comfortable walking to our house whenever they felt like it. My son teased them, as boys do; they shrieked and retaliated, as girls do, but the lack of tension among the adults made it easy for them to feel relaxed in our home.

The call came midday, without warning, from a neighbor. My husband's ex-wife was having a psychotic break; I needed to come get her daughters right away. This wasn't her first episode, but it was the first the girls witnessed in its entirety. When I arrived, instead of our usual hugs and chatter, they stood—two white-faced frightened children tightly clutching each other—waiting for me. I hugged their stiff bodies, reassuring them as best I could: their mother would recover as she had after previous bouts. In the meantime, they'd be staying with me, my son, and their father.

Dinner that night was difficult. Despite my making the girls their favorite foods, neither of them could eat. My son was eleven, the girls, twelve and thirteen. In the past, we'd had conversations about growing up that had interested the girls but bored my son, who, when he could, would leave the room. Now, despite my urging them to talk, the girls remained silent, pushing food around their plates, filled with misery, their mother's threats and screams still resonating, their father not knowing how to help.

Then, my son, not known for his compassion or for talking about his feelings, spoke to the girls in a tender voice I'd never heard. "I think you need to talk about what happened with your mother. I know she said terrible things and scared you, but if you don't talk about it you'll only feel worse."

The girls continued to push food around their plates. My son kept talking to them, gently trying to comfort them. "I know what you saw was horrible, and it's hard to talk about it, but you need to tell what happened. Who better than us?" He kept looking at them with such concern I was teary-eyed. I'd never seen him so caring.

After more urging, the older of the two began to talk, her voice barely a whisper, frequently stopping to look at her sister, encouraged by my son. "She said she wanted to kill us. To save us from the danger. She kept yelling and screaming and threatening. We didn't know what to do. We ran outside. The neighbors heard her. Someone called 911. We saw the ambulance people carrying her out. She was strapped to a board, but she was struggling and shrieking until they gave her a shot." In a comforting voice, my son kept encouraging them to talk about how they were feeling. I was filled with love and astonishment and gratitude. His surprising kindness was making it possible for the girls to begin to let go of the worst of the day's horror.

When they stopped talking, I asked their father and my son to clear the table. For once they didn't object. When the girls stood up, I hugged them. Although they were initially rigid and unresponsive, I kept hugging them until the tears came, followed by loud sobs and desperate hugs. That night, I tucked them into bed and sat with them until they fell asleep.

Their mother did recover. The horrific memories lessened in intensity. The girls and I continued to talk.

How do you release feelings after being in a nightmarish situation?

❧ ❧ ❧

A BOLT OF LIGHTNING

In 2017, I was hiking up a steep incline, almost to the top of the mountain, when I felt a surge of energy like a bolt of lightning charge through me, starting with my feet, moving up and out the top of my head. Dumbstruck, unable to move, I stood in the path, wondering what the hell just happened. A man and his dog appeared. The man asked if I was okay. I couldn't speak but I motioned for them to walk past me. The man did, but his dog, big and shaggy, stopped and began nuzzling me.

The man stared at his dog moving around my body. "I've never seen him do anything like this." He called the dog, but the dog continued his soothing rubbing, offering comfort. The man called the dog again, but the dog ignored him. Not wanting him to leave, I stroked his fur. When it seemed pretty clear the dog wasn't going to stop any time soon, the man came over to him and said, "Time to go," and nudged the dog up the path.

I couldn't get my body to move. Hikers passed, asking if I was all right. "Fine," I answered, though I was anything but fine. Then, with no conscious decision to do so, in my mind's eye I began seeing friends who had hurt me, family members who'd blamed me, people with whom I'd continued to interact despite having been treated unkindly. No matter who I thought about, what incident I remembered, there was no charge—no anger, no bitterness, no frustration. Only calm.

Confused, still not able to get my body to move, I consciously remembered insults, accusations, offensive remarks and actions. Nothing. More people passed me. Then, somehow, without effort, I began hiking, feeling lighter, free of negativity, sensing a new inner spaciousness. My feet moved faster despite the increasingly steep incline. I felt a rare sense of joy and wonder as I reached the top, but it also felt mysterious and unexplainable.

I don't know what happened as I hiked up the mountain. What I do know is pent-up difficult feelings dissolved. Now I could think about people with whom I had troubled relationships and feel peaceful. I could wish them well, but no longer want to interact with them.

In the following days and weeks, I found caring ways to cease contact with people with whom I could not be myself. It was as if we had been on one path up until the incident on the mountain, and after it our paths diverged; I moved on to a healthier way of being in relationship. How could decades of negative feelings dissolve in seconds? I can't explain it, and yet, they did.

Are you open to unexpected shifts in how you deal with difficult relationships?

13

WORLD TALE

The Power of Song

RUSSIA

Singing has power. The stories, Complaints into Arias, From Fear to Courage, and How Can I Keep From Singing, describe how singing changed feelings and behaviors.

• • •

THE POWER OF SONG

There was once a king and queen who lived happily together until the king and his men were captured in battle. After three years, the king found a way to send his wife a message, commanding her to raise a large army and money for ransom to secure his release as well as the release of his men.

The queen disliked the plan. Too many months would pass before she could raise the money to fund an army and pay the ransom. She decided to make her own plan. Without telling the king's advisors, she transformed herself from queen to troubadour. Taking only her lute, she started to walk. After a short time, she met up with a band of pilgrims who invited her to join them.

When her path diverged from theirs, she joined a group of merchants, leaving them to climb the steep mountains that surrounded the kingdom where her husband was being held captive. She approached the castle playing her lute, singing in a sweet voice. She soon attracted the attention of the guards who took her to the king of that kingdom.

At his command, she sang songs of love and loss. The king was much taken with her music and asked, "Sweet troubadour, from where do you come?"

The queen answered in a man's voice. "From far away. I wander as I will, earning my way by singing and playing for those who would listen."

The king was so entranced by her performance, he said, "Play for me for seven days, and when you must leave, ask what you will of me. I will grant your request."

When seven days had passed, the queen said, "The mountains are steep. The way is often dangerous. Perhaps you would allow me to take one of your prisoners to keep me safe company." And so, when the queen was ready to leave, she was taken to the dungeons where she found her husband. Because she was dressed as a man he did not recognize her.

Safely home, the queen changed back into her womanly garments and welcomed her husband home. He was displeased. "You did nothing to secure my release. I asked you to raise an army and a king's ransom. You ignored my command. Had it not been for a brave troubadour, I would still be languishing in a cold, dark prison.

The queen excused herself and changed into her troubadour's clothing. She approached her husband, who greeted her with grateful ceremony. Then the queen removed her disguise to reveal her true identity.

The king did not understand.

The queen sang a song about the time and effort the king's plan would've required. She sang of missing him too much to wait so long. She sang of the plan she'd devised to rescue him with no loss of men, time, or money.

The king bowed his head in shame and begged her forgiveness.

The king understood.

COMPLAINTS INTO ARIAS

In 1952, I was a junior counselor whose primary job was to take care of the girls in my bunk—inner-city kids, around twelve years old, from poor neighborhoods. Although they were tough in some ways—dealing with rats, cockroaches, marginal housing, uncertain meals, and human predators—they'd never used a latrine, hiked in woods, or seen raccoons enter their bunk to eat food they weren't supposed to have. What they complained about most was being told what to do by me, their counselor, only a few years older than them.

One night, as they were getting ready for bed, a fight broke out. When I went to intervene, they turned on me, telling me how much they hated camp and hated me even more. Their histrionics reminded me of opera, so I told them they could say how much they hated me, but they had to sing it. Their look of incredulity made me laugh. Some of them laughed as well at the absurdity of what I'd just said, but one girl took me seriously and sang how much she hated me. Others joined in, their words and sounds clashing, making a rather satisfying cacophony.

When they stopped, one of them told me it was my turn. I can barely carry a tune. Still, I sang how much I loved being their counselor, how much I wanted to take them hiking and swimming, and wanted to help them make plays and dances, ignoring all their words of hate. I sang how much I loved hearing their complaints in song.

When I finished one girl asked, "How can you sing about loving us when we sang about hating you?"

I shrugged. "How you feel about me has nothing to do with how I feel about you. You're entitled to your feelings."

Another girl admitted, "We don't really hate you, but it was fun to sing about it, especially because you didn't get mad at us.

A third girl said, "We should do this more often."

An idea occurred to me. "What if we ask the director to make space after Sunday lunch so anyone who has a complaint can share it with the camp, only she has to sing it."

They were absolutely sure the director would not allow this. I said I'd ask anyway. The next morning, I told her what had happened and made my suggestion. "My girls will volunteer to show the rest of the camp how to do it." It took a bit of persuasion, but she finally agreed to try it.

The next Sunday, after lunch, the director told the campers, "Anyone with a complaint can express it, but you have to do it singing." She invited my campers to begin. They had decided what they would complain about, so they were prepared in ways other campers weren't. But a lot of them had complaints and were willing to sing them. The director took note, and responded in song. What began as a way to defuse a fight became a Sunday ritual.

How might singing what you feel, rather than speaking it, affect you?

❧ ❧ ❧

FROM FEAR TO COURAGE

My mother told me we were going to join the march to protest the executions of Julius and Ethel Rosenberg. I was terrified. I'd heard about the violence perpetrated by angry bystanders against people protesting outside of Sing Sing Prison. If I could have figured out a way to say no, I would have, but my mother framed it as a moral obligation. I knew, despite my fear, she was right.

We took the subway into Manhattan and joined a crowd already marching. Just as I feared, people, mostly young men, were shouting curses and anti-Semitic remarks, hurling bottles and cans, threatening to kill us all. My mother, angry at the injustice of the execution and taunts from bystanders, but speaking from years of experience attending protest marches, said, "Ignore them. They feed on your fear."

Easier said than done. I couldn't stop trembling, especially after a bottle hit the man marching next to me. Blood gushed from his head. A woman put her handkerchief against the wound and suggested he leave, but he refused. "I'm not letting those bastards win."

My shaking got so bad I could hardly walk. I felt like I was going to throw up. Then, from behind, I heard singing. I knew the song. Knew the words. "We shall not, we shall not be moved. Just like a tree that's standing in the water, we shall not be moved. "

People around me sang, their voices strong and clear. I joined the singing. As my voice found its power, my fear disappeared. I felt proud to be part of history, part of thousands of people protesting injustice. For the rest of the march, I walked with newly found resolution. When I saw a can coming toward me, I deflected it. As the curses and yells grew stronger, and the bottles and cans more numerous, my courage strengthened.

I squeezed my mother's hand. She squeezed back, smiling her approval. One of the few times in my life that my mother and I were in accord, doing what we knew was right, in the company of thousands who were marching for justice.

What gives you courage in a difficult situation?

❧ ❧ ❧

HOW CAN I KEEP FROM SINGING

In 1955, I'd been hired as the associate waterfront director at a camp in Massachusetts, but a hurricane wiped out the waterfront, leaving me with nothing to do. The camp director, knowing how much I loved the arts, suggested I go to a Pete Seeger concert in a venue near Jacob's Pillow, about twenty miles from camp. He thought my depression was about the destruction of the waterfront. I didn't tell anyone I was feeling bad about my boyfriend not writing, disliking the teacher's college I was attending, detesting what I was studying, wishing I was smart enough to attend a liberal arts college. I had no friends. At nineteen my world was filled with misery and disappointment, which I didn't know how to fix or change.

I hitched a ride to the area where the concert was to be held, arriving too early to do much except buy my ticket and wait for the hall to open. I found a soft mound of earth shaded by a huge oak tree and sat, watching people, mostly couples and small groups, move through the area, feeling alone and unlovable.

I was too deep in misery to notice the man walking toward me until he was close enough for me to sense his presence. I looked up and saw a tall, skinny man with a banjo strapped across his chest. *That looks like Pete Seeger,* I thought, *but why would he be walking over to me?*

He knelt down and said, "You look like you could use a friend." I nodded, realizing it probably was Pete Seeger. "You look like you could use a song," he said. "Never found a time when a song didn't help." I nodded again, too shy to speak.

"Mind if I sit down?" he asked. I nodded, feeling stupidly mute. "Mind if I sing a little tune?" he asked. I nodded again, thinking I should say something, but no words would come. He took his banjo off and cradled it against his body.

He started singing the song, "How Can I Keep from Singing." I knew the words and began, softly, to sing with him. Some people heard and gathered around us. Suddenly there were a lot of people standing and sitting around, singing with Pete. He grinned at the ever-increasing numbers of people, singing the song several times with increasing enthusiasm and passion.

When he finished, people clapped and asked for more. "Well," he said, "I have to get ready for the concert. Hope you all will join me. We've got lots of singing to do." He looked at me and said, "Don't we."

I found my voice and said, "Yes, we do." As he got up to leave, I said, "Thank you so much."

"You feeling better?" he asked. I nodded. He chortled. "Told you. Never found a time when a song didn't help." I watched his tall, lanky frame disappear. He was right. Nothing had changed. Yet I did feel better. A lot better.

What power does song/music have for you?

14

WORLD TALE

The King Who Would Be a Rooster

EASTERN EUROPEAN

A prince decides who he wants to be. The stories, Attending a Revlon Workshop and Big Sur Weekend, explore personal authenticity.

• • •

In a time long ago and a place far away, there lived a king, queen, and their son. The king and queen made sure the prince had the best teachers and most knowledgeable sages to instruct him in all he needed to know in order to be a wise and kind ruler when he became king.

One day, the prince began to act like a rooster. He took off all his clothes, flapped his arms as if they were wings, began to crow, and stopped speaking the language of the kingdom. He refused to eat anything but corn from the floor, under the table, all by himself.

The king and queen called in the best doctors and healers, begging them to treat the prince, to turn him back into a man, but nothing anyone did made a difference. The roosterprince continued to crow and flap his arms, hop around the palace, and eat under the table.

Just when the king and queen had given up hope, an old man, dressed simply, came to the palace and said, "Your Majesty, I would like to try to cure the prince."

The king asked, "Where are your medicines and potions? What is your plan?"

The old man replied, "I have my own ways. Allow me seven days with the prince. All I ask is that you leave us alone and make no comment, even if my requests appear strange." Reluctantly, the king and queen agreed. They brought him to the prince and left the room. The first thing he did was take off his clothing, jump under the table, and sit opposite the roosterprince, who stared at the old man for a long time. He was patient and said nothing.

"Who are you and what are you doing here?" crowed the roosterprince.

"I'm a rooster. Can't you see that?" answered the old man using the prince's language.

"Oh, I'm a rooster, too. Welcome," replied the prince. Time passed and the two companionably crowed and flapped their arms.

In time, the old man got out from under the table and began to walk around, a little straighter each time he circled the table. The roosterprince had grown so fond of the man, he began to follow him, hopping wherever they went. The next day, the man put on a shirt and a pair of trousers. "What are you wearing, my friend?" asked the roosterprince. "Roosters don't wear clothing."

"You're right, dear prince, but I was a bit chilled. However, I assure you, you can still be a good rooster, even with clothes on. Try it." The roosterprince put on a shirt and a pair of trousers and continued crowing and flapping his arms.

On the third day the man sat at the table and ate corn from a golden platter. When the roosterprince joined him and started eating, the man signaled to the servants, and soon the table was set with silverware, goblets, golden plates, and platters of delicious food. When the old man began to eat, using a fork, a knife, and a spoon, the roosterprince imitated him. And after they had eaten a whole meal, he crowed happily.

The following night the man went to sleep on a bed, once again assuring the roosterprince, "Don't worry, my prince, you can be a good rooster even if you sleep in a bed," so the roosterprince slept each night in a bed and ate at the table.

Soon after, the man began to discuss a philosophy of life with the roosterprince, but the roosterprince objected. "Wait a minute! Roosters don't have to think, and they certainly don't have to debate the merits of a way of life."

"You may be right," agreed the old man, "but you can be a good rooster and still engage in discussion. After all, you know you're a rooster and that's what matters." The roosterprince thought this over and began to discuss philosophical ideas with the man.

On the seventh day, the old man bid farewell to the roosterprince. Before he left, he said, "Please remember: roosters are fair game for hunters, so always pretend you are a human prince. This way you will live a long and interesting life. Act wisely and help others. Farewell, dear roosterprince." In time, when the prince became king, ruling over the kingdom, no one beside himself knew he was still a rooster.

❧ ❧ ❧

ATTENDING A REVLON WORKSHOP

My father was a pharmacist in a store that also sold cosmetics. Although he knew I never used any kind of makeup, he decided to send me to a cosmetic workshop designed to show cosmeticians the newest products and demonstrate how to use them. I questioned his sending me, but he said he wanted me to go. I went.

The workshop convenors made no attempt to hide their displeasure at my appearance. Since they didn't ask why I was attending, I could shrug off their comments; selling makeup was their livelihood, not mine. Besides, I didn't find the women particularly attractive. To me they looked like painted dolls.

The agenda was clear. Participants used the new products on themselves in order to be able to sell them to customers. My lack of proficiency led one of the convenors to intervene. In a patronizing tone, she said, "You look like you're having trouble, dear. Let me help you." Without waiting for my consent, she proceeded to apply makeup on my face and polish on my nails.

I endured the process, more amused than annoyed. When she finished, she cooed. "You look so lovely. What a difference from before and after. We should have taken photos." I tried to fake a smile of appreciation, but it wasn't easy. My facial muscles felt encased in gunk.

She handed me a mirror looking extremely pleased. I tried not to gasp. All I could think was: Who is this person? I ignored the various admiring oohs and aahs; the face I saw in the mirror belonged to a stranger. The makeup obliterated my sense of self. How could creams and gels and coloring make me unrecognizable to myself? I watched the woman: her pride in her work, obvious; my discomfort, unnoticed. As the women made suggestions about the best use of the products, the best way to sell them, all I could think about was how soon I could clean my face.

I left the workshop with hundreds of dollars' worth of makeup on my face and headed for the nearest bathroom where I did my best to wash it off. To get rid of the alien in the mirror. To recognize my face. To be the person

I was—someone who didn't wear makeup or dress up, who preferred to play sports, not flirty games. I couldn't ignore the red nails that looked like drops of blood, so on my way home I bought nail polish remover, sat on a park bench, and restored my nails to their natural state.

When I came home, I gave the cosmetic kit to my father, who was pleased to have it. My mother asked how the workshop went. "Great, if you enjoy looking like a painted doll." She sighed. I was not the daughter my mother wanted me to be.

What do you do if how you look is not acceptable to others?

BIG SUR WEEKEND

In 1972, I was attending a theatre conference and leading a movement workshop in San Francisco, not far from the Esalen Institute in Big Sur, a place I'd wanted to visit for years. It's gorgeous, with hot springs, ocean, and fascinating courses. I didn't want to take any of the workshops focusing on consciousness-raising, trauma, etc., using the techniques of Fritz Perls, Carl Jung, Carl Rogers, and others. I wasn't interested in becoming more vulnerable in front of a group of strangers who would disappear after the workshop, leaving me to deal with the emotional consequences. Then I noticed an ad for a weekend course in aikido. The timing was perfect—I could go after the convention and workshop ended.

As part of creating and teaching movement for actors, I'd attended courses in circus skills, stage combat, and some martial arts, but I was particularly captivated by aikido, a Japanese martial art that uses opponents' energy, strength, and momentum against themselves. No violence of any kind. Although acting students wouldn't have much opportunity to use aikido in a play, I thought the practice had metaphorical possibility. A woman playing a part in which she is faced with a threatening man might use the practice of aikido to inform her reaction, stepping aside to let his energy do him in. At the very least, I'd be learning a new physical skill.

When I walked into the registration area, people were anxiously seeking, asking, talking, gesturing . . . I felt uncomfortable, an outsider who shouldn't have come. I told myself this was just nerves. I had every right to be here, having paid for the workshop. As I stood in line, a woman asked what course I was taking. "Aikido," I answered.

She frowned. "Why would you sign up for that? It doesn't have much to do with becoming more conscious." I stared at the woman, unable to think of a retort. She wasn't the only one. When other people asked about my choice of course, they had similar responses, which left me feeling unsettled and out of place.

I decided to go for a swim. The sign said bathing suits optional. Although I've done a lot of skinny dipping, I didn't feel like doing it just to fit in, so I wore a suit. Judging by the negative comments, optional was only for the sign. Ignoring the others, I dove into the water and swam, soothed by the gentle ocean waves. My stay at Esalen was forcing me to make choices based on what I wanted rather than what others thought I should do—or be.

In the morning I walked to the aikido room. I was early but the door was open. A tall man was moving gracefully, his eyes closed. "Come in. Join me," he said in a deep, welcoming voice. Embarrassed at being noticed, I took off my sandals and positioned myself behind him, slightly to his right. I don't know how long we moved together; his eyes remained closed, but when other students arrived, he sensed their presence and invited them to join us.

When he opened his eyes, he smiled, welcomed the group, talked a little about aikido, formed us into pairs, gave us brief instructions, and then we began. At one point he murmured to me. "You're trying too hard. Let go of wanting to 'get it right.' Think of your energy as water flowing freely—no obstructions."

All my life I've tried to "get it right," to avoid abuse, to be liked, to achieve a goal, always with stress and anxiety, never ease. As the session continued, I felt less tense, as calm as I ever remember being, yet at the same time, paid attention to the form and content we were learning. His teaching was different from other martial arts teachers. He spoke sparingly, in a soft voice, never correcting, only suggesting. He exuded serenity and caring. I felt the energy in the room shift in a way that's hard to describe, as if all of us were letting go of expectations, of "getting it right," yet moving with relaxed energy. He had created an oasis of calm without effort. At the end of the morning, with no words, he invited us to form a circle. Again, without instruction, we bowed to him and then to each other. He bowed to us and left the room. I felt new and clear, internally spacious.

The woman with whom I'd been partnered asked if I'd like to join her for a walk before lunch. She led me to a place at the edge of the cliff where the underwater plants swayed to the rhythm of the water's movement. The sun sparkled on the ocean's surface. We stood in silence for a few minutes. "I came here to figure out who I am," she said. "You'd think at my age I'd know."

I didn't ask her age. I guessed she was in her midforties, like me. Although I knew who I was as a mother, wife, and professor, I often wondered who I would be without the roles. "Something happened to me in the workshop," she said. I asked her to tell me, if she felt comfortable doing so. "After we'd been moving for a while, I began to have a new sense of me—not as a lawyer, wife, mother, daughter . . . but an undefinable me. It's a strange and wonderful feeling. Do you think it can last after the weekend is over? I like who I am right now."

What she said described my experience as well. I said, "I think the power of the workshop for me won't be the aikido movement, although I'm enjoying it immensely. Somehow, his way of teaching is so quieting and spare, it's allowing me to stop worrying about 'getting it right,' and to let go of expectations. Who knows if it will last? At least I know something now I didn't know before."

She held my hand and said, "I think the gift of the workshop is knowing we can be who we are no matter who people think we should be. It's a new feeling for me." Both of us experienced such a surge of joy and energy, we ran to lunch, eager to see if we could be who we were, regardless of the anxious, searching, seeking, distracted energy all around us.

The sense of being authentic deepened as the sessions continued. Each time I entered the room it was like moving into a world without judgment, comment, negativity—just ease and grace. After the second day, I hardly noticed the chaotic energy swirling around me when I left the workshop. I was moving from an internal, centered sense of self; I told myself to remember what it felt like when I returned to my "real" life.

My internal calm was quickly challenged by the life to which I returned, but the memory of the aikido teacher—his grace and ease and serenity—became a touchstone in times of stress.

How do you differentiate between an authentic self and a public persona?

15

WORLD TALE

The Wisdom of Children

AFRICAN

The smallest and youngest succeed when others do not. The stories, Big Sister and Head Start Children, explore ways children act in surprising ways.

• • •

THE DAY BEGAN LIKE any other in the small village. People worked, ate, and talked to their neighbors, but they were not too busy to notice the arrival of a beautiful bird no one had seen before. Then, life changed quickly. Whatever people planted during the day was gone the next morning. Each day there were fewer chickens, goats, and sheep. Even during the day, the huge bird found its way into the storehouses and ate its fill of grains. Would there be anything left for people to eat in the winter? Now no one and nothing was safe.

The villagers were shocked. Afraid. No one knew what to do. The bird was so quick it evaded arrows and stones and traps. The Headman of the village told the strongest and wisest men, "Sharpen your axes and machetes. Go cut down the tree on which the huge bird perches." At first all went well. The sharp blades cut into the tree. It began to shake. Suddenly the bird emerged, almost too beautiful to look at, and began singing a song so sweet, so full of stories about places the men had never been and would never go, they fell to their knees, enchanted and bewitched.

The men's hands could no longer hold their axes and machetes. They lost their urge to kill the bird. When the sun went down, they returned to the Headman and told him they could not harm a bird that sang so beautifully.

The Headman was furious. He gathered the young men together. "Go and do what the stronger and wiser men could not. Surely you are brave enough to outwit this bird."

The young men set out, pleased to be asked to do what their elders could not. At first, their axes and machetes bit deeply into the trunk of the tree. Then, as if by magic, the bird appeared, more beautiful than the day before, singing a song of love and courage, of wondrous adventures the young men would never have. As before, entranced by the bird's song, the young men's hands became weak, they dropped their axes and machetes. When the sun went down, they too returned to the Headman, embarrassed and ashamed.

The headman was beside himself with fury and worry and fear. Now who could he send? Certainly not the women—they would marvel at the beauty of the bird, the wonder of its song. They would feel sorry for the tree. This left only the children. Perhaps if they worked together they could defeat the bird.

Early the next morning, the Headman took the children to the forest to the tree where the bird lived. He told them to shut their ears, not look up, pay attention, and do what he told them to do. The children lifted the heavy axes and machetes and went to work. When the beautiful bird emerged from the leaves, the Headman heard its song, and his hands grew too weak to hold his ax.

Intent on what they were doing, and proud to be asked to do what the wisest and strongest men could not, what the brave younger men could not, the children did not look at the bird, nor did they listen to its song as they chopped away.

When the tree fell to the ground, the bird crashed with it, crushed by the weight of the branches. People heard what the children had done and rushed to the forest. A great feast was held to honor them. In years to come, people told stories about the children who saved the village when the wisest and strongest and bravest could not.

BIG SISTER

I was almost six, super excited when my baby sister was born. Although I loved playing with dolls, now I had a real live doll to hug and kiss, who would hug and kiss me back. I watched my sister like a hawk, making sure she was safe from harm and had plenty of hugs from me since our mother wasn't affectionate.

When my sister was about five months old, we moved to a first-floor garden apartment. Upstairs was a young couple who quickly became friends with my parents. The husband adored my sister—me, not so much. Maybe it was because of the diaper incident.

When my mother wasn't home, she couldn't hurt me, so I was always devising ways to get her out of the house. The easiest was to find movies showing at local theatres, especially if it starred either Joan Crawford or Bette Davis. One day I scored a double play—two movies showing back-to-back, each starring one of them.

Even though I was only six, I reminded my mother she'd seen me feed and change my sister's diapers, and that I'd taken care of the baby when she'd had a headache. I assured her if there was a problem, I would ask the upstairs couple for help. My mother wanted to go; it took little persuasion on my part for her to agree. Armed with her favorite chocolates, she left. Now I had at least three hours free from her unprovoked anger.

When my sister woke up, I fed her a bottle, burped her, and after a long cuddle, put her back in the crib. About an hour later she woke up crying. I realized she needed a diaper change and was getting things ready when the man from upstairs came into the apartment. He said he'd heard her crying. "She just needs her diaper changed. There's nothing wrong," I told him. I got out a clean diaper and was taking off the dirty one when he pushed me aside.

"I'll do it. You're only a kid. Besides, your mother told me to take care of your sister if she cried."

I was furious. What right did he have to come in and mess with my sister? She'd stopped crying as soon as I undid the dirty diaper. I didn't need his help, but he was bigger and older and a friend of my parents. There was nothing I could do to stop him.

I watched his clumsy moves, knowing I could do better. We had to use pins to secure the diaper, and as he was preparing to pin the two ends of the diaper together, he accidentally stuck the pin in my sister's stomach. She howled.

With all my six-year-old sense of righteousness, I pushed him aside. "See, you hurt her. You should have let me do it. I know how to change a diaper without making her cry." I pinned the diaper ends then picked her up and calmed her down. She gurgled as I cuddled her to my chest and kissed her. I could feel the man from upstairs watching me, but I kept going. I resented him taking over when I'd been doing everything right, though I was more than a little worried about what he'd tell my mother.

When I was sure she was okay, I put her back in her crib, put the blanket over her, and rubbed her back until she fell asleep. I wanted to tell him to leave, but he stayed for a while, sitting in the chair by the crib. Since he was my mother's friend, not mine, I didn't say what I wanted to say: "Why don't you go upstairs where you belong?" I stood by the crib, waiting for him to go.

I breathed a sigh of relief when he finally left. I told my sister she was a good girl, and I loved her, went into the kitchen, poured myself a glass of milk, put it and two cookies on a tray, and went into the living room to read until our mother returned.

When you were a child, what assumptions did people make about you?

HEAD START CHILDREN

In 1966, I'd been teaching dance and movement for adults and teens but needed a summer job. I was hired to teach a Head Start class of fifteen children ages four to six, although I had no credentials to teach young children. I was given a room housing a kindergarten during the school year, but was told the only equipment I could use were the blocks. I protested. The administration reluctantly gave me permission to use the easels as well as a bit of program money to buy paints and clay.

On the first day of class, fifteen boys and girls, accompanied by an aide, ran into my classroom laughing, crying, pushing, shoving, screaming, although a few hung back looking frightened. I had no idea how children were assigned to teachers, if my kids were more given to acting out than others; what I did know was the turmoil had to stop. Immediately.

All thoughts of having the children paint or sculpt disappeared. I had to use my most authoritative voice to get them to sit. When they were mostly quiet, I told them, "I have no capacity for chaos." They looked at me as if I were speaking a foreign language, and I suppose in a way I was. I explained we needed to be kind and considerate and caring and respectful. More bewildered looks. They lived in a nearby housing project—radios and televisions blaring, people yelling, fighting, hitting . . . I couldn't expect them to understand what I meant immediately, so I decided to start with an activity that wasn't messy. I showed them where the blocks were and invited them to play with them.

Oy! As soon as a child built a tower someone knocked it down. Hitting. Crying. Throwing blocks. Some took a few blocks, and concealed them behind a screen.. Others took blocks and hit any child who tried to snatch a block from them. This had to stop. Immediately.

I asked them to bring all the blocks to the middle of the room and then to sit in a circle around them. This took so long it was time for snacks. As they were sitting, drinking juice, I said, "We're going to have a meeting where everyone can say what they think and feel." Silence. I was still talking a language they didn't understand. I began, "Who likes to build with blocks?" Every hand went up. "Who likes to have someone knock down what they've built?" No hands went up. "Well," I said, "we have a problem. You like to build, but you don't like someone to knock down what you've built. What are we going to do about this?"

They stared at me. Bewildered. Eventually, one child said, "You the teacher. You tell us what to do."

"Yes, I'm the teacher, but I'm not the one building with blocks, and I'm not the one knocking them down. You are, so you have to figure out a solution. What should we do so that everyone can build without worrying someone is going to knock it down?"

For the first time, there was complete silence. Once again some ventured to suggest I tell them what to do. Once again I explained why the solution had to come from them. The silence was uncomfortable. Maybe I was asking too much of them too soon. At least they were sitting quietly, not hitting or squirming or yelling. It looked as if they were thinking about what to do. Maybe this was as good as it could be for now. I was trying to think what to do next when a pigtailed girl ventured to speak. "Maybe we should ask if it's okay to knock someone's blocks down?"

I grinned. Jubilant. "Right! What you're saying is you want people to ask permission to knock something down." She looked confused. Permission wasn't a word anyone knew, so I defined it and asked them to repeat the word, which they did, with great gusto, yelling it several times. Just for fun, I asked them to use it in sentences, which took some time, caused lots of giggles, and resulted in a few interesting sentences like: "Do I have your permission to fart?" which made them laugh so hard I couldn't help laughing. When we were able to stop, I said, "Okay, now we have a plan, but what happens if someone knocks down the blocks by accident? Then what?" More silence. I could see they were thinking about the question, which pleased me.

One boy said, "I know. We say 'Sorry. Can I help you build?'" The children shouted their approval.

"Right," I said. "Let's practice what you've decided. There are enough blocks for everyone, so build what you want. If someone wants to knock something down, what are we going to do?"

"Ask for permission," they shouted.

"What if the person says no?" I responded.

There was a silence before a number of them shouted, "We don't knock it down?"

"Yes," I shouted.

And so they didn't.

Did you ever experience finding a solution yourself rather than someone telling you what to do? What was that like?

16

WORLD TALE

The Lightkeeper's Box

VENEZUELA

A tale of unexpected kindness. Comfort in a Hospital Bed and Hugs and Cuddles on a Trail, reveal effects of compassionate acts.

• • •

IN THE BEGINNING, NEITHER day nor night existed. No one knew about dreams. No one could bask in the warmth of the sun or watch the moon wax and wane. People didn't miss what they didn't know, yet not everyone was satisfied with the way things were.

In one village, there lived a chief who heard that somewhere in the distance there was a man who kept the light. Deciding on a plan, the chief said to his oldest daughter, "Find the man who keeps the light and bring some back to me." He blew on her face so that the *hebus* of the bush, water, and sky would keep her safe.

The young woman packed a small sack and left. When she came to a place of many roads, she didn't know which to take, nor did she know how to choose. She walked down a tree-lined road and came to the house of Deer, who greeted her warmly. She stayed with him, enjoying their time together, but soon remembered her father's request and went home. She told her father she had not found the Lightkeeper.

The chief decided to send his younger daughter. "Find the man who keeps the light and bring some back to me." He blew the hebus on her face, played his flute, and wished her well.

The younger daughter left and, like her older sister, came to the place of many roads. She stopped, not knowing which one to take. In the distance, she thought she heard the sounds of her father's flute. As she listened, she began to have feelings about the roads, as if they had faces. She chose the one that seemed strong and old. After walking for a long time, she came to the house of the Lightkeeper.

The Lightkeeper was as young as the road seemed old and just as strong. "Who are you?" he asked.

"I am the younger daughter of a village chief. I have come to get some light from you."

"I have been waiting for you," he replied. "Please stay with me for a while and I will show you the box of light. He picked up a box woven of *itiriti* leaves.

He opened it carefully so the dreams inside would not spill out. The young woman, seeing light for the first time, was awed by its brilliance. When the Lightkeeper closed the box, he offered her a meal.

For many days, the Lightkeeper opened the box made of itiriti leaves so they could enjoy themselves, but in time the young woman remembered her promise to bring back light from the Lightkeeper's box. As a present, he gave her the itiriti box filled with light and dreams.

Taking great care of the box, the chief's younger daughter traveled home to a joyful welcome from her sister and father. After showing them the dreams and light contained in the box, their father decided it should be shared and hung the box from the highest roof beam.

People from nearby villages heard about a family near the river who had light and came to see it. At first, they were welcomed and fed and given places to sleep, but, in time, the chief and his daughters grew tired of the throngs of people who gathered in and around their house. They decided everyone everywhere had a right to the light. The chief flung the box of woven itiriti leaves into the sky. The body of light flew to the East and became Sun. The box tumbled to the West and became Moon.

Thus were light and dreams brought to the world for people to enjoy.

❧ ❧ ❧

WOMEN IN LONDON HOSPITAL

In January 1985, I was in London, England, working on a book with a colleague and leading workshops for teachers and recreation workers when

I was beset by a cough that wouldn't quit, hemorrhaging for no discernible reason, and hardly able to eat or drink. After a colleague asked how I was, I reluctantly admitted, "Not so well." She called the Warden (person in charge of the post-graduate student housing where I was living for five weeks). The Warden called a doctor, with a lovely Scottish accent, who examined me, told me one of my lungs had collapsed, my pulse was extremely high, and I was very sick. Stunned by her findings, I tried to tell her I'd be fine in a few days, but she ignored my protestations. "It's off to the hospital with you, my girl. Right now!"

Even after being examined by several doctors, who did all kinds of tests, none of them could diagnose my illness. I had three days of treatment in a four-bed ICU-type room and was then, in spite of pleading I needed to be in the smaller room, wheeled to a huge ward filled with twenty-eight women, all of us critically ill. Even after I no longer needed oxygen or blood transfusions, and despite being treated with seven different kinds of antibiotics, I was still hooked up to an IV filled with various medications, prescribed by doctors who were trying their best to keep me alive.

When two doctors discussed my case as if I weren't in the room, I couldn't bear it and blurted out I couldn't bear it and blurted out, "You act as if I have leukemia." As soon as I saw their surprised nodding, I realized this was exactly what they were thinking. Me? Leukemia? Cancer? I wished I'd kept my big mouth shut.

In order to diagnose the type of leukemia I had, the doctors ordered a bone-marrow biopsy, which was more painful and less diagnostically useful than predicted. When the second one was ordered I asked for an anesthetic. As I felt the jab of the needle, I noticed the time—a few minutes past eleven.

When I next looked at the clock, it was a few minutes past five. A group of women, all hooked up to IVs, were clustered around my bed. "Oh, Luv, you're awake." "We've been so anxious." "You've been crying all day." "Telling us how hard your life has been."

I looked at them, unable to comprehend what they were saying. What were they doing huddled around my bed? Where had I been the past six hours? A sister (nurse), noticing I was awake, shooed the women away, took my vital signs, noted something in the chart at the end of my bed, and left without a word.

When the women were sure sister was gone, they returned to my bed, full of concern. "We've been really worried about you." "We tried to comfort you." "You've been crying ever since the doctors left." Others chimed in with more expressions of caring.

I looked at the women, feeling a jumble of embarrassment, disbelief, curiosity—mixed with wonder at their concern, sick as they were.

One of the women said, "We should let you rest," and started to wheel her IV away.

"Wait, please," I begged. She stopped. "Could you tell me what I said?"

It seemed they were upset about my crying but hadn't known what to do except listen. Although none of them had stayed with me the whole time, they told me what they remembered. "You said you had a really hard life." "You talked about your mother beating you." "You said she broke bones and dislocated your jaw and shoulder, and they didn't take you to a doctor." "Nobody loved you." "Nobody helped you." "You said you wanted to die." "Why didn't they let you die?" "Some of it we couldn't understand. When sister came round, she would tell us to get back into our beds."

I couldn't believe I'd been crying and talking about my life for six hours, or that women as sick or sicker than I was would stand by my bed trying to comfort me. "Thank you so much," I said, not knowing what else to say, overwhelmed by their compassion.

"Don't worry, Luv," said a woman too young to be dying. "We do what we can. It's an awful time in an awful place."

"I really appreciate your caring."

"We know," said a white-faced, wrinkled woman. "You help us too."

"I do?"

"When we have to sit around the table and eat, and none of us likes the food or feels hungry, the jokes you make about 'our fine dining,'—you make us laugh." This didn't seem like much to me, but another woman added, "And the way you talk to the sisters, like you aren't afraid—that's really good."

"All I did was ask sister to turn off the overhead lights when everyone said they hurt their eyes. As you pointed out, we all have lamps by our beds."

"Well, none of us dared to do it. And when sister asked who turned off the lights, bold as brass you were, telling her you did it. You took her by surprise. They're not used to anyone challenging them. Bold as brass you were." We started to laugh, remembering the shocked look on sister's face.

"See, I told you, you make us laugh," grinned one of the women. Then a sister entered the room, and they hobbled back to their beds, deftly steering their IV poles. We might be sick and dying, but we hadn't lost our sense of caring or our ability to laugh.

Think about a time when you were in a difficult situation and someone's caring helped you.

❧ ❧ ❧

HUGS AND CUDDLES ON A TRAIL

I was hiking down a steep trail, lost in thought. Sometimes, if I allow myself to feel what I'm feeling without judging, a memory will surface, and I can connect the past with the present and let it go.

As I hiked, too many memories surfaced, none of them good. Annoyed at myself for only remembering bad times, I forced myself to think of something good. In the process I forgot to look where I was going and tripped on a loose stone, falling headfirst, narrowly missing jagged rocks as I let go of my hiking poles and twisted my body to protect my head. Cursing my carelessness, I surveyed the damage. Blood on my legs and arms showed only surface cuts, easily taken care of. My hip was bruised, but moving my arms, legs, fingers, and toes revealed nothing was broken. I sat for a moment, drank water, took arnica pellets (a homeopathic remedy that helps reduce bruising and swelling), ate a bit of protein bar, and stood up.

My options were to go back up the steep trail to the trailhead for two and a half miles, or keep going down the steep trail and hike the four and a half miles to the trailhead. I decided to keep going down, focusing on the trail, watching for loose stones, sending energy to the hurting parts of my body.

I stopped suddenly when I realized a woman was watching me, a smile on her face—her dog, a collie, I think, sitting quietly beside her, looking at me, its tail swishing back and forth. Embarrassed, I apologized. "I'm sorry. I was so lost in thought I didn't see you."

"No problem," she said. Maybe it was her tone of voice, or mine, but the dog got up and gently pressed its body against me, tail wagging. I petted its head, the tail swishing even faster. It's not the first time a dog on a trail has nuzzled me, but this dog seemed to want my attention. The woman smiled. "My dog obviously likes you. Is it okay that she's snuggling you?"

"It's more than okay. It feels great. I had to help my cat die a couple of months ago, and I miss her cuddling."

We talked for a few minutes about her dog and my cat. We both lived alone and depended on our animals for hugs and cuddles."

"Are you getting another cat?" she asked.

"Don't know. Mia lived seventeen months beyond what the vets thought she'd live, and the last five or six months were pretty difficult. I'm not ready to take care of another animal, but it's hard living without her snuggles, particularly at night when she used to drape herself around my head after I turned out the light. Sometimes her paw would rest gently on my cheek." I could feel myself tearing up. The dog continued to nuzzle me.

"I think my dog knows you miss your cat," she said, grinning.

I nodded, grateful for the woman's caring. Usually, when I meet people on the trail, we say hello and continue hiking. She seemed in no hurry, perfectly happy to share her dog with me.

"You need a hug?" she asked.

"I do," I admitted, startled by the unexpected question.

She moved toward me just as I moved toward her. We hugged. Two strangers on a trail, her dog caressing us both. A soft landing after a hard fall.

How would you react if a stranger offered to hug you?

17

WORLD TALE

You Never Can Tell

EASTERN EUROPE

An event ends unexpectedly. In the stories, Boys and Blueberries, Softball, and Interview, what seemed like probable endings turned out surprisingly differently.

• • •

A LONG TIME AGO there was a farmer who loved horses. When his favorite mare ran away, he was sad, but when villagers came to sympathize, he told them, "Yes, I lost my horse, but who knows what will happen. All we can do is wait."

A few months later, the mare returned with a stallion, and his neighbors congratulated him on his good luck. "Yes, this seems like good fortune, but who knows?"

One day, while riding the stallion, he fell and broke his hip. People gathered around to help him, commiserating, lamenting his bad fortune. He shrugged. "No one can tell the future."

Shortly after, the area was attacked by marauders and all able-bodied men were conscripted to serve, but the farmer's bad hip kept him safe from the fighting. Few returned home.

In years to come, whenever someone sympathized or rejoiced with him, his only response was, "Let us see what happens. You never can tell."

BOYS AND BLUEBERRIES

I was a waterfront counselor unable to work because the waterfront had been destroyed by a hurricane. I was restless. The campers were restless. Five nine-year-old boys were causing so much trouble the director asked if I could help. "They need an adventure," I told him.

"You're right," he agreed. "Why don't you take them out of camp and keep them busy for a couple of days." He took my silence as a yes. It was blueberry season. I remembered how my mother and I had picked buckets of wild blueberries and made pancakes, jam, cakes, and muffins. Maybe I could do some of this with the boys.

When the director told them they were going on a two-day camping trip with me, but that if they were having a good time, they could stay out for three days, Max told the director, "Camping with a woman won't be any fun."

I rolled my eyes. "How many women have you camped with?" I asked. Silence. "Maybe you'd rather stay in camp?" Silence.

The director was so anxious to get the boys out of camp, he agreed to whatever I asked for. Rucksacks, canteens, and sleeping bags were found. It was warm. We'd sleep out in the open. I packed supplies and hung them in a bag from my rucksack. The boys would carry food, water, and camping gear. I had them practice carrying their packs and immediately they complained their packs were too heavy. I told them I had no interest in their whining—they could carry their packs or stay in camp. "You're no fun," muttered Alex.

"Neither are you," I snapped back. "Stay or go. Your choice." Why had I said I'd take them camping? I didn't expect gratitude, but I thought they'd be excited about leaving camp and sleeping out.

As soon as we left camp, the boys began arguing about who was carrying the most weight. Soon they'd taken off their packs and were fighting, cursing, and hurling insults, just as they had in camp. Furious, I yelled, "You're a bunch of spoiled brats. If you want to come, put on your packs and join me. If you don't, go back to camp. And, if you think your backpacks are too heavy, you're welcome to carry mine." Without looking to see what they'd do, I started walking. Fast.

I could hear footsteps behind me, but I was still so mad I just kept going, only stopping when I heard one of them yell, "Nancy, stop! Jeff fell!" The blood made it look worse than it was, but I treated it with care.

"How far do we have to go?" whined Jeff.

"About three miles," I said, not feeling sympathetic.

"How long will it take?" he asked, looking less cocky than when we started.

"Depends on how fast we walk, how many pit stops you need. Maybe we should go back and forget about camping," I said, wishing I hadn't agreed to take them camping.

Kenny picked up his backpack. "I vote to keep going. Anything's better than camp." The other four reluctantly nodded. I handed out small chocolate bars to cheer them up.

We arrived at the campsite, the boys tired and sweaty, more than ready to put their packs down. I gave everyone a job while I prepared the firepit. When we finished, I told the boys to follow me. Picking up on my excitement, they walked through brambles, tripped over rocks, and pushed their way through high grass without complaint. Not one of them asked why we were no longer on a path.

"Here we are," I announced. Gasping with pleasure, they could not believe their eyes. Bushes and bushes of ripe blueberries. Even eating as much as we could, we quickly filled the bucket.

"What are we going to do with all the berries?" asked Dan, his tongue and lips bright blue.

"You'll see," I teased.

Back at camp, I put the blueberries, a bit of water, and sugar into a metal pot and set it over the fire. While the boys took turns stirring, I mixed up a thick batter and put some around sticks the boys had cut and stripped of bark. When the blueberries had cooked and thickened, I took the bowl off the fire so the boys could bake their batter until it was nicely browned. I helped them slide it off their sticks onto tin plates and spooned blueberry jam over it. The boys ate with gusto, asking for more.

"I guess it's not so bad camping with a woman," I said.

"Who knew," quipped Max.

How open are you to new experiences?

❧ ❧ ❧

SOFTBALL

I was 13, ignored by the girls in my bunk, unable to play sports with the boys who wanted nothing to do with me. Lonely and frustrated, I walked to the camp bulletin board and wrote: "This camp is chauvinistic. It doesn't allow girls to play softball with the boys." I didn't sign my name. A few hours later, two counselors who'd seen me writing found me in the dining room. The male counselor said, "You're right. Girls should be able to play with the boys."

The female counselor said, "We've talked with the boys and told them it's wrong to exclude girls." I instantly regretted what I'd written, even if it was true. With a sinking heart, knowing how much the boys didn't want me to play with them, I agreed to join them at afternoon practice.

I was a pretty good ballplayer, as good as most of the boys, but not as good as the best. And it was hard for me to play well when I wasn't wanted. The boys definitely did not want a girl on their team.

The two counselors walked me down to the field. They reminded the boys I had every right to play with them. There was no welcoming committee. They glared at me, making negative comments. If the counselors heard, they didn't show it. Knowing the counselors were watching, the captain of the team asked what position I wanted to play. I told him I was a pretty good pitcher. Not bothering to hide his displeasure, he told the boy on the mound to go sit on the bench. As the boy glowered at me, the captain motioned for me to take his place. I didn't have a glove. More displeasure. The male counselor found a glove that more or less fit me. Nothing to be done but to throw the ball.

I struck the first two batters out despite their jeers and snide remarks. I was beginning to relax a little when the next batter hit a hard line drive straight to me, and I fumbled the ball. He made it to third base. The jeers got louder. The comments nastier. I told myself I could do this, I could keep going, but the increased jeering didn't improve my playing ability. The next player hit an easy popup that I barely caught. As I left the field, the second and third basemen let me know I was unwanted. I managed to last the rest of the game, but their hostility was too much. I quit. No one tried to convince me to keep playing. I was a failure.

Six years later, I was a recreational therapist in a large mental hospital where the men had a softball team. I was told the women didn't want one, but when I asked some of my patients if they'd like to form a softball team and play women in other mental hospitals, as the men did, everyone said yes. I remembered my failure at thirteen. This felt like a chance to redeem myself. If the men could have a team, so could the women. It was difficult to persuade the director to let me form a women's team. He kept insisting they didn't want one and didn't need one; they were women. "What's that got to do with it? They want to play."

We were at a standstill when his secretary told him his next appointment was waiting. He shook his head and said, "If you want to start a women's softball team you can try. I doubt you'll find women who are interested." He showed me the door.

Almost every woman wanted to play. Everyone practiced with great excitement. The head attendant chose who could play the women's team at another hospital. I was warned: the director had said the team had to win in order to continue playing. This was bad enough, but I was shocked to learn the attendants who accompanied the men's team were good ballplayers and always stepped in when the men were losing. I told myself I would never do that.

And yet . . . It was our first game. The women were enjoying themselves, but at the top of the ninth inning, my women were losing 3-1. I asked the pitcher if she was tired. As a patient, what she heard was that I wanted her to leave so I could take over. She gave me her glove. I struck out all their players. In the bottom of the ninth, with two players on base, I hit a home run. We won 4-3.

The women were furious. They'd wanted to win or lose on their own. They didn't care if losing meant they couldn't play other teams. They cared about autonomy. For them, as for me years ago, what mattered was having the right to play.

Have you faced obstacles doing what you wanted to do? What was the outcome?

INTERVIEW

In 1964, my husband took a new job, which meant moving from Rhode Island to Delaware. At the time I was teaching dance at Mary C. Wheeler, a private girls' high school, and subbing at Pembroke College. I hoped to find similar work in Delaware and applied for the position of dance instructor in the Physical Education Department at the University of Delaware. I was pleased to be granted an interview.

Arrangements were made. About a week before I was scheduled to leave, my son was diagnosed with mumps. Three days later, my husband was diagnosed with mumps. No way could I leave. I called the faculty liaison and explained the situation. He was polite but clear. "I'm sorry your family members are ill, but we do not postpone interviews. We will cancel the classes you were scheduled to teach. Good luck."

I tried to tell myself I might not have gotten the job. Getting sick was no one's fault. Still, I was angry and frustrated and worried. It had taken a lot of effort to find teaching positions in Providence. How would I find work in a city where I didn't know anyone?

We moved to Wilmington. Eventually I found piecemeal work teaching dance and movement classes at a YMCA and community centers, but none of it felt satisfying. I mourned the loss of the opportunity to teach at a university. In hopes of finding a way to make my work life more meaningful, I started a children's theatre, writing and directing plays, casting people who lived in the city and suburbs, white and Black, young and older. The plays were a success; we played to full houses, yet I felt something was missing.

I was credentialed to teach physical education and junior high school science, but the thought of doing either made my stomach hurt. In a fit of desperation, in the fall of 1966, I enrolled in a university course in theatre, hoping I could find the money to complete the degree. Everyone told me I'd never find a job with such a "useless" degree.

Catastrophe lurked everywhere. My husband and I divorced. With no child support, the money I earned from summer federal grants, to create theatre with street kids, and from teaching as many classes as I could, just about paid expenses. Then, out of the blue, the Theatre Department Chair asked if I would fill an unexpected opening to be a teaching assistant for the spring semester. I agreed, but it wasn't enough to live on. As a thirty-year-old woman, I applied for a school loan and had to fight the loan officer who demanded a male sign the agreement. I refused and made such a fuss he eventually granted the loan just to get rid of me. This meant I had enough to live on at least through the summer. Barely.

Frustrated, depressed, and upset about having no money to finish the degree, I arranged to teach dance in a variety of places. Two days before the fall semester began, the Chair called. The student who'd had a teaching assistant position had left to teach in Vietnam—would I like to take her place.

In May of 1968, as a single mother, I received an MA in theatre from the University of Delaware. In September 1968 I became a part-time instructor at the University of Delaware. In February 1969 I was hired to teach full time. As I began the semester, the dance program I so wanted to teach in was cancelled.

You never can tell.

Has there been a moment in your life that turned out differently from what you'd hoped? What was the outcome?

18

WORLD TALE

Curious Peculiarities

CHINA

Curious Peculiarities. What could they be? Each story, Playing Tennis and Taking a Walk, delineates a curious peculiarity.

• • •

An old woman went to visit her daughter who lived with her husband's family. Everyone was out except for her daughter and her daughter's mother-in-law. The mother was invited to stay for supper, and the three women had just begun to eat when a gust of wind blew out the lamp, leaving the room in darkness. The mother-in-law said, "Sit still. I will relight the lamp," but even as she said this, the daughter quickly took the lamp and left the room.

The mother, thinking the mother-in-law had gone, said, "Guests should have the best of the meal and be served first." She continued to talk about the poor service and food until her daughter appeared with the light. Horrified to realize she'd been talking to the mother-in-law, the mother said, "I have a curious peculiarity that has affected me my whole life. If a light goes out, suddenly my mind wanders, and I talk without making sense until the light reappears."

"Ah," responded the mother-in-law. "I totally understand. I too have a curious peculiarity. Whenever the light goes out, I become deaf and only recover my hearing when the light returns."

ஃ ஃ ஃ

PLAYING TENNIS

As I was leaving to play tennis, I noticed my doubles partner had left a message on voice mail saying she couldn't play and had gotten a sub, not saying who the sub was, which was odd. Still, I headed to the court, looking forward to playing.

Fortunately for me I saw her before she saw me. I stopped. Trying to control my anger. My partner knew better than to pair me with a woman who had done her best to isolate me from other players, telling lies about me, accusing me of cheating, criticizing me in front of others. I thought about leaving, but this wouldn't be fair to the other two with whom I played regularly.

When the woman saw me, she smirked. I took a deep breath and made a quick decision. I'd kill her with kindness. I returned her nasty look with a fake smile, deeply satisfied by her puzzled expression. When I hit a ball out, she scolded me for not running fast enough. Normally I might've responded with a dirty look or a defense. Not this time. I said, "You're right. I'll start sooner next time." Another bewildered look.

When she hit a ball out, I said, "Good try." When she hit a hard line drive, I said, "Well done!" No matter what she did or how she played, I reacted with feigned caring and support, enjoying her confusion.

I could see her staring at me as we changed sides. Hostility had given way to incomprehension. I grinned when she couldn't see me. When one of the other two women tried to console me about having to play with her, I told them it was fine. In a weird way it was. She was a good tennis player and with every compliment she played better

Much to my astonishment, after I hit a hard ball to the far left of the opposite court that won us a game, she muttered, "Good shot!" I thanked her.

We ended up winning two of the three sets. As we were about to leave the court, I said, "Thanks for playing with us today. You're welcome to sub any time." She nodded, looking baffled.

When I got to my car I couldn't stop laughing. Who knew reacting to hostility with smarmy kindness could be so much fun.

Have you reacted in a way that contradicted how you felt? What did you do?

❧ ❧ ❧

TAKING A WALK

The mountains and city trails in Santa Fe were closed for almost two months due to fires, drought, and high wind. Since I need to hike regularly, all that was left was a four-to-five-mile walk around where I live. As roads go, it's not bad, winding up and down, with well-designed houses, lots of trees, shrubs, and flowers providing pleasant vistas. There are enough hills that I get somewhat of a workout, but it doesn't lift my spirit the way hiking in nature does. If I go after nine and before four, there's not much traffic—just a lot of parked contractors' trucks.

Since the road is free of rocks, stumps, roots, and drops, it's easy for me to space out as I walk, deep in thought, although if another walker says hello, I respond, and then can't remember what I was thinking about. It's as if I'm transported into a different space and time,

I recognize my "spacing out" is nothing new. I think it's a habit I developed as a coping mechanism during a childhood filled with abuse and violence. The problem is, I don't have control over when I space out. If my sensory system is overloaded, it's not uncommon for me to bump into someone or something. Overwhelmed by embarrassment, all I can do is apologize.

One day, I was walking, deep in thought, when I heard a man's voice yell, "Cuidado! Cuidado! Careful!" I looked up and found myself about two inches from a white truck where a man was standing in the bed, his arms out, ready to catch me before I bumped into the back of it.

Shaking his head, he said, "I was watching you walk. Right to my truck. I couldn't believe you didn't see it." I couldn't believe it either.

Shaken, I thanked him for watching out for me. We talked for a few minutes. He was obviously upset. Almost every sentence he spoke was punctuated with references to how I'd almost walked into his truck. "I couldn't believe you didn't see my truck. You just kept walking like a blind person. You coulda got hurt." He was right.

I was too embarrassed to tell him it wasn't the first time I came so close to walking into a parked truck or a person on a trail or a shopping cart. I also knew it wouldn't be the last time I'd space out, despite telling myself I need to pay attention. Thank goodness for kind people.

Have you ever spaced out and found yourself in a peculiar situation? What happened?

19

WORLD TALE

The Artist

INDIA

What does it take for an artist to make art? The stories, Weaving My Way and Page 91, reveal ways to create personally meaningful work.

• • •

THERE WAS ONCE AN emperor who was so in love with the peacocks he saw roaming around his palace—their beautiful colors and graceful shape—he asked the court artist to paint him a picture of one. For more than a year his request was not fulfilled. One day, in a rage, the emperor stormed into the studio demanding the painting.

Frightened by the emperor's anger, yet calm, the artist slowly brought out paper, paint, and brush. In a few minutes, a perfect picture of a peacock emerged.

Now the emperor was purple with outrage. "If you can paint a perfect picture of a peacock in five minutes, why did you keep me waiting for over a year?"

"Come with me." The emperor followed the artist to the storage room. Paper was piled from the floor to the ceiling. On every sheet was a painting of a peacock.

"Your Majesty," explained the artist, "it's taken me more than one year to learn how to paint such a painting in five minutes."

⁂

WEAVING MY WAY

When, in 1968, a man in my neighborhood "sold" me a tapestry loom for a can of cookies, a loaf of bread, and a future weaving, I had no idea how this would change my life.

Despite dealing with a difficult child, intense work as a teacher, playwright, director, and writer, and later, another challenging marriage and divorce, I now had something of my own to satisfy my need to create, which wasn't subject to people's opinions, schedules, requirements, or wants. I wove with my fingers and a fork, quietly, simply, without a plan.

In March of 2022, the Afghani father of the man who owns the rug cleaning company I use, who knows everything there is to know about rugs from the Middle East, saw the fork near my loom and asked what it was for. "I use it as a beater," I told him. (A beater is used to tamp down the yarn as its woven.)

"A fork?" He didn't try to hide his incredulity.

"Well, I have three beaters, but none of them work as well as my fork." I showed them to him. He shook his head in disgust.

"I'll bring you a beater," he offered, looking with disdain at my fork. I thanked him, not believing he would follow through given the amount of time between his picking up and returning my rugs.

Months later, after he brought my newly cleaned and repaired rugs into the house, carefully placing them on the floor, he went to his van and returned with something in his hand. With sparkling eyes, he said, "Here's your beater."

I was stunned. The beater was handmade, perfectly balanced, beautifully crafted. I thanked him profusely, amazed he would give me such a special gift. "Show me how you plan to use it," he grinned.

I sat on my stool and wove for a few minutes, with him watching, hoping he approved, in spite of my early decision not to care what anyone thought. I did care what he thought, not only because he was an expert in weaving, but because he cared enough to give me a priceless tool.

He didn't say anything as I wove, but when I stopped and looked up at him, he was smiling. "Good," he said. "Very good."

I thanked him again and again until he put up his hand to stop my words. "It's enough thanking. I'm pleased you're so happy with it. I'm happy you're finally using a proper heater."

After weaving for a while, I was amazed to learn, after fifty-four years of weaving with a fork, how much easier and more efficient it is to weave with the right tool.

What do you make that's important to you? Do your tools matter?

❧ ❧ ❧

PAGE 91

I moved to Santa Fe in 2001 with many unfinished writing projects, including 90 pages of a book, *Dancing With Wonder*. Since I was no longer teaching, no longer having to meet with students, no longer dealing with committees, I had all the time I needed to finish writing about my work with stories in the US and abroad.

I wrote. Rewrote. Good thing I was writing on a computer, so at least I wasn't wasting paper. Despite countless hours of writing, I hated what I wrote and could not get to an acceptable page 91. Desperate, I even took a nonfiction workshop, something I'd never done. None of the instruction proved useful.

I called my friend Claudia, a poet and storytelling colleague, told her what was happening and asked for a suggestion. She was quick to respond. "You wrote the first 90 pages when you were a professor, even though you used stories in your books and essays. Now you're no longer a professor; you're a storyteller. Throw out the 90 pages and start over—as a storyteller."

Dumbfounded, I asked, "How do I start?"

She sighed. "With the women of Kazakhstan, of course." I threw out the 90 pages, feeling weirdly relieved, and began anew, with the experience of working with the Kazakh women.

A few years before, I'd led an all-day session with women from Kazakhstan, using two translators from the US State Department. The women, who didn't know each other, were invited to the US by the American Friends Service Committee because they had developed creative solutions to combat violence in their country.

I began with a story from India, about how Ant, the smallest creature, outwits Elephant, the largest creature, using nonviolent means to get him to treat others well. The story resonated with the group, but one woman demanded to know, "What good are stories when your husband is beating you? For no reason. Because he can."

I gasped. "No good. The beatings have to stop. But, afterward, telling your story might help in healing the trauma."

"Okay," snarled the woman, "I tell you my story." As she talked, the women nodded, clearly relating to her experience. After she finished, she challenged me: "I tell you my story. So what?"

Hoping I'd made a wise decision, I handed out small squares of paper and asked the women to paint a small image of healing and give it to her with a blessing. When they finished, one by one, they offered her their images and blessings. I had to have my blessing translated, spoken out loud, which worried me. What if I said the wrong thing? Thankfully, she nodded thoughtfully as my words were translated. For the rest of the day, we explored the power of stories to create community, support healing, and deal with difficult circumstances.

Later, after dinner at my house, one of the translators asked her how she was feeling, having told her story. "At first," she said, "I was furious, but I tell my story. Then I think, what good is telling? What good are pictures and blessings?" She paused, smiling. "But then, I begin to feel better."

"How are you feeling now?" asked the translator.

"Is still feeling better," she said.

Remembering the session helped to unlock whatever had been locked inside me. Words flowed. Stories poured out. Page 91 came and went as I finished the book. *Dancing With Wonder: Self-Discovery Through Stories* was published in 2005.

Seventeen Years Later

In 2022, a Frenchwoman working with Ukrainian refugee children in Poland emailed to ask if I could send her a copy of *Dancing With Wonder.* She thought it would be useful in her work. I sent her a PDF, along with suggestions as to how she might use storymaking with young people who have experienced multiple horrors and are now exiles in a country whose language they do not speak.

The words that were unlocked by a friend's advice to work with a group of women from Kazakhstan, are now helping young refugees tell their stories, deal with their trauma, and, I hope, begin to heal.

Have you experienced a time when something seemed impossible? What was that like?

20

WORLD TALE

Why the Akha Wear Black Dresses

AKHA/THAILAND

A young woman and man solve a problem of difference. Hate, Dismissed, and Disbelief are stories that explore challenging relationships.

• • •

A LONG TIME AGO, an Akha man met a beautiful, kind, and caring woman. He wanted her to be his wife. However, she was not Akha, and he knew her parents would not approve. Still, he loved her very much and asked, "Will you be my wife?"

The woman loved the man and said, "Yes. But what shall we do about my parents? They will never agree to this marriage."

The man said, "Let us try. We can marry in secret and perhaps they will not come to our wedding."

But the parents did come, they saw their daughter in her brightly colored clothing, and took her home.

Still, the woman and man were determined to be wed. They sat and thought. The woman looked at the man and said, "I have an idea. In my village, the women wear clothes of many colors. You must ask the women in your village to wear black to our wedding. I will wear black. If my parents come, they will not know who I am."

Once again, the parents came to the village to take their daughter home, but they could not find her. There was no woman wearing brightly colored clothes. All the women looked alike in their black clothing.

The couple were happily married.

To this day, all Akha women wear black, just to be safe.

❧ ❧ ❧

HATE

When I was in fifth grade, every Wednesday at two in the afternoon, Catholic kids were dismissed to attend catechism at the local Catholic Church. This meant Carol and I were left. Two girls. Two Jews. According to our teacher, Carol was the smartest kid in the class. I was the second smartest. The way the teacher made this pronouncement, for no discernible reason, made me cringe. I wasn't even sure it was true—about me. Every Wednesday she let us know she could have left school early had it not been for us. The hour passed painfully slowly, with the teacher's disapproval patently obvious.

There was always tension between the kids who left to go to catechism and the two of us who didn't. The teacher's assertion about how smart we were didn't help. When I overheard some of the Catholic kids talking about us, using a word I didn't know, I asked my father what it meant. He said it was derogatory; those who used it hated Jews. I knew the kids in my class didn't like me, but it never occurred to me it was because I was Jewish.

One afternoon, as they were getting ready to leave, I asked one of the girls, "Why do you hate Jews?"

She didn't hesitate. "Because you killed Christ."

"But Jesus was a Jew. Why would Jews kill him because he was a Jew?"

She responded with absolute certainty. "Jesus wasn't a Jew, he was a Christian, and besides, it says in my catechism Jews killed Christ."

I couldn't believe it, so she showed me the passage where it said the Jews killed Christ. She smiled triumphantly, as if the matter was settled, and left.

My father said Jesus didn't become a Christian until hundreds of years after his death, that he was born, lived, and died a Jew. My mother said the kids in my class were taught to hate Jews, and there was nothing I could do about it.

A few months later, when our teacher talked about decorating the class for Christmas, I asked if we could put up Chanukah decorations. "No," she said, "there are only two of you."

"What's that?" asked one of my classmates, curious in spite of the teacher. I told him about the fight for freedom, the miracle of the oil, that we celebrated by lighting a menorah and eating latkes. It was the first time I'd talked about anything to do with Judaism. Since they were listening, I emphasized the delicious food we ate to celebrate the holiday.

That night I told my parents how I'd talked about Chanukah, and my mother said, "We should invite your class to come and eat latkes."

"There's no room for everyone in the kitchen," I said, horrified by the idea. But my mother was intrigued. The next day she sent my teacher a note inviting the class to come eat latkes.

The latke party was scheduled to start around five o'clock. I hoped no one would come. I was afraid no one would come. About half the class came, not bothered by the need to squeeze around the kitchen table. They loved the food, especially the latkes and homemade applesauce. They listened to the story again as I lit the menorah. At the end, I gave everyone a tiny bag of Chanukah gelt (money), chocolate coins wrapped in gold foil. As they left, some of them even said they'd had a good time.

The next day in class, one of the girls who hadn't come said she'd heard how everyone who came to the party enjoyed it. She was sorry she couldn't convince her parents to let her attend. "They should have let me go. Some Jews are okay."

Have you faced discrimination? How did you react?

❧ ❧ ❧

DISMISSED

In 1971, I was in Denmark with my Danish husband, visiting his family and friends. I didn't know much about his parents since he never talked about them. One of his sisters told me their mother was the Protestant daughter of a postmaster, with only a grade-school education. Their father was from a rich Jewish family, with a PhD from a fine university. Their mother spoke Danish, French, and German, but no English. Their father spoke Danish, French, German, and English. When my husband and I were together with his parents, only English was spoken, leaving his mother out of the conversation. I tried, with no success, to get the two men to speak Danish and then translate, but they ignored me.

When his mother and I were alone, we had a good time. Despite her initial shock at my offering to help with meal preparation, we began communicating in sign language and mime, coupled with my pidgin French. We didn't always understand each other, but we laughed a lot, especially at my awkwardness filling the balls of dough with apples, which she called aebleskiver and cooked in a special pan.

I enjoyed being with her. She seemed happy to have whatever relationship we could make given our lack of a common language, living oceans apart. As soon as my husband or father-in-law entered the room, her laughter stopped. Her demeanor changed to that of a servant, responding to requests with a subservience that hurt my heart. At dinner, she didn't sit or eat until everyone else had started.

When we visited his wealthy, sophisticated paternal aunts and uncles, everyone spoke perfect English. They ridiculed my mother-in-law, with no complaint from my husband or hers. When I spoke up in her defense, they shook their heads and changed the subject. Later, when I talked with my husband about how bad I felt for his mother, he shrugged and said, "She's used to it."

We spent time with some of my husband's friends, all of whom spoke good English, but my husband answered them in Danish, and pretty soon everyone was speaking Danish. I watched them talk and laugh as if I were not in the room. I imagined this was how his mother felt.

In the days that were left of our visit, I decided to do what I could to include my mother-in-law in conversations, or at least make it obvious I wanted to hear what she had to say. I studied the Danish/English phrasebook I'd brought with me, knowing my attempts to use it in the past had not been well-received by my husband. "You don't need to bring the book," he'd told me. "I'll translate for you." He didn't.

During dinner the next evening, using the book, I said, in Danish, "The food is delicious." Everyone, including my mother-in-law, burst into laughter. I understood. Danish is difficult to pronounce correctly, but after the laughter subsided, my father-in-law took a bit of time to help correct my pronunciation. Even this evoked laughter, but at least the conversation didn't leave my mother-in-law out. When I said, "Thank you for dinner," in Danish, she responded in Danish. I figured out, sort of, how to say, "You're a good cook, and thank you for dinner," which gave her another opportunity to respond.

For the rest of the visit, I carried my Danish/English phrasebook wherever I went. When it was time for the visit to end, my mother-in-law took my phrasebook and found the words she wanted to say, in English. "Thank you for the visit. I enjoyed meeting you." I took back the book and repeated her words in Danish. Just before we left for the airport, she hugged me, saying once again, "Thank you for coming," in English. I responded in Danish: "Thank you for a wonderful visit." We didn't have words in common, but we found a way to create a warm and caring relationship despite all that we didn't share.

Have you seen someone being treated badly? If so, how did you respond?

❧ ❧ ❧

DISBELIEF

In 2001, shortly after I moved into my house in Santa Fe, I called an electrician to come and figure out why so many lights didn't work. When I was a theatre technician running the light board, we had a rule: if one light is out, replace the bulb. If two lights are out, check the system. When the electrician came, he found a lot of frayed and broken wires as well as many burned-out bulbs needing replacement. When he was ready to leave, he said, "Everything's working. Good you called."

Some weeks later, I was putting a not completely dry pan away in a bottom kitchen cabinet when suddenly there was a burst of flames. Too shocked to think, I put out the fire with my hands. After taking care of the burns, I called the electrician who'd checked all the wires and outlets when I first moved in.

When I told him what had happened, he reacted as if I were hallucinating. "Have a drink. Take a nap. You'll feel better."

"No! You need to come. Now! I don't know what caused the fire."

"Calm down. It's Saturday afternoon. My son and I are drinking beer and watching a ball game on TV. I'll come Monday."

"No," I said, "you have to come now."

I could hear him muttering something about a crazy woman to his son. I didn't care how weird he thought I was as long as he came to check out what caused the fire. "Okay," he said, "but it will cost three times the normal price. Maybe four times." His tone was patronizing. I could tell he didn't believe me.

"I don't care what it costs; you need to come now." After a few more rounds of his telling me to calm down and me telling him he had to come right away, he finally, reluctantly, agreed.

When he and his son arrived, he said patronizingly, "Show me where the *fire* was." I ignored his disbelief and pointed to the bottom cabinet. When he saw the charred wood, his attitude changed. He got down on his knees, looking at the area with a flashlight. When he finally spoke, his tone of voice was serious—no joking, no telling me to calm down. "Okay, tell me what happened—from the beginning. I want to know exactly what you did."

"I washed a pan and sort of dried it, then I put it in the cabinet. Suddenly there was a burst of flame."

He shook his head and turned to his son, an apprentice electrician. "Take a good look at this. You'll probably never see anything like it."

No longer questioning my sanity, he told me to kneel down beside him. He pointed his flashlight on an electric outlet. "What you have is a live feed. If you hadn't acted so quickly the whole kitchen would have been in flames. Do you mind if I disconnect it?"

"I'd mind if you didn't," I said, relieved he'd found the problem and knew how to fix it. "What's a live feed?"

"It means that any contact, even a single drop of water, could ignite the charge because the electricity is flowing. Your house could have burned down if you hadn't been here to put the fire out."

I was stunned. Just the thought of how easily the fire broke out was scary.

"By the way," he said with a grin, "I do not recommend putting fires out with your hands." Then, more seriously, he told me, "You need to have home fire extinguishers, especially in the kitchen."

"I'll buy some tomorrow. Thank you so much for coming. I know you thought I was crazy."

"You're right. I absolutely thought this right up until I saw the charred area and the unprotected outlet." He shook his head. "Who leaves a live feed in a house?"

I got out my checkbook and asked how much to pay. "Just the regular charge," he said. "It's really good you insisted I come."

Have you been in a scary situation where you asked for help and weren't believed? If so, what happened?

21

WORLD TALE

Journey of the Stream

SUFI

What does it take to be open to new possibility? The stories, Special Treat and Me and the GRE, explore what might change a pattern or situation.

• • •

THERE WAS ONCE A stream that came to life in the highest of the high mountains, moving through dense forests, wide plains, and deep valleys until it came to a huge desert. No matter how hard the stream tried to pass through the desert, its waters always evaporated beneath the hot sands.

The stream was afraid it would disappear if it did not find a way to cross the desert yet was soon exhausted by its futile efforts. While the stream was resting, a voice whispered, "The wind crosses the desert and so can you."

"How?" asked the stream. "I am not like the wind. I cannot fly. I make my way along and under the ground."

"This is true," said the voice. "But the wind can help you cross if you are willing."

"How? I am water, not wind," protested the stream.

"Let the wind carry you over the desert. Allow yourself to be absorbed by the wind. If you continue as you have, you will disappear forever," answered the voice.

The stream did not like this idea. It had always been its own master. It did not want to change into something else, not even for a short time. How could the stream be sure it would find itself again, once it had traversed the desert, carried by the wind.

The stream did not believe the voice. It kept trying to cross the desert and continued to disappear. The voice whispered again, "Do not be afraid. You will once again become a stream if you let the wind carry you across the desert."

Too tired to keep fighting the sand, the stream, which was now just a trickle, sadly agreed to be absorbed by the wind. Gently the wind cradled the stream across the desert, onto the top of a very high mountain where, as raindrops, it fell softly onto the welcoming ground and transformed itself once again into a swiftly flowing stream.

SPECIAL TREAT

My father was a pharmacist who formulated his own cough medicines, syrups for various ailments, and creams for an assortment of skin conditions. Once a month he went to New York City's Chinatown to buy herbs, tinctures, and spices, using them to make the formulas. After he'd bought what he needed, he would go to a nearby restaurant for lunch. When he told me the menus were in Chinese and the waiters spoke no English, I asked, "How do you know what to order?"

"I don't," he said. "When I come in, they give me food."

"But how do they know who you are?"

"The man from the herb and spice shop wrote the restaurant owner a note."

"What did it say?"

My father shrugged. "I couldn't read the Chinese writing. I think it was something about me being a good customer who liked to eat good food."

It all sounded tremendously exciting to my ten-year-old self. A restaurant where you can't read the menu, and you can't ask the waiter to explain what something means, and you can't decide what you want to eat? Imagine! A restaurant where food is served with no choice or explanation?

"But when the waiter brings you food, how do you know what you're eating?"

"I don't," he admitted. I was totally intrigued. I wanted to go.

I begged him to take me with him. He refused. "I don't want you to embarrass me by not eating what they bring." For him, this was the end of the conversation. For me, it was the beginning. My urge to go with him was working overtime, and I wasn't about to accept no. After every month's visit, I would barrage him with questions: What did he eat? What did it taste like? What did he do if he didn't like what they served him? How did he know what to pay? What was it like to go to a restaurant where he was the only person who wasn't Chinese?

I knew when he'd gone because he'd come back with new spices, herbs, and tinctures for my mother to use in cooking and baking, but I didn't know when he was going, so I couldn't ask to go with him. Each month my desire grew.

Years before, when I'd gone with my parents to eat in a foreign restaurant and balked at eating something strange, my mother admonished me: "Nancy, don't you want to be cosmopolitan? Eat!" I didn't know what *cosmopolitan* was, but it sounded like something I should be. I ate. Although nothing I had said changed my father's mind, I remembered my mother's words. When I thought it might be close to the time for his monthly visit to Chinatown, I said, "Dad, don't you think you should let me go with you? Don't you want me to be cosmopolitan?"

He shook his head. "Nancy, you never give up, do you." I promised I'd eat whatever the waiter brought. I promised I'd be good, whatever that meant. I was ready to promise whatever I needed to promise. Finally, he agreed to take me the next time he went.

The shop where he bought the spices, herbs, and tinctures was a feast for the senses. Smells and shapes and colors—all labeled with lettering I couldn't read. My father and the owner used a lot of words I'd never heard, making decisions by pointing, smelling, and tasting. The owner gave me a bit of sugar cane, with a sparkle in his eye, which I guessed meant it was a treat. It smelled terrible and tasted worse, but I remembered my promises and pretended to love it. I began to wonder what I'd let myself in for if this was a taste of what was to come. As soon as we were outside, while my father talked to the shop owner, I threw the sugar cane into a waste bin, hoping no one saw me.

We entered the restaurant, barely bigger than our kitchen at home. I hoped the food would taste as good as the delicious smells welcoming us. There were four tables, three with people crowded together, sitting on mismatched chairs. A waiter came with napkins and chopsticks and sat us at the last empty table. Within minutes he brought us plates of steaming food, none of which I recognized. My father looked sternly at me. I nodded. I had never seen or used chopsticks before, but I managed to copy what my father did. I noticed the other people put food into a bowl filled with rice and brought it up to their mouths, so I did the same. What a relief! So much easier than bringing food from my plate to my mouth using chopsticks wiggling out of my grip.

The food was hot, spicy, and mostly delicious, although I had to force myself to eat something gelatinous that threatened to come back up. I kept it down by drinking a continuously refilled cup of hot tea. When we finished, the waiter took our plates, nodding approvingly, then brought dessert, which I thought was a sweet bun. I bit into it and, by sheer dint of will, kept from spitting it out. Whatever was in it was sour and tasted awful, but this too I managed to finish. When the meal was over, the waiter brought the bill with the numerical amount my father had to pay. I guess numbers are universal. The waiter put his hand on my shoulder and asked, "Good?"

"Good," I responded. My father paid. The waiter came back with a stick of sugar cane, a big smile on his face as he gave it to me. I smiled the best smile I could muster and said, "Thank you." We left the restaurant, me trying to ditch the sugar cane without my father noticing. I felt like I'd been in a foreign country, yet I'd never left the city in which I was born.

At dinner, he told my mother how well I'd behaved. "Can I go next month?" He nodded. Thereafter, I was his lunch companion for the next few years. Surrounded by people who looked, dressed, and talked in ways I'd never seen or heard, and who ate foods I'd never seen or eaten, was a continuing adventure like no other I'd experienced. A time to accept what was new and strange without judgment.

Are you cosmopolitan? How do you know?

ME AND THE GRE

In the spring of 1966, when I decided to get an MA in theatre, one of the nonnegotiable requirements for admission was passing the GRE (Graduate Record Exam). I'd been out of school for years and dreaded having to take any exam, much less one determining my fitness for graduate school. I kept putting it off until there was one chance left to take it if I wanted to enroll for even a single course in the fall of 1966.

Although I usually wasn't good at talking about my feelings—sometimes I didn't even know how I felt—I had no hesitation when it came to complaining about the exam. The last time I'd taken a math class was in junior high school, decades ago. My only current connection to math was balancing my checkbook, and sometimes I had trouble doing that. In spite of my worries, resistance, and fears, I signed up for the exam to be held in early summer.

I moaned. I groaned. I whined. As the time to take the exam drew near, I was a one-note complainer. Why did the university require an exam? Why weren't my credentials enough? On and on I went, spewing my misery on any person unfortunate enough to be within hearing distance.

Some members of the community where I lived told me I needed to go out the night before the exam, have a drink, relax, and think about something else. Hah! This was as possible as not breathing. Besides, I don't drink much. No matter. Three people made the decision among themselves to take me out, despite my protesting that I needed to have a good night's sleep before the exam. They pointed out it was highly unlikely I'd sleep given my tension level. A drink would do me good.

The night before the exam, before they picked me up, I was so tense I couldn't stand myself. I was willing to do anything to ease my anxiety. We had cocktails before the meal, wine with dinner, and, they insisted, brandy afterward. They drove me home, laughing, telling me I was sure to be relaxed tomorrow. I set the alarm clock and passed out.

The exam was held in a local high school. On Saturday morning, the sunshine was too bright, the traffic noise too loud, too many people in the exam room. When I finally made myself take a seat, the proctor brought me the test, handed me two sharpened pencils, and walked to the front of the room. "Begin," he said.

I looked at the paper. The words were spinning. I forced myself to focus. I had to work to clear the fog from my brain, cursing myself for agreeing to the night out. The room was cool, but I was sweating and thirsty and hungry. I'd been unable to force myself to eat breakfast, and drank only a small cup of coffee before leaving my house. I looked at the math problems, which looked like scribbles in a foreign language. Feeling overwhelmed, I decided to do the language part of the test first. At least I sort of understood what I was reading. With more difficulty than I could have imagined, I finished the language arts part.

Dreading what was next, I looked at the math section. Nothing made sense. I tried to figure out some of the problems, but the answers I came up with didn't appear in the blanks to be filled out. Hoping I'd guess the right answer, I blacked in a blank after each problem, but soon gave up even trying and filled in the remaining blank circles arbitrarily. I handed in my exam, certain I'd failed. Graduate school was not a possibility. I would have to keep teaching dance and movement, scraping together enough work to pay my bills and support my son.

When the Chair of the Theatre Department called to tell me he had the exam results, he was laughing, which made me cross. Why would he laugh at my failure? I was about to tell him how much I wanted to get a degree in theatre and ask was there any way he could help me bypass the exam, when he said, "Nancy, you got 100 percent."

"What? How . . .?"

He interrupted, still laughing. "You scored 93 percent on the language part, which is great, and 7 percent on the math. Imagine, only 7 percent of the people taking the exam knew less than you, but this doesn't matter. Your total score means you passed the GRE with one point to spare. Welcome to graduate school."

What do you do to prepare for a stressful experience?

22

WORLD TALE

The Dreamer and the Dream

EASTERN EUROPEAN

A man travels a far distance only to make an important discovery. In the stories, An Impossible Dream, Magic Circle Theatre, and The Stories Project, dreams become real in unexpected ways.

• • •

THERE WAS ONCE A man who lived in a small village far from the nearest big city. He and his wife worked hard, but they often went to bed hungry in order to feed their children. One night, he woke his wife and said, "I have had the most marvelous dream. I want to tell you what it was, so I won't forget it."

His wife said, "I have never known you to have such a dream. Tell me. I am listening."

"I dreamt I went to the city and walked to a bridge spanning a wide river. Next to the bridge, guarded by a soldier, was a little hill and at the bottom of the hill, buried deep, was a bag of gold."

Neither he nor his wife knew what to make of the dream, but after he dreamed it for a third time, they decided he should go to the city. Maybe there was gold buried beside the bridge. The couple saved and scrimped until the man had food and a bit of money to walk the long distance to the city.

When he arrived, tired and dirty, he saw the soldier guarding the bridge. It was all as he had seen in his dream. As he approached the side of the bridge, the soldier came up to him and said, "I have to tell someone about my amazing dream." When the man nodded, the soldier began: "I dreamt I walked a far distance to a small village where there is a large tree shading a small house. Tangled in the roots is a bag of gold." The more the soldier described the village, the more astounded the man was. It seemed the soldier was describing his village, the tree beside his little house. The soldier sighed. "If only I could get leave, I'd go to the village. I'd dig up the gold, and no one but me would know."

The soldier seemed so sure the gold was in the small village, near the house, sounding exactly like where the man lived, the man, who was afraid of the soldier, decided to leave.

When he arrived home, he told his wife about the soldier's dream. Together, toward dusk, when no could see them, the couple dug carefully around the tree's roots. And there, before their incredulous eyes, was the bag of gold.

❧ ❧ ❧

AN IMPOSSIBLE DREAM

In 1955, I was a junior in college studying to be a physical education and dance teacher. The dance part was fine, but I intensely disliked team sports. The thought of teaching them was depressing, although I chose the college and major precisely so I could support myself after graduation. When I heard a psychologist was doing occupational testing, free to students, I signed up. Many of the questions made no sense to me in terms of possible occupation. For example: Did I prefer to be with large groups or small? Actually, I preferred to be in no groups, but there was no place to say this.

When I met with the psychologist two weeks later, she looked at me, puzzled. "Your results make no sense. You like being alone, yet you're good with groups. You're studying physical education, yet you want to work with all the arts—visual, dance, theatre, music—and you don't like to perform. I can't think of a job where you could use all the arts. The best you could do would be a teacher specializing in one."

What she said echoed my mother's judgement. "Nancy, you're a jack of all trades and a master of none."

I didn't give up on the dream as much as I stopped thinking about it. I was too busy being a mother and a wife, married and divorced, twice. In 1984, I began teaching in the University of Delaware's Honors Program, creating courses with titles such as: Creating Theatre from Myth; The Text, the Self, the World; To Walk in Someone's Shoes . . . One day, a student said, "I love your courses. It's wonderful to be able to use all the arts in class and to feel free to choose whatever medium seems right to me rather than having to use just one, like I have to do in every other class I take."

"Huh!" I was dumbfounded. He was right. Why hadn't this occurred to me? My students sculpted, painted, wrote, moved, created music and drama, and role-played as a way to understand characters so different from themselves—all in the service of exploring whatever book we were reading. In the process they were learning a lot about who they were—their ideas, feelings, assumptions, and biases.

After the student spoke, others joined in, expressing their pleasure, and how satisfying it was to explore world literature using all the arts. Their comments reminded me of the psychologist's conclusion—what I wanted to do was impossible. How wrong she was.

Yet it didn't happen consciously. In the process of trying to use all my interests and provide a rich learning environment for my students, I ended up making my dream come true.

Have you had a dream as a young person, then, many years later, found, without realizing it, you'd made your dream come true?

❧ ❧ ❧

MAGIC CIRCLE THEATER:

In 1964, my then-husband, son, and I moved to Delaware from Rhode Island where we had both been involved in creating theatre for children. The plays were well-done, but left me emotionally unsatisfied. I wanted to create a theatre for children where kids as well as adults participated, where actors with varied points of view helped create emotionally and psychologically empowering theatre. I dreamed of making theatre with people from the city and suburbs, interracial, young and old, where what I wrote developed from the actors' interests, bringing who they were into the creation and performance of my plays.

While looking for teaching jobs, I volunteered at Peoples' Settlement, an organization in inner-city Wilmington, serving a mostly Black community, teaching dance and movement, invigorated by the children's enthusiasm.

One day I asked the girls in my dance class if they'd been to the theatre. Some shook their heads; others didn't know what theatre was. I decided to bring theatre to them.

I talked with the director of the settlement house and received his permission to write a play with characters formed around whoever showed up for the audition. His only condition was that I use some local people. At 6:45, the night of the audition that began at 6:00, the room was empty except for my husband and me. I was upset, but told myself I'd done what I could. I was packing up when people started coming in. Pretty soon I was answering questions about the play, casting, rehearsals, and performance dates—almost none of which I'd thought about. I told them I would make a scenario, and we would build the play together; they would be part of the playmaking. I asked how many were interested. All hands went up. I told them they were all welcome to participate.

One man, who looked as if bending any joint was painful, told me he loved theatre and felt bad he couldn't be in the play. "Why not?" I asked.

"I'm like a stick. How can I be an actor?"

"I'll write a part for a man who moves in his own way. You have a lovely voice. You'll do fine." He was incredulous. I kept telling him he could be in the play. He kept thanking me. I think he would have thanked me all night had the janitor not told us it was time to leave.

I took note of who had come, what they looked like, and how I might create a drama to fit their capabilities. I titled the scenario Showdown at the Hoedown, a sort of western theme, organized rehearsal times around their schedules and, with their input, set the performance dates. My dream of having an interracial, mixed ages, urban and suburban cast was now a work in progress.

Early on I decided I wanted to have live music but didn't know how to make this happen. At each practice I invited local kids to watch rehearsals to give me feedback as to what they thought. One day, a boy came with a flute. I asked if he'd like to play when we needed music. He said he didn't want to do it alone but had friends who played—could he invite them? I was thrilled.

One afternoon, when the boys (all Black, between eight and twelve years old) and I were working on a theme for the play, there was a knock on the door of the house where we were practicing. I opened the door and my heart sank. There stood a very large white policeman asking to come in. I couldn't think of what I'd done wrong, yet I was a white woman in a room with a group of Black boys—not a common occurrence in this neighborhood. Were we making too much noise? Had I broken a law I didn't know about? "Can I help you, sir?" I asked, my voice trembling.

"I heard music and thought I'd check it out," he said, walking into the room, filling the space with his uniformed presence.

The boys were unfazed. I explained about the play and the band's contribution. Joshua, the boy who acted as leader said, "This is the theme we're working on. It's improvisation, you know." They played for a couple of minutes, then stopped.

The policeman was visibly impressed. "You guys sound great. Seems like it's gonna be a good show. I'll bring my kids and wife to see it."

After he left, the boys looked at me, grinning. Joshua was laughing as he pointed his finger at me. "You were scared. I could tell; you were really scared." They thought it was funny I'd been so tense. The rehearsal continued for another hour.

Word got around. People offered to help. We made tickets out of donated ice-cream-cup covers. Twenty-five cents for adults, ten cents for kids. The afternoon of the first performance, no one in the audience laughed. I quickly realized they didn't know it was okay and rushed upstairs to get an administrator with a booming laugh to attend. Once kids heard him laugh, they joined in.

The performance was a big success, but afterward, the audience wouldn't leave. Joshua said, "I know what to do. Don't worry." The musicians, like the pied piper, began playing as they walked up the stairs, the audience following them, giving us time to set up for the second performance.

Half an hour later, the second performance began, with many from the first audience coming again. So many people wanted to attend—we had to stay within the limit set by the fire department—we added performances, promising that everyone who wanted to attend would have the chance. At the end of the evening, cast members, helpers, settlement staff, and I enjoyed a potluck dinner arranged by women in the community. With tears in my eyes, I told them how grateful I was they'd made my theatre dream come true.

What do you dream of doing?

THE STORIES PROJECT

I saw him from across the busy street—a young boy crying—no adult in sight. I walked over to him and asked what was wrong. "I'm tired of being told I'm stupid."

"Who says you're stupid?"

"Everyone. I'm eight years old and can't read. I'm stupid. "

"Not being able to read doesn't make you stupid; it means you need special help."

"Lots of people try to teach me but nothin' works. I'm just stupid."

As we were talking, a woman came up to him. "Teddy, I've been looking all over for you. Why did you run away?" He didn't answer, moving closer to me. I guessed she was his mother. If she asked who I was, what would I say? A woman who saw her son crying and tried to comfort him?

That was many years ago, but I never forgot him. While I was working with children in other countries teaching English as a foreign language, using stories in different ways to help children speak and read, I decided to devise a program to help children attending The College School, a school for children with learning differences housed on the University of Delaware's campus.

The University Honors Program has a service-learning component, which means students, in addition to class meetings, do some kind of service. I decided helping children learn to read was a worthy service-learning project. When I contacted the Director of the College School, she said they already had undergraduate tutors teaching reading. I told her my students wouldn't be tutors; they'd be *Storypartners*. She asked me to develop a program.

I devised "The Stories Project," a service-learning course pairing an undergraduate and a child in a partnership relationship. Over the course of ten sessions, each would both tell and write stories, beginning with my student telling a world tale to the child. The child would then create an image arising from the story and write a story the undergraduate would collect. At the end of the ten sessions, my students would write a story for their Storypartners, and each child would write a story for an unborn grandchild. My students would make a book from the images and stories. The books would be given to their Storypartners at an authors' celebration.

It took time to arrange—meetings with the director to get her and her staff's approval, setting up an undergraduate course, putting it in the course catalogue, working up a syllabus, hoping children would volunteer, hoping undergraduates would register for the course, which required class time, ten hours of working one on one with a child, plus time to collect the images and stories and make them into a book. A lot of pieces had to fall into place. And yet, it happened. Children volunteered. Undergraduates enrolled.

Each class period, students talked about the troubles and joys of working with the children, each with different learning problems. During one class period, a student complained about the murderous violence in the stories her Storypartner had written. What should she do? He had titled his book,

"People Killing Other People." The cover was a photograph of him shooting a toy gun. The males in the class pooh-poohed the violence, saying it was just "male stuff." Then a mass shooting occurred, shocking everyone, including the males in my class who began to rethink their positions. I suggested my student ask her Storypartner how he felt about what had happened and, depending on what he said, ask if he wanted to write a story about those feelings. I called the Director of the College School, told her what he'd done, and asked for her support in encouraging all the children in the school to reconsider the effects of violence on people.

My student returned to class after meeting with her Storypartner. "Ben was crying. He felt terrible. He said he wanted to write all new stories and make a new cover. There's not enough time for us to write ten new stories. What should I do?"

In the end, with her encouragement, he wrote some new stories and modified those he had written, changing the murderous violence to various kinds of disasters. His story for an Unborn Grandchild read: "*It's all right to be small because there are advantages like being flexible and not having old bones, plus it's easy to sneak around and hide.*" He told my student, his Storypartner, he'd been bullied a lot and didn't want his grandchild to feel bad if he was small.

Like the little boy who felt stupid because he couldn't read, Ben felt bad about himself because he was smaller than his classmates. When he told my student about the bullying, she asked the male students in class how she might respond. They gave her many suggestions, which she told Ben came from "big boys," in college. Knowing "big boys" cared about him helped Ben feel better about himself.

He titled his new book, "Ben's Book." The cover image was a white roundish shape on black background. Ben told my student, "It's a special kind of egg. It hatches good things and people."

My dream of helping children learn to read also enabled children to tell their stories. Not only did their reading and writing improve, but they also found ways to feel good about themselves.

Have you ever had an experience that spurred a dream? If so, what happened?

23

WORLD TALE

Location of Wisdom

AKHA/THAILAND

The community faces the loss of their history. In the stories, Poem Power and Hailstorm, solutions to problems depend upon the wisdom of more than one person.

• • •

In former times, the Akha had letters that contained all the wisdom of the tribe, but one year, they were swallowed by the water buffalo. The Akha moved every year and when it came time to move, the water buffalo's skin was too big and too heavy for the people to move it. They were perplexed. Although they did not want to leave their letters and wisdom, they could not find a way to move the weighty skin.

They went to the Headman. He thought about the problem, then spoke. "If we cannot move the water buffalo's skin, we must eat the water buffalo's skin. This way, we will keep the letters and our wisdom inside us, forever."

And so, the water buffalo's skin was cut up into the number of people in the group. Each person swallowed a piece. Thus was wisdom kept within the tribe forever.

POEM POWER

The principal's normally calm voice on the phone was unusually distressed. "When I took this position, I was warned about the fourth-grade teacher. She disciplines the class through fear. In the past, parents put up with her, but now a vocal group of parents want her fired or fixed—their words, not mine. I can't fire her because she has tenure; yelling at students is not cause to terminate a contract. I've tried to suggest alternative ways to discipline her class but nothing's worked. I've run out of ideas. Can you come? If anyone can help her, it's you."

"Flattery will get you everywhere," I teased. We made arrangements for my visit, with me wondering what I could do, given all the principal's suggestions, none of which had worked.

The teacher had been told I was coming and agreed to my visit. When I opened the door, the noise and chaos stopped as if a movie director had yelled, "Cut!" I introduced myself. She left the room. How was I supposed to help her if she didn't stay in the room?

Before the kids could start up again, I grabbed a pile of paper and sat down on the floor. "Please come and join me," I said, "and bring something to write with." I tore each piece of paper in half.

Warily, not knowing what to expect, they slowly formed a circle around me. I asked them if they liked poetry. Some nodded, others shrugged. "Have any of you ever written a poem?" A few hands went up. At least they were listening.

"I'm going to give each of you half a sheet of paper. I'd like you to write one sentence describing how you feel about something. Okay?" They nodded, clearly uncertain. "Don't write your name on the paper—just the sentence."

I passed out the sheets of paper. "What should we write?" asked a pigtailed girl.

"Anything you like about how you feel," I said.

"You gonna grade it?" asked one of the boys, who'd been throwing a paper airplane when I entered the classroom.

"No. All I want is for you to write one sentence about how you feel."

"Why?"

"You'll see." I grinned. "You have a couple of minutes to write, so go to it."

After they finished, I collected the papers, mixed them up, then handed them out. "I'd like you to read the sentence on the paper you picked. Who wants to start?"

Still puzzled, each in turn read their sentence: "I hate school." "I feel bad when I have to read out loud." "I feel horrible." "I hate being yelled at." "I feel scared when someone yells at me . . . "

None of them mentioned the teacher. "Okay," I said. "Now we're going to put the sentences in whatever order you like, and we'll make a group poem."

"How can it be a poem?" many asked simultaneously.

"I'll show you. Who thinks their sentence is a good beginning?" One girl raised her hand. I took the paper from her and marked it #1.

Soon someone said, "I think this goes next." I numbered the papers as they handed them to me, so we'd know the order the class thought worked best. When I had all the papers, I read out what had been written.

"Gosh," said airplane boy, "it sounds like a poem."

"It is a poem, and you all wrote it. What should we title it?"

"I feel . . ." suggested the girl sitting next to me. The group looked pleased.

When the teacher returned, joined by the principal, I asked airplane boy to read their poem. The teacher looked shocked. The principal looked pleased. "Would someone like to tell our guests about our poem?"

One child volunteered. She talked about what they had done and ended with, "It was fun. I'd like to do it again." I asked the teacher if she'd be willing to type up the sentences and give everyone a copy of their poem. She nodded.

I thanked the children for their good work and stayed while they got ready to leave. When the teacher and I were alone, I told her how much I appreciated the opportunity to work with her class. She started to cry. This was not the hard-nosed woman I'd been told about. I waited for her to feel ready to speak. She wiped her eyes, said "Thank you," and left the room.

When I met with the principal, all he would tell me was she'd asked for leave without pay. He asked if I could teach the class for two days while he hired a sub. I agreed.

The kids asked if they could write more poems together. At the end of my two days, one of the boys said, "I'm poemed out but I feel good."

How would you have dealt with the situation?

HAILSTORM

The skies were clear. The sun was shining. A friend and I started down the mountain. Minutes later, black clouds blotted out the sun. The temperature fell. It began to hail—large hard balls of ice pummeling our bodies. Soon, along with the hail came drenching rain quickly filling the arroyos and trail with gushing, rushing water, making it impossible to make our way down the trail. How could weather change so dramatically?

We put on our rain gear and stared at the once-familiar landscape now barely recognizable. We had to bushwhack our way down on the highest ground we could find. She pointed out what looked like a way—it was, for a minute or two, before a wall of rocks blocked our way.

I saw an opening in the trees and suggested we head there. This worked for a while, but we soon came to an arroyo with water moving so fast and deep we were afraid to cross it.

With the rain and hail unrelenting, we continued exploring ways to get to the trailhead. I'd been in a similar situation a few weeks earlier, but my friend had yelled at me, as if the weather were my fault; as if I should've known a clear way down even though the trail and arroyos were rampaging waters. I was grateful the friend I was with remained calm. Like me, she recognized the only way to get back to the car was for both of us to figure out a possible path.

It was increasingly difficult to find our way as every little indentation in the earth was filled with branches and rocks pushed on by torrential water. But we were willing to try each other's suggestions with no judgment when they didn't work.

We commiserated with each other. The hail hurt. The rain made it difficult to see. We were cold. Water was seeping down our necks and socks even though our boots were waterproof. What normally would have taken us about an hour now seemed like an endless trek.

Cold and wet, we kept working our way through brush, over rocks, and under barbed wire fences. We were hiking in unknown terrain. We knew we had to go down, not up. Eventually we came to a big arroyo, normally easy to walk in. Now there was no way we could cross what was a roiling river filled with debris.

There was a bridge across the arroyo, but it led to a private house. We trespassed until we came to the road leading to the parking lot. We walked to the car, drenched, freezing, exhausted, and grateful. Together, the two of us had managed to find our way. Two heads were definitely better than one.

Have you experienced an unexpected event requiring a resourceful solution? What did you do?

24

WORLD TALE

The Lion and the Woodcutter

CENTRAL ASIA

A gift turns into a potent lesson. The stories, Street Scene and Wordwound, describe the impact of thoughtless words.

• • •

THERE WAS ONCE A poor man who cut and sold wood in order to earn a living, but no matter how hard he worked, he never made enough money to buy all the food his family needed. Day after day, watching his children grow pale and thin, he became so discouraged he decided to end his life.

He went to a cave where he knew a lion lived and stood outside of it. "Lion, please come eat me."

The lion, amazed at the request, asked, "Why do you ask such a thing of me?"

The man told him of his plight and added, "If I die, perhaps my wife will find a new husband who can take better care of her and the children."

The lion listened, then said, "If it is only money that keeps you from wanting to live, take this gold coin."

He threw the man more money than he usually saw in a year. Thanking him, the woodcutter rushed to the market and bought as much food for his family in one day as he'd been able to buy in a month. Though his wife was careful, eventually they spent all the money. Once again, there was not enough food to feed the family.

Once again, the woodcutter went to the lion, begging him to eat him. Once again, the lion threw him a gold coin. In time, the man's wife said, "The lion has been so good to us. I think we should invite him to dinner to show him how grateful we are."

The man was not so sure. "He's a lion. We don't know what he likes to eat. Perhaps we should think of another way to thank him."

But his wife persuaded him. The next day the woodcutter went to the lion. "My wife and I would be very pleased if you would come to our home for dinner."

"Thank you. I shall be delighted," said the lion with such joy the man forgot his misgivings. The next day his wife spent all day preparing the most delicious meal she knew how to cook. The children cleaned the house. The man chopped enough wood to make a splendid fire.

At the appointed time, the lion knocked on the door and was ushered in by the family, who kept telling him how grateful they were for his help. The meal was a great success, and the man began to relax, thinking how good it was his wife had thought to invite the lion.

As the husband was showing the lion to the door, he overheard someone say, "He's a very nice lion, but he doesn't smell very good." Shocked, the man hoped the lion had not heard. When the lion did not react, the man sighed with relief.

Outside, the lion said to the man, "Tomorrow, come to see me. Please bring your sharpest knife. I have a favor to ask of you."

"With pleasure," said the man. "After all you have done for me and my family, I am happy to help you."

The next morning the woodcutter stood in front of the cave waiting for the lion. This time, after the lion gave him a gold coin, he said to the man, "I want you to take your knife and slash my face to ribbons."

The woodcutter recoiled in horror. "I can't do that. You've been so good to me and my family. Why would I want to hurt you?"

"You promised you would do as I requested," reminded the lion. "Are you going to go back on your word?"

With a heavy heart, the man slashed the lion's face until his face was a bloody mess. "Now, leave me," said the lion. "Return in two weeks."

When the man returned, the lion said to him, "My head heals. My heart still hurts."

❧ ❧ ❧

STREET SCENE

In 1941, I was five years old, just back from living with an aunt and uncle for almost a year. I didn't know any of the kids on the block, so when a girl from across the street invited me to play with her, I skipped to her house, filled with excitement.

She invited me to go down to the basement where a group of girls was waiting. The smiles on their faces didn't feel good. The girl who invited me said, "We're going to play a game. We'll make a circle. Go into the circle. You're *it*."

Not knowing what the game was, I hesitated, then went into the middle as the girls joined hands and started to circle around me. Suddenly they changed, "You killed Christ. We're gonna kill you."

Terrified, I broke through the circle, ran up the stairs, out the door, across the street, up the stairs to my apartment, opened the door, ran into my room, and hid under the bed, crying.

My mother came in, pulled me out from under the bed, and asked why I was crying. Through my sobs I managed to say. "They told me I killed Christ. I don't even know who he is."

"Oh, for goodness sakes," said my mother. "Don't be such a crybaby. No wonder they don't want to play with you. They were only teasing." My mother left the room in disgust, leaving me no wiser as to who Christ was.

I stopped crying but I didn't stop worrying. Who was this man? Why did they say I killed him?

Have you experienced prejudice? If so, what happened?

❧ ❧ ❧

WORDWOUND

In college I studied modern dance, performed with the dance club, choreographed works, and taught dance at a local YMCA. I hoped to become a professional dancer. The summer after my college graduation, I attended Connecticut College Summer School of Dance on a scholarship. Afterward, I planned to attend the University of Wisconsin, majoring in dance.

The classes were taught by professionals whose performances I'd seen in New York City. To be so close to such famous, talented dancers was awe-inspiring. Watching them demonstrate movements was like attending a private performance. Some of their techniques were harder than others. Some teachers were more focused on demonstrating than teaching, but I was entranced and fully absorbed in learning new movements and developing my ability.

One morning there was an unusual amount of excitement. Dancers were extraordinarily busy warming up. I was about to ask what was going on when Martha Graham walked in. I had seen her perform many times. Being so close to her was exciting and scary. She was short, barely five feet, but she filled the space with incredible ease and power.

She began class by demonstrating the sequence, then we lined up, her eyes focused on each dancer as we moved across the room. I was nervous. Being in her presence felt overwhelming, yet I took my turn, relieved when I reached the safety of those who'd already gone.

Standing next to another dancer, I saw Ms. Graham looking at me. Staring. "You there," she said to me, "the one who can't dance."

All thought of becoming a professional dancer vanished. Fifty-seven years later I still remember the way she looked at me, pointing her long, bony finger as she spoke.

Have you been wounded by words? If so, what was that like?

25

WORLD TALE

How Much is Enough?

PERSIA

What is enough? To Read or Not, To Ski or Not, and A Lesson or Not, explore the value of considering what is sufficient.

• • •

THERE WAS ONCE A wise man who went to a house of learning to offer his wisdom. He expected many people to attend, but, though he waited for a long time, only one person showed up. The wise man was thinking of leaving, but being polite, he asked the man, "You are the only person here; should I leave and return another time, when more people might attend?"

"Sir, I am not a wise man like you, but if I entered a stable and there was only one horse, I would still feed it."

The wise man nodded and began to speak at great length. When he paused to take a drink, he asked, "Shall I continue?"

"Sir, I am not a wise man like you, but if I entered the stable and discovered there was only one horse, I would not feed it all the grain in the stable."

❧ ❧ ❧

TO READ OR NOT:

My second novel, *Morning Light,* was published to good reviews, and I'd been invited to do a book signing and reading at a well-known bookstore in Albuquerque. I drove down in high spirits, looking forward to sharing my work. The staff assured me they had done enough publicity to expect a good number of people to attend.

I arrived early, signed copies of my novel, and helped the bookstore staff arrange them on a table. It was my first bookstore reading, and I was excited and apprehensive, relieved when a woman walked in, took a seat in the second row, and patiently waited. I smiled at her, inwardly worried when no one else appeared.

I checked with the bookstore staff. They said they would tell the woman the event was cancelled. "No one wants to do a reading with just one person in the audience," said the manager.

The woman began gathering her things, looking as tense as I felt. "Seems I'm the only one who's come tonight," she said to me. "Guess I'll leave."

Something in me felt this wasn't right. She'd come. I'd come. Why didn't this matter? "You're here," I said. "Why don't I tell you a little about my novel, and then, if you like, we can have a conversation."

"Are you sure?" She looked uncomfortable but didn't move to leave.

I sat down next to her. "The title, *Morning Light,* comes from a Yiddish proverb: You can cry, cry, cry all night, but smile by morning light. The novel is about a woman who doesn't know how to stand up for herself. She's bullied by her mother and her boyfriend, and cares too much about the preschool children with whom she works."

"Sounds like my life," said the woman, not looking at me. I moved my chair so it was easier to have a conversation, not quite facing each other, but it felt cozy. "So," she asked, "did writing the novel make a difference in how you felt about yourself?" I sensed she was looking for answers to whatever she was going through.

"Takes more than writing a novel to change deep trauma, but it did help in some ways."

"How? If I may ask?"

I didn't know this woman, but I felt she needed something from me. I hoped what I said was the right choice. "I wrote countless drafts, except for one part, where Anna, the protagonist, remembers her father sexually molesting her. It poured out of me. I could never rewrite that section. And the whole time I was writing it, I was shaking, as if I were writing about my life rather than Anna's."

"Was it your life?" She was leaning into me as if we were old friends.

"I don't know. The writing came from a place deep inside me and opened up a slew of memories. It made me realize most of the stories told about me by my family were lies. The few times I was able to ask questions, what I got was denial, blame, and shame."

"I know about that," she said bitterly, her face contorted by misery. She told me a little about her life.

I was uncomfortable about the conversation—too raw for strangers who needed to leave soon. "Look," I said gently, "people who are abused don't ask to be hurt. Children don't ask to be treated badly. Whatever happened to you is not your fault. If people were unkind or hurtful to you, please be kind and caring to yourself."

The woman asked if she could tell me a bit more about her life. I nodded. After talking for a few minutes, she stopped, smiled, and patted my knee. "Thank you for taking the time to talk with me. You're a good listener. Although I'm sorry I'm the only one to come to your reading, in a way I'm glad. I know it sounds selfish, but we wouldn't have had this conversation if there'd been a full house. What you've said and how you listened means a lot to me. Could you sign three books for me? I'll tell you who they're for."

When she left, the bookstore manager apologized for the poor turnout. I shrugged. "It's okay. We sold three books." Selling books matters to me. A lot. Connecting with a reader in a heartfelt way is why I write.

Would you have stayed? Why or why not?

TO SKI OR NOT

I signed up for a series of group ski lessons, wanting to increase my confidence and hone my skills. There were five of us at the first lesson—four men and me. The instructor chatted and joked with the men, leaving me to wonder whether I should quit the class and ask for my money back. I decided to stay and followed the men who followed the instructor, which in itself was sort of a victory as they were more skilled, and their pace was faster than mine.

It snowed the next Monday, with a fierce wind, making driving conditions hazardous on the road to the ski basin. There was a blurb on the Ski Santa Fe website: Winter road conditions. four-wheel, all-wheel, snow tires highly recommended. I could not force myself to drive up to my ski lesson. Missing one class out of five didn't seem terrible.

The next Monday, there was an even more formidable snowstorm. I told myself I should stay home. I told myself I should not miss another lesson. I told myself I should face my fears about driving up the ski basin road in bad weather. To stop the voices in my head, I got ready and headed up the winding snowy road, driving as carefully as I could, praying I wouldn't have to face a car blocking the road.

By the time I parked, I was a sweaty mess, grateful I'd arrived in one piece. After coffee and time to calm down, I skied over to where my instructor was waiting. He did not look pleased to see me. No other students showed up. "No point in having a class for one," he said.

I was furious. For this I risked my life driving in horrible weather? "I'm here," I told him. "What difference does it make if you teach one or five? You still have to teach." He suggested we wait to see if anyone else showed up. Minutes later, shaking with cold, I said, "No one else is coming, could we please start?"

Clearly annoyed, he agreed. We skied to the lift. No line. Normally people chat on the way up. I had nothing to say. He had nothing to say. I could feel my tension rising—not a good way to ski.

By now there were about six or seven inches of powder on the slope, and visibility was close to zero. "Have you skied in powder?" he asked.

"I tried a few times, but I kept falling. I guess I don't know how," I admitted.

He sighed. "Okay, follow me. I'll make sweeping turns. Stay in my tracks." He took off, faster than I would have wished, but I was afraid to lose him in the whiteout conditions, so I followed as best I could. He stopped, looked at me, and yelled, "Breathe!" I laughed. How did he know? He took off again. This time I hummed a song that mirrored the rhythm of the turns. Breathing made a difference. I began to enjoy myself. I got so close to him he stopped. "I feel like you're stealing my soul," he said, somewhat good-humoredly.

"I have enough trouble dealing with my soul; I don't need to deal with yours as well." He laughed and started down. His laughter relieved my tension. I followed him, now enjoying the sense of freedom and ease as we made our way down to the lift.

"Let's do a few more runs and call it a day," he said. "This snow isn't going to let up any time soon, and I know you're nervous about driving back down." True.

The rest of the lesson was a joy. We joked and chatted on the lift. I followed him, filled with pleasure and a sense of accomplishment as he carved turns in the falling snow. When the lesson was over, I thanked him. "Well, you were right," he said. "Teaching one is just as good as teaching the full class."

Driving down the mountain was a nightmare. I skidded more than once, but each time I managed to keep the car facing the right direction on the right side of the road. When I was safe at home, I felt proud I had faced my fears, more than pleased I'd asked for what I wanted and had managed to have the best ski lesson ever.

What makes you stand up for yourself?

❧ ❧ ❧

A LESSON OR NOT

We meet regularly in a local park for an hour's tai chi class. Usually five or six people participate. Having to remember complicated sequences of physical moves irritates and frustrates me, yet it's a centuries-old technique, and part of me appreciates the age-old activity and tradition.

One morning, when I arrived for class, the teacher was going through one of the sequences. I followed his motions, waiting for people to show up. After a while, the teacher stopped moving. No one else had appeared. He did not look happy. I offered to leave. He agreed. I put my sweater back on, picked up my bag, and walked away, feeling like I didn't matter.

I was just about to my car when I heard him yell, "Nancy, wait up." I turned around. He was waving at me to come back. He met me halfway. "I'm sorry," he said. "You came. We should have a class."

"Are you sure?" We paid by the session, so having only one student meant he was teaching for a lot less than usual. I didn't offer to pay for a private class.

"I'm sure," he said, walking toward where his things were. I put my stuff down and waited. He began to move, and I followed, so intensely focused on him that after a while it felt like there was no space between us even though I was more than five feet away. I had no thoughts, no worries. I was pure movement.

When he stopped, I stopped, still feeling connected. He broke the silence by saying, "Thank you." I had no idea what he was thanking me for, but I thanked him for the session. We stood quietly, looking at each other.

I sensed it was wrong to leave. My teacher made no move to pack up. When he spoke, his voice was soft, filled with emotion. He told me about a time he'd worked with a shaman who spoke no English, yet somehow managed to convey important principles. "After the group session was over, when I started to leave, the shaman told me to stay. When the others had gone, the shaman began to chant and move in unfamiliar ways, nonverbally inviting me to join him. I chanted and moved with him, just the two of us, with no explanation. I felt he'd given me a gift, but today I understood the power of his choosing to teach just me. When you were the only one, I thought there was no point teaching a class for one person, but then I remembered the shaman's words at the end of our session: '*Para ti*'" (for you).

Simultaneously he and I bowed to each other. It was the right time to leave.

How do you decide how much/many is enough?

26

WORLD TALE

Coyote Keeps His Name

OKANOGON/ NATIVE AMERICAN

Coyote wants a new name. The stories, Blind Date and The Price of Fame, illustrate the power of identity.

• • •

Great Spirit gathered all the Animal People together to tell them New People were coming. All the Animal People were going to have forever names, handed down to future generations. The Animal People were told to come to Great Spirit's lodge the next morning at dawn and each in turn would receive their names. First come, first served.

Coyote hated his name. He didn't want to be known as Trickster or Imitator. He wanted a great name, one the Animal People would respect and honor. He wanted to be called Grizzly Bear for his strength. If that name was taken, he would be called Eagle, for his swiftness. If that name was taken, he would be called Salmon, the powerful swimmer. Satisfied with his plan, he stayed awake all night, putting twigs in his eyes to keep them from closing. He intended to be first so he could have the name he chose.

The next morning, he was pleased to see no one was around. Surely he was first to appear before Great Spirit. Joyfully, he asked to be called Grizzly Bear. Great Spirit spoke: "Grizzly Bear was already here. He has taken his name."

"Oh," said Coyote, delighted he had a strategy, "Then I will be Eagle."

"Eagle has come and gone. He has taken his name," said Great Spirit.

"Then I will be Salmon," responded Coyote.

"That is impossible. Salmon has taken his name," said Great Spirit.

Coyote was too upset to think of another name. "What name has not been taken?"

"All the Animal People have come and gone. You are the last to appear before me. No one wanted your name." Coyote looked so miserable, Great Spirit said, "I made you sleep so you would be the last to come. I need you to be who you are. Coyote."

"But I don't want to be who I am. I want a new name."

"I need you to keep your name. I need you to be who you are. I have important work for you to do. The New People who are coming do not know anything. You know how to laugh and cry. You are brave and cowardly, wise and foolish, hard-hearted and kind. I need you to teach the New People how to be fully human, for that is who they are—human beings."

Coyote was not convinced. "But if I am foolish, they will laugh at me. When I am cowardly, they will not respect me. How can I teach them?"

Great Spirit reassured him. "When you are foolish and wise, cowardly and brave, mean-spirited and kind, they will understand that no one is always foolish, always brave, always uncaring. You will see them through bad and good times. To help you do your work, I give you special gifts. You can change into any shape you choose. You can understand and talk to all who speak to you. If you die, you will be reborn. Shape-changer, go and do your work. You will do it well."

Coyote felt his heavy spirit lighten and his heart fill with joy as he went out into the world to meet the New People, ready to do the work of Great Spirit.

BLIND DATE

In 1954, I was a college sophomore, the only one in my part of the dorm who never had dates. A girl, I'll call her Sally, offered to fix me up, in all senses of the word—lend me clothes, make up my face, and provide me with a blind date. My initial reaction was no, but for reasons I'll never know, she was too excited about the "project" to take no for an answer. I told her I had a boyfriend back home, but she dismissed him as irrelevant since he'd never visited. She insisted it was time for me to start going out. I don't know why I agreed, but it probably had something to do with how long it took my boyfriend to respond to my letters.

On the night of the date, I went to her room to get ready. We were about the same size, so her clothes fit me, but I wore loose clothes—she liked clothes that clung to her body. When I put on the dress she wanted me to wear, I said it was too tight. She countered that I looked great. Fortunately, my feet were bigger than hers, so I couldn't wear her high heels. Dismayed by my "poor" taste in shoes, she found a hall-mate with a pair of heels, not as high as hers. At least I could walk in them, though I wasn't sure for how long.

Pleased with what she'd done so far, she sat me down and covered the front of the dress with a towel. I could feel stuff being smeared on my face, lines being drawn under my eyes and over my eyelids, more stuff smeared on my cheeks and lips, then a pad patting my face. She handed me a mirror, her pleasure in her work clearly evident. I looked at myself but couldn't find me.

If I was uncomfortable wearing her dress and someone else's shoes, the makeup covering my face made me even more so—something I didn't think possible.

We left her room and walked toward the common room filled with males and females eyeing and cooing. While we headed for the two guys who were waiting for us, she prattled on about how good I looked and what a fun evening we were going to have. Her enthusiasm made me nervous. She introduced me to my date, a guy who looked familiar. "I think you're in my English class," I said.

He stared at me for too long then nodded. "You look so different I didn't recognize you." He added, "You look great."

Before I could think of something to say, Sally took charge. "Let's get out of here. I'm thirsty." Her boyfriend put his arm around her, fondling her breast, which made her laugh. She pushed his hand away and kissed it. My date and I followed the two of them, walking down the hill to the main part of town where we headed toward a bar with music playing so loud I could hear it from a block away. I hoped we weren't going there. We were.

Sally's date led us to an empty table and grabbed a fourth chair from the next table, seemingly occupied by the look of glasses and plates of half-eaten food. She and I sat down. The two guys left and made their way through the crowd. Sally gushed about her boyfriend, but it was so noisy I could hardly hear her. I nodded every now and then, which seemed to satisfy her. They returned with a large pitcher of beer and four glasses. Sally's date filled the glasses and handed them out. He put his glass out and toasted, "To a wonderful evening with gorgeous gals." I winced. Gal? A man from the next table came back, grumbling about a missing chair. Sally's date ignored him and said, "Let's party."

The three of them downed their beers before I'd taken a couple of sips. My date filled the others' glasses and looked at mine, then at me, grinning: "Hurry up and finish, woman. Time's a-wasting."

Too much noise. Too many people. Sally and the two men laughed and bantered. I nodded, as if I were part of the conversation but couldn't think of anything to say. When my date put his arm around me, I could smell his beery breath. I watched his hand move down the front of my dress. I stood up and said I needed to use the restroom. No one noticed I carried my purse and sweater. It took a while to get through the crowd and even longer to find the ladies' bathroom. One stall was empty, and I went in and locked the door. I must have been there longer than I realized because I heard Sally call my name. I flushed the toilet, waited a few seconds, then came out.

"You've been in there forever. You okay?" Her lipstick was smudged—from kissing I guessed.

I said the only thing I could think of: "I just got my period, and I don't want to ruin your dress. Besides, the cramps are pretty bad. I better go back to the dorm. Tell the guys I'm sorry I had to leave."

Sally looked disappointed, then shrugged. "Okay, maybe next time." She left. I waited until I couldn't see her, then found a side door, which led out to an alleyway and the street. I practically ran back to the dorm. It was a relief to take off her dress and her friend's heels. It was even more of a relief to scrub my face until I recognized myself.

I dislike being in bars, being with people drinking, with music so loud it hurts my ears, yet I'd agreed to do this, wearing someone else's clothes and shoes, with makeup that created a person I didn't know. I felt ashamed for agreeing to be turned into someone I was not and never wanted to be. Sally didn't offer to fix me up again. My date didn't ask for another date. A painful lesson I promised myself never to repeat.

What is it like to listen to your true self's needs?

THE PRICE OF FAME

I was at a family Seder in 1963, talking to an aunt about the women's exercise classes I was teaching at a local Jewish Community Center. When I said I'd started with one class of four and was now teaching three full classes with a waiting list, a cousin's husband who'd overheard our conversation asked if he could talk with me, privately.

While we sat outside on the porch, he told me he worked in publishing and asked a lot of questions about what I was teaching the women, how the number of classes had increased, and why I thought the women were so responsive. I told him they generally had bad feelings about their bodies, were not in good shape, and thought the classes were helping them feel better in a lot of ways. "We have a lot to talk about," he said, giving me his card. "Call next week so we can arrange a time to meet at my office."

He met me at the elevator, greeting me with a hug and smile, unsettling me. I barely knew him, yet he acted as if we were close family. His office was impressive—lots of windows, healthy looking plants, comfortable chairs—but the walls were filled with framed magazine covers, mostly young women with glorious figures posing in bathing suits and various stages of undress, which made me wonder why he wanted to talk with me. What was he wanting me to write?

His secretary brought us coffee and pastries and left. He didn't waste time on pleasantries. "I know you're a teacher and teachers don't earn much. If we work together I can make you a lot of money." He grinned. "A whole lot of money. Here's the deal. Women want to look good. That means they have to know what to do to look their best. You write a softcover book with exercises and diet suggestions, as well as tips on how to attract men. I provide the photos and the publicity. We call it The King Method in big print. In small print we say something about how the book can help you live the life you choose. We put it on shelves near grocery checkouts, in gyms, fitness studios—any place women go. You offer workshops and seminars, which we'll organize, and sell copies of the book." He grinned. "Great idea, right?" I couldn't help thinking he sounded like a used car salesman.

He drank coffee, watching me as he said I'd get a five-figure advance.

I was stunned. He was offering me a huge amount of money to write a book—money for an idea, not even a written proposal. It was more money than my husband and I together earned in a year, multiplied many times over. He mistook my silence for wanting more money and said, "Look, if it's too little money I might be able to get you a bigger advance. Just think about it. The King Method will make you famous . . . as well as a lot of money. What could be better?"

Fantasies of being a famous author filled my imagination.

At least I was clear about the title. "We can't name the book The King Method. What I teach is based on anatomy, physiology, and kinesiology." He shrugged. I kept seeing the gorgeous female bodies on the walls. "The women in my classes will never look like the women on your covers no matter how hard they work. They're not in their twenties and they don't wear bikinis."

"So what? They can't dream? You're selling them a sense of who they could be. And who knows? Maybe they can. You're telling me they're stuck with how they look forever?"

He had a point. Was I underestimating the possibility of women to change how they looked? Could what I write help women feel better about themselves? What he said sounded good, and yet, something felt off. Maybe it was all the babes in bikinis staring at me. "Suppose I write this book, and you don't like it. Then what?"

"No chance of that. You send me what you write chapter by chapter and I make the necessary changes."

"What if I don't agree with the changes?"

"You will," he said. "We both want the same thing."

"What's that?" I asked.

He ignored the question and began telling me once again what he could do for me and how great it would be to work together. "So, ready to sign a contract?"

I wanted to be an author. I liked the idea of earning a lot of money by writing a book, especially a lot more money than my husband earned. When I'd told him I was thinking about writing a book, he'd responded, "What do you know?"

I liked the idea of writing a book that might help women change their lives in ways they chose, so they could feel better about themselves. I imagined being on talk shows, leading workshops all over the country, having money to hire babysitters, so I could have a life apart from my son and husband. I drank a cup of coffee, which he refilled, smiling as if he knew my answer.

I thought about the photos of svelte young women covering the walls of his office, about his rewriting what I wrote with me having no chance to object or rewrite, yet my name would be on the cover.

I thought about the book I was thinking about writing, about women who were looking for ways to feel better about themselves, who appreciated not only what I taught, but the class's camaraderie, how they supported each other. We were talking about two entirely different books, only one of which I could possibly write, which wasn't the book he was describing.

My wanting to be famous and rich danced with my conscience. If I made a lot of money writing the book he was proposing, I could then write the book I wanted, but would I have credibility? It seemed the choice was between money and self-respect. Either or, but not both.

Reality took hold. If I accepted his proposal I would earn a huge amount of money, but I'd have no control over what was published. No chance of taking my name back if I didn't like the book.

Conscience won. "I appreciate your thinking of me. It was good to talk with you. The offer is more than generous—"

"But . . .?" he said, interrupting me.

"I can't do it. What you want me to write, it's not who I am. It's not how I work. It's not even how I think. And there is no King Method."

"There could be," he said, looking puzzled.

"Maybe, if it's written by someone else with the name of King, but not by me."

He shook his head. "You're making a big mistake. Think again. Besides the money, this is a great opportunity for you to make a name for yourself. You'll be famous."

"I appreciate your thinking of me, but the book you're proposing isn't what I want to write." There was no way I could sign the contract and live with myself.

How might you react to an experience where your conscience and checkbook collided?

27

WORLD TALE

A Woman's Wisdom

INDIA

A woman reacts to danger in an unexpected way. The stories, Surrounded, Uninvited Guests, and The Visit, explore ways to navigate unforeseen situations.

• • •

IN A SMALL TOWN in India, a bunch of thieves had terrorized everyone. It was so bad they would tell people which house would be raided that night. If people tried to hide their valuables or call the police, they suffered dire consequences.

One day, Bapurao, a rich man, received word his house would be raided and was given the usual warning. Shaking with fear, he told his wife Parvatibai about the thieves' plan. He said he would gather their servants and arm them so they could fight back.

His wife shook her head. "Many people have tried this, and no one has succeeded. We need to think of a way to outwit the thieves."

"What can we do?" asked her husband. When she told him she needed to think about it, he left to collect as many men from the village as would join him.

When her husband had gone, she went into the kitchen and said to the cook, "Prepare the best meal you can for fifty people. Set the tables with our best dishes and finest tableware. I need everything to be ready by midnight."

Just before midnight, she dressed in her most beautiful sari and took off all her jewels except her wedding ring and the necklace her husband had given her in honor of their marriage. When she heard the noise of approaching horses, she told the servants to be ready to serve. Taking a deep breath, she opened the door, terrified but calm.

Before her stood many men, ready to storm in. Without waiting, Parvatibai said, "Welcome brothers. Please come in. I have been waiting for you. Please wash your hands. Dinner is ready."

The head thief wondered if it was a trick, but he could smell the food and saw that the woman welcoming him seemed unafraid.

When they were all seated, the servants attended to each man. Parvatibai made sure they all had enough to eat and drink. After dinner, she brought the head thief a dish filled with jewels and placed them before him. "Brother, this is what I have to give you. I have kept back only the necklace my husband gave me when we married and my wedding ring. Please, I beg of you, let me keep them."

The head thief looked at her, then said, "Of course I will spare them. We have eaten your meal, and we are always faithful to those with whom we share food. You have called me brother and given me a brother's welcome. From today you are my sister, and I will see to it that you and your family come to no harm." He returned the jewels and ordered his men to free her husband, their servants, and the men who had come to help and bring them back to the house unharmed.

Even today, people talk about how Parvatibai outwitted the thieves.

SURROUNDED

In 1971, I had just finished attending an international conference on drama in England—a week filled with tension between me and the leader, an upper-class Englishman who didn't bother to hide his racism and misogyny—as well as spending a day taking care of a psychotic woman. I decided to visit Stratford-on-Avon to relax, as well as attend a performance at the famous theatre.

I bought a ticket for the evening's performance without paying attention to what was playing. Just being in the famed playhouse was a treat. After a light dinner, I made my way to the theatre, settled into my comfortable seat, and waited for the curtain to rise. The renaissance play, *The Duchess of Malfi*, contains scene after scene of murder, betrayal, lust, torture, madness, guilt, and everything in between. I left the theatre stupefied, filled with the powerful emotions that had played out over the hours-long play.

I'd walked in daylight to the theatre, from the small hotel where I was staying, in about fifteen minutes. Now it was dark, no moon, few overhead lamps, and I wasn't exactly sure how to get back. I had gone a few blocks when I noticed a group of males not far from where I was walking. I crossed over to the other side of the street. They not only crossed over but walked toward me. I thought of running back to the theatre, but they were too close, and I wasn't a fast runner. As they came nearer, I could feel my heart beat faster. My mouth went dry. There were four of them. One of me. They did not look friendly. No other people in sight.

One of them crooned, "Hello, sweetheart. How about a bit of fun?" His cronies laughed.

"No thanks," I said, hoping they'd take my no for an answer.

Grinning, they cooed how I wasn't being friendly.

"I'm not in a friendly mood, so please leave me alone."

One of them moved toward me, his eyes cold and scary. "Why not? We're all out for a good time. Don't spoil the party."

I was so filled with emotions from the play, my response came without thinking. "You'll have to party without me. I've had my fill of rape and murder. Hours and hours." All the murder and mayhem I'd vicariously experienced spoke for me. "If you want a party, go see *The Duchess of Malfi*."

"What's that?" one of them asked.

"It's a play, at the theatre. If you want a good time, go watch it. Plenty of rape and torture. Right now, you've got the wrong woman." I felt a surge of energy—anger at the way the heroine in the play was treated. Anger at the four males wanting what I wouldn't give them. Anger at the way men have used their strength and power against me for too much of my life.

I surged into a space between two of the men and walked fast, taking them by surprise. I kept walking as fast as I could without running, not knowing if they were following me, but when I found what I hoped was a safe place to hide, I huddled and waited. When I couldn't hear anything, I poked my head out from behind the barrel nestled against a wall where I'd hidden. I couldn't see anyone. I decided it was safe to keep going.

I had lost all sense of direction and was relieved when I saw two women walking ahead of me; I asked if they knew where my hotel was. They did and cheerfully offered to walk me there, an offer I gratefully accepted. "It's too dark for you to be out and about by yourself, dearie," said one of them. "You never know who you'll meet."

Have you ever been in a dangerous situation? How did you deal with it?

❧ ❧ ❧

UNINVITED GUESTS

As part of a three-day conference on drama, I was in a community center gym, welcoming a group of junior- and senior-high-school English teachers to my workshop, "Exploring Imagination and Creativity Through Drama." I was unusually nervous because a group of internationally respected drama leaders were watching me conduct the session from the bleachers. Suddenly, a group of kids burst into the gym, bouncing a ball between them, playing some kind of game, laughing and shouting to one another.

My first reaction was to tell them to get the hell out of there; the space had been reserved for the conference. I had enough to worry about. I didn't need uninvited kids to add to the mix. I could feel the participants scrutinizing me. I was too aware of the drama teachers in the bleachers observing me. I wanted the participants to enjoy the workshop. I needed the drama leaders to think well of me. I had to figure out how to deal with the situation. Fast.

I walked up to the group, and, as luck would have it, intercepted and caught the ball. "This gym has been reserved for a three-day session on creative drama." I waited to see if this was enough for them to leave. It wasn't. I had their ball and their attention. I didn't know how to politely ask them to leave, and I didn't want to start a confrontation, so I said the only thing I could think of. "Would you like to join our drama workshop?"

"We don't know nuthin' about drama," said one of the guys, whose name I later learned was Alex.

I threw the ball to him. "You don't need to know anything. You're welcome to participate." I hoped I sounded sincere. I hoped I seemed welcoming. I hoped they'd say no thanks and leave. The silence while they looked at each other seemed to last forever.

Alex asked, "You sure?"

Trying to look as if I meant it, I said, "Yup, I'm sure." He put the ball down near the bleachers, huddled with the rest of his buddies, and then, I guess by mutual consent, joined the participants.

The three-hour session loomed long and problematical. What I had planned to do depended in part on the participants being familiar with educational terms I'd be using, as well as knowing about my work. Now almost a third of the group were kids whose attitudes and reasons for agreeing to join were unknown. I scrapped the plans I'd made, observed the group, and spontaneously created a plan in my head.

Whether teaching a class or leading a workshop, the first activity I do is to create a sense of community by telling a world tale. Right now, this seemed more necessary and important than ever. After the introductions, I asked the group to sit comfortably while I told them a story, centuries old, passed down from generation to generation. The English teachers would be familiar with this story, but I counted on their understanding my need to find a way to integrate the kids with the adults.

The group listened with rapt attention, giving me a sense that everyone could work together, which, much to my surprise and relief, they did.

For the rest of the session, it was as if the kids had been specially selected and specifically invited. The English teachers treated the kids as peers; the kids treated the teachers with respect. My newly hatched plans worked well, better than I'd hoped.

At the end of a class, I always leave room for reflection. That day was no exception, yet I worried what the kids might say, given that they'd come into the room to play ball and had ended up creating drama, which they'd never done, with adults they didn't know.

Alex was the first to speak. "This was the strangest experience I ever had." I couldn't tell if he meant it as good or bad, so I asked him to tell us more. "Well, we ran in, ready to play ball, and there were a bunch of adults on our court. I was mad. 'What the hell are they doing here?' I asked Grady. 'This is our space. We always play here.' Then you invited us to join in and that was even weirder." He scratched his head, looking puzzled. "But it was fun."

One of the participants asked, "So what was this afternoon like for the rest of you?"

Moira volunteered. "I never been with a group of adults who treated me like a person. I kept expecting you all to make fun of us, but it was like we were the same as you, even though we aren't."

Some of the participants admitted they were initially annoyed at the intrusion and wondered how I was going to handle it. Some even admitted they would have thrown the kids out. They laughed. Jamie said, "I expected to be thrown out once I saw all of you staring at us, like who the fuck are you?"

Lilly raised her hand, then put it down. I encouraged her to speak. "I never done creative drama. I was scared someone would make fun of me, but the group I was in kept encouraging me to say what I thought. I never expected grownups would want me to do stuff with them."

One of the English teachers said, "I don't know what Nancy planned to do before you joined us, but what we did, and your participation, made creative drama come alive for me in a new way. Being with you"—she looked at the kids who were sitting together—"was a new experience. It gave me a chance to appreciate the power of making drama with young people, as a peer rather than a teacher."

The session ended with Alex getting the ball and throwing it around the group. He invited us to come back after the conference and play with them. A fine note to end on.

What do you do when your first reaction is anger, but you know it won't solve the problem?

❧ ❧ ❧

THE VISIT

I returned from being hospitalized in London in mid-February 1985. My mother, her sisters, and my sister kept calling me to say I needed to visit my mother. Her cancer, first diagnosed in 1983, had returned, and she was now paralyzed from the waist down. By mid-March, although my illness was still undiagnosed, I felt well enough to visit and asked a friend who my mother adored to drive me. A few days before I was scheduled to leave, my mother's youngest sister called to reassure me my mother would be alive when I visited.

My aunt explained my mother had asked my uncle to buy pills. She would take them just before my visit so when I arrived, I would find her dead. When I was re-reading..I could not make this make sense for myself... maybe this paragraph needs to end, "But the family had convinced her not take her life before I could get there."

"What?" My mother hated me so much she wanted me to travel four hours just to find her dead? I cancelled the visit.

No matter my reasons for not going, I was barraged by phone calls from my mother, aunts, and sister telling me I needed to visit. I was assured by my aunt, my uncle had not bought the pills, and my mother would be alive when I arrived. I kept saying no until I was worn down and said yes.

My friend and I drove to my sister's house, about a mile from where my mother lived. As we drove, I entertained my friend by imagining worst-case scenarios. When we arrived, I called my mother's nurse to tell her I needed a nap and would come afterward. I could hear my mother screaming in the background, "Tell her to come NOW!" The nurse told me to call when I was ready to visit.

When my friend and I arrived, my mother was furious. "I told you to come by yourself." She was not mollified by the presents we brought. Her years-long adulation of my friend vanished, despite her efforts to pacify my mother. When my friend saw my anguish and my mother's increasing rage, she volunteered to sit outside on the steps while I visited.

To prepare for the visit, I had followed a friend's suggestion and worn a red silk scarf around my waist to ward off anger and emotional abuse. I decided ahead of time I would not defend myself, nor would I confront or challenge my mother. I was tired and sick. What I wanted was kindness.

What I got was a two-hour diatribe: what a terrible daughter I was, what a terrible person I was, what a terrible mother I was. The intensity of her fury astounded me. The session was ended by the nurse coming in, a horrified expression on her face. "Mrs. Rubin, your daughter is ill. She needs to rest."

"She's not sick. I am. She's just pretending," snapped my mother. The nurse said it was time for my mother's pills and told me to leave.

I met my friend on the stairs, and we drove to my sister's house in silence. My sister excused our mother's behavior as she'd always done. I asked her to leave me alone while I took a walk, thinking about what I wanted to do. I decided I would briefly visit my mother the next day, just before we drove home.

In the morning, as we were about to leave my sister's house, my brother-in-law said, "Nancy, for once in your life think about someone else besides yourself." I left without acknowledging his words or presence. However, if looks could kill . . .

I told myself to forget about everything and to do what I came to do, which was to have as good a visit with my mother as possible. En route, I planned what I would say, knowing the words were lies, but words were all I had to try to end the visit in a better way than it had begun.

When I entered her bedroom, I gave her the coffee and doughnuts my sister and I had bought on the way. Without emotion, I said, "Mother, you and I are both sick. I don't know how much time either of us has, so I want you to know I forgive you."

Her response was quick and venomous. "There's nothing to forgive me for. You're the one who caused all the trouble. You're the one who was so horrible."

"We're both ill. This might be the last time we see each other."

"You're not sick. You're just pretending so people will feel sorry for you."

I decided this would be the last time I'd see my mother no matter what. I also decided to keep saying what I didn't feel: "I love you."

I needed my last visit with my mother to be one without accusations and arguments. I'd had enough of her vitriol. We'd run out of time. I just kept saying, with whatever pretended feeling I could muster, "I love you."

After what felt like hours but was probably less than half an hour, she said, without feeling, "I love you too." This was good enough until she added, "I love you more than your sister." I didn't want to be loved more than my sister. I didn't want to be loved less than my sister. I just wanted to be loved.

As my friend and I drove home, I thought about the scenarios I'd imagined on the way up. The reality had been so much worse, and yet, despite my feelings, I'd chosen to behave lovingly. A decent enough way to end my relationship with my abusive mother.

How do you prepare for a situation you know will be difficult?

28

WORLD TALE

The Cracked Pot

AFRICAN

Something broken may create opportunity. The stories, The Art of Stapling and Spilled Paint, explore how challenges or failures can transform a situation.

• • •

THERE WAS ONCE A water bearer who carried two pots of water on opposite ends of a long pole across the back of his neck. One pot was perfect, the other had a small crack. By the end of the water bearer's trip, the pot with the crack had lost half of its water.

The perfect pot sneered at the cracked pot. "The poor man works so hard to fill you up, and then you can't even keep all the water inside you. Drip. Drip. Drip."

The cracked pot felt terrible. One day it said to the man, "I am so sorry. Because of me you lose much of your hard work. I am filled with shame."

"Why?" asked the water bearer.

"There is a small crack in my side and water slowly drips out. By the time you reach the end of your journey, I am only half filled. You do not get the full value of your hard work."

After hearing how the cracked pot was suffering, the water bearer said, "There is no need for shame. You do what the perfect pot cannot do."

The cracked pot was incredulous. "How can this be? I do not understand."

The water bearer smiled and said, "As we walk, look to your left and then to your right. Tell me what you see."

The cracked pot thought this was ridiculous. How was looking going to erase shame? But it did what it was told. To the left there was nothing. To the right were lovely flowers lining the path. "What do you see?" asked the water bearer.

"I see nothing on the left and flowers on the right. What does that have to do with me?"

"When I saw water dripping from you, I planted seeds along the right side of the path. Water seeping from you waters the seeds. Now there are lovely flowers along the side of the path. Had you no crack, there would be no flowers."

❧ ❧ ❧

THE ART OF STAPLING

In the early 1960s education system in Providence, RI, Black children went to an all-Black school, separate and unequal from schools for white children. When the school building for Black children was condemned, the city of Providence was forced to close it and integrate Black children into previously all-white schools.

An article in the local newspaper described a project the city had created titled Cinderella, and was asking for volunteers to help "improve Black children's academic skills." Despite my feelings about the need for such a project—years-long educational neglect—I volunteered to work with a group of fourth-grade girls, planning to use the story of Cinderella as part of my strategy to develop their language arts abilities. I volunteered because I cared about the kids. Privately, I worried the program was too little too late.

Although the school building where we met was condemned, some rooms were deemed safe for the volunteers and students. I protested, but we were given no new places to meet—one more sign of how little the authorities cared about Black children. We volunteers figured out ways to manage being in the building safely, but I never stopped being concerned. The girls in my group had no worries when they entered the classroom, eager to participate.

After brief introductions, they listened intently when I told them the story. They instantly agreed they'd like to make a play from the story. They even agreed on the characters: mother, two sisters, Cinderella, fairy godmother, and prince. However, when it came to deciding who would play the mother and two sisters, no one offered. No one wanted to be the mean mother or an ugly sister.

They told me I should cast the play. I refused. "It's your play. You have to decide who you want to be." They argued with me and among themselves, furious because I wouldn't make the decision. We sat in silence. Stalemated.

Then, Alicia said, "I know, I know." We all stared at her. "Maybe the reason the mother and stepsisters are awful is they feel unloved. Maybe when Cinderella meets the prince, there's so much love, the mean mother and ugly stepsisters get filled with the love and become kind and beautiful."

I gasped in amazement at her wisdom. The girls giggled. Delight filled the room. The play was cast. Rehearsals began. The sessions were going smoothly until Tamisha said, "We want to perform our play and we gonna need costumes. Can't have a play without costumes." Oy! I had no money to buy costumes, but even if I found material I could afford, I can't sew. I knew the girls' mothers worked, often more than one job, so I didn't feel I could ask for their help. I told the girls I'd try to figure something out.

I went downtown to a shop that sold material and sewing supplies. I thought if I found inexpensive material, I might be able to find a volunteer to sew the costumes. I told the man about the girls making the play and asked about material for six costumes. No matter what he showed me, it was all too expensive. Then he said, "I have a lot of felt in a variety of colors and lengths. You can have the felt, and when the play is over, bring it back, but you can't cut it." *Huh?*

I went home with six bolts of felt in six different colors and lengths, wondering what the hell I was going to do with them. Still, it was material. The next time we met, I lugged the six bolts into our room. When I told the girls we couldn't cut or sew the material, they burst out laughing. Every time one of them stopped, another would start. Jenina asked, "You got material we can't cut or sew? How we gonna make costume that fit us?"

Until that moment, I had no idea how to use the material, but it was all we had. Sometimes desperation is a good motivator. "We'll unroll the material and whoever is smallest gets the least amount of fabric. We'll distribute it according to size." This made the girls start laughing again, looking as me as if I'd gone crazy. Lena asked, "How we gonna keep the material on us if we can't sew it?"

"We'll drape it and then I'll staple it in whatever shape you want."

"Staple?" they asked in chorus. "Staple?" More fits of laughter.

"Let's rehearse the play," I said. "Next time I'll bring my stapler and show you." Shaking their heads as if I was crazy for sure, we spent the session focused on fine-tuning the play. They were going to perform it in two weeks for white students at one of the schools Black children would be attending in September.

I knew their mothers worked, yet much to my astonishment every one of them appeared at our next session, prepared to meet their daughter's weird teacher. Lord knows what the girls told them. "You gonna staple my girl into a costume?" asked one of the mothers. I explained my predicament. "The man told me I couldn't cut the material, but he didn't say anything about stapling."

So began one of the funniest times in my teaching experience. The girls and their mothers decided who would get which bolt of fabric based on the girl's size and the length of fabric. Then the girls stood still while their mothers draped the fabric around them as artistically as they could. I stapled the fabric in place amid continuing laughter. When everyone was "costumed," the girls performed their play for their mothers. They were an enthusiastic audience, and the girls proudly bowed at the end. Afterward, Tina asked, "How we gonna get out of our costumes?"

"We'll undo whatever staples you need to take off the costume. I'll roll it so it won't crease, and we'll know how to restaple it." With their mothers' help, the girls carefully undid their costumes. I put a name on each one.

I thanked the mothers for coming. One of them said, "I haven't laughed so hard in years. Worth missing a day of work." The others agreed, big smiles on their faces.

The girls' performance was a big success. The staples held. The costumes were fine. The local television station filmed part of the performance and used it as their lead story that evening. I returned the bolts of fabric, thanked the man, and hoped ironing the felt had covered the staple holes well enough.

How have you improvised in a problematical situation? If so, what did you do?

❧ ❧ ❧

SPILLED PAINT

In 1990, I taught a seminar at an International Conference on Innovative Teaching that was held at Janus Pannonius University in Pecs, Hungary. In 1991, while leading a seminar in an international program for teachers of language arts at the University of Delaware, I met one of the Hungarian university faculty members, a participant in the course. Intrigued by what she called "my unusual teaching strategies," she persuaded her Chair to invite me to teach a similar course for graduate students studying English as a foreign language. I accepted the invitation and prepared to teach in Pecs at the university.

When I meet students for the first time, I introduce myself, then ask members of the class to introduce themselves. In the many countries where I've taught, it's never been a problem, but the Hungarian students stared at me, unable to comprehend what I'd asked them to do. When I explained the importance of us getting to know each other, one of them said, "What you're asking us to say is personal. This is a class. Who we are is not important."

Despite their five years studying to be English teachers, none of them felt comfortable speaking. I hadn't expected such resistance and explained: "Who you are is important. If you don't feel comfortable in class, you won't feel comfortable speaking, which is as important as reading and writing. This will be our focus. I will not correct mistakes until everyone feels so at ease speaking you will ask for corrections."

After an awkward silence, a few people volunteered: "I have a brother." "My mother is a nurse." "My grandmother is good cook." Simple declarative sentences with no emotional content and nothing to start a conversation.

The first few sessions were extremely difficult. I told stories, had them sculpt and paint images in response to abstract prompts such as: make an image of a moment in the story that is important to you, then write a few words that come to mind. I had them share their images and words, but they did so reluctantly, visibly distressed, bewildered by my "strange" methods. They were used to authoritarian education, and since I was the authority, they did what I asked, as minimally as possible.

Slowly, encouraged by my refusal to correct, they began to talk a little more, a bit less wary. They got used to painting and sculpting and sharing. The atmosphere was slightly less heavy. Teaching became a little easier, but not much.

One day, as I was preparing the tray of finger paints, the students rushed in and accidentally bumped into me, spilling the paints on the newspapers I'd spread on the floor. They looked at me. Horrified. Terrified. Waiting for me to yell at them for being so clumsy. I looked at the mess of paints on the floor and all I could think of was Jackson Pollack. So I yelled, "Jackson Pollack!"

They stared at me. At the mess. Then Elisia said, "Jackson Pollack, the artist?" I nodded and asked her to tell the class who he was and what she knew about him. They forgot about making mistakes, began speaking and asking questions—who he was, why I said his name, what she thought about him.

I took advantage of the moment. "Since the paint is spilled, I'll give you paper. Use the paint on the floor to make your own painting. When you're finished, write how you feel. Create a story. Make as many as you like in the next five minutes."

By now they had reluctantly accepted my odd way of teaching. With no hesitation, they dipped their fingers in the spilled paint and began painting and writing, many of them laughing at the absurdity of the situation.

When it came time to share their work, we sat in a circle around the newspapers splotched with paint. The mess and my reaction seemed to alleviate their habitual discomfort. They talked and laughed with the first real ease I'd seen. When a few of the students stopped talking after realizing they'd made a mistake, or when they couldn't find the right word, others chimed in with suggestions. Words flowed freely. I breathed a sigh of relief.

After the last student finished sharing, she asked what I planned to do with the paint-covered newspaper. I hadn't thought about it. I asked her for a suggestion. "Well," she said, "I think we should let the papers dry. Then we can tape them all together and hang it on the wall. We could title it, 'Hungarian students make a Jackson Pollack painting.'" That's what we did.

For the rest of the course, whenever a student hesitated to speak, or apologized for making a mistake, someone in the class would yell, "Jackson Pollack." It became our class's code word for "no worries about speaking."

How do you react when something unexpectedly absurd happens?

29

WORLD TALE

Catherine's Fate

SICILY

Catherine is forced to make a harrowing choice. The stories, Casting the Snow Queen and Naiveté, explore decisions and their consequences.

• • •

CATHERINE, A LOVELY, INTELLIGENT, kind, gentle young woman, with wealthy parents and an adoring fiancé, living in a beautifully landscaped mansion, was sitting in her favorite place when she saw the strange woman. "Who are you? What are you doing in my garden?" The woman did not move or speak. Catherine ordered her to leave immediately.

There was a fraught silence before the woman said, "I am your Fate. It is your choosing time. Will you be happy when young and unhappy when old, or unhappy when young and happy when old? You must choose. If not, I will choose for you. Decide now!"

Catherine wished she were dreaming, but knew she was not. "Wrinkles and age make poor companions. I choose to be unhappy when I am young and happy when I am old."

Suddenly there was a fierce wind. The strange woman disappeared. Catherine was alone. All she'd known was gone. She decided to walk until she came to a town where she might find work that would give her food and lodgings.

When she passed a house and saw a woman looking out the window, Catherine told her she was looking for employment. The woman replied, "I have need of a servant. I think you will do well. Come in."

Catherine learned quickly, and the woman became fond of her, each day trusting her more. One day, she told Catherine she had to leave for a few hours, to take good care of the house. Once the woman left, Fate appeared. "So, Catherine, did you think you could escape me?" With that, Fate began to wreck the house. Horrified, Catherine begged Fate to stop.

"My mistress will be furious. Please, go." When Fate refused to stop, Catherine gathered her few belongings and fled. Unbeknownst to her, as soon as Catherine had gone, Fate restored order and left. So it was for seven years. Every time Catherine found a place to live and work, Fate followed her, destroying the interior, forcing her to leave.

In time, Catherine traveled to a city far from where she'd ever been. Tired, hungry, and discouraged, she walked by a house where a woman was watering flowers. "Please, Ma'am, might you be so kind as to give me a bit of food and a place to rest. I am willing to work."

"You have come at the right time. I will feed and give you lodgings, but every morning you must climb the mountain with bread and cheese and leave it in front of the cave at the top."

After a few days, Catherine worked up her courage to ask about the strange task. The woman said, "I must feed my Fate to keep her content. I dread to think what she might do were I to stop." When Catherine heard this, she began to weep. She told the woman how she had spent the last seven years, how she had lost everything. The woman said, "Do not despair. When you bring my Fate her bread and cheese, ask if she might speak with your Fate. Perhaps she can help."

The next morning, after giving the woman's Fate the food, Catherine asked if she might help her make peace with her Fate. "Your Fate is sleeping. I will not wake her. Tomorrow, when you come with my bread and cheese, bring her a gift. If she is pleased, she will give you something. Thank her graciously and leave."

Before climbing the mountain at dawn, Catherine made a bouquet of flowers to give to her Fate. After her mistress's Fate received the bread and cheese, she took Catherine to her Fate and asked her to stop tormenting Catherine. An arm appeared, took the bouquet, gave Catherine a skein of purple thread, then disappeared.

Puzzled, Catherine showed her mistress the curious gift. She told Catherine, "Keep it safe. There might come a time when it will be of use."

Sometime later, the king of the country discovered his royal robe had ripped. None of the country's tailors had the right color thread. "Issue a proclamation," he ordered. "Whoever has silk of this color must bring it to the court."

That afternoon, Catherine went to the palace. She showed the skein of purple silk to the guards who immediately took her to the king. He thanked her for the silk and put it on one side of a scale. On the other side his advisor placed gold. No matter how much gold he put on the scale, the skein weighed more. Exasperated, the king placed his crown on the scale and the scales balanced. "Who are you?" he asked.

Catherine told the king about her meeting with Fate and what had happened since. "It is clear," he said, "Fate has brought us together." As was the custom, they married. For the rest of her life, Catherine continued to bring gifts to her Fate.

❧ ❧ ❧

CASTING "THE SNOW QUEEN"

In 1978, I created a play for children based on Hans Christian Andersen's story, "The Snow Queen." The main human characters are Gerda, Gerda's grandfather, Kai, and the Snow Queen.

The story is well-known, and many students auditioned. I asked each person what mattered most to them in the story and why they wanted to play a particular part. Some shrugged, not prepared to answer with any depth. A few loved the story and wanted to be in the production. I chose the most talented students who clearly had thought about their participation.

When I posted the cast list, I was stunned by the barrage of outraged students, a few townspeople, and even some colleagues. How could I do such a thing? Why had I cast a Black male as white Gerda's grandfather and a Black female as the Snow Queen? "Because they were the best for the parts," I responded, an answer not well-received.

Letters. Phone calls. Angry looks. Threats of a production boycott. I chose to ignore them and focused my energy on directing the cast I'd selected.

At our first rehearsal I welcomed them, wondering if any had heard about the racist reactions. They had. Both Black students offered to leave the production. I told them, "We want you in the play. I chose you because I thought you were the best for the parts. That's all that matters." They agreed to stay.

The production was complex. I used still and moving images, canned and live music, small and large puppets—all integrated into the actors' words and actions. Rehearsals were complicated, and yet it was a play for children, and I always invited children to watch rehearsals to gauge their interest and the power of my writing.

After one rehearsal, when I asked the children what they thought about the play, and if they had suggestions or questions, a child asked, "How can a white girl have a Black grandfather?"

Before I could respond, another child asked, "How can the Snow Queen be Black? She's made of ice and ice is white."

I took a very deep breath while I thought about my response. Deliberately not looking at the two, I asked the audience, "Who believed Grandfather loved Gerda, his granddaughter?" All hands went up. "Who believed the Snow Queen was icy and cold?" All hands went up. "Well, this is what theatre is about—creating characters who touch the audience's emotions and feelings. According to all the hands that went up, it seems you were sure Grandfather loved Gerda, and the Snow Queen was cold and regal."

I decided not to ask the two if my response to their question satisfied them. I felt they needed time to think about what I'd said, but it pleased me to notice they were among the group of children who chose to talk with both characters afterward.

The play was well-received and was nominated to perform in Washington, D.C., as part of a children's play festival. "The Snow Queen" received a standing ovation.

What choice have you made that created conflict? How did you deal with it?

NAIVETÉ

In April 1959, I answered a newspaper ad written by an internationally renowned folk-dance teacher. He was looking for people to join him teaching folk dancing in a variety of European countries for eleven weeks during the summer. I'd been longing to go to Europe. This seemed a great way to go since I'd been folk dancing for years. His timetable coincided with my public-school teaching schedule—it would be during my summer break—which made it possible to apply. I responded immediately.

During the interview, R. showed me a record he'd made. I noticed the list of countries he'd taught in and read some testimonials from groups he'd worked with. He asked about my dance and teaching experience, then put on a record. The first piece of music was to a dance I knew, so it was easy to follow him. When he led dances I didn't know, I followed as best I could. I guess I was good enough, because he invited me to join him in Vienna where the work would begin. Once in Europe he'd pay all expenses. I'd leave the day after I finished teaching and return two days before the start of the new term.

I applied for a passport, told my parents, and answered their questions as best I could. They wanted to know more about him, what countries we'd be going to, who we'd be teaching . . . Mostly they worried about me going to Europe by myself. When my mother kept hounding me about traveling alone, I reminded her she'd hitchhiked to the Grand Canyon with a girlfriend when she was nineteen. "I'll turn twenty-three while I'm on the plane to Europe," I told her, "and I'll be working with a group."

Once in Vienna, I immediately learned there would be no group, just R. and me, but the first week was such a heady mixture of learning new dances and teaching large groups of enthusiastic participants I gave it no thought. R. spent a lot of time with his girlfriend, a lovely young woman who danced like she was made of air. I asked her how I could improve my dancing. "Think of dancing as floating," she said, happy to help. When I asked R. why he hadn't chosen her to be his teaching partner, he changed the subject.

When it came time to leave Vienna, I arrived at the train station and saw R. and his girlfriend hugging passionately. She was crying. I looked away. When our train was announced, R. met me as I walked to where we had to board. Once the train started moving, he got up from his seat across from me and sat next to me, putting his arm around my shoulder—too close for comfort.

I tried to move his arm, but he tightened his grip. "What are you doing?" I asked, annoyed.

"Getting to know you," he said, his tone seductive and demanding.

"You have a girlfriend."

"So what? She's in Vienna. You're here with me. That's all that matters." Something in his tone of voice frightened me. Against everyone's advice, I'd signed up to teach with a stranger for eleven weeks. Now all their warnings seemed to be coming true. To calm myself I told him I had to use the bathroom. He reluctantly released me, managing to stroke my body as I left.

That night he came into my bed. I fought him off, but he was bigger and stronger. I froze inside myself and let him do what he wanted, just as I'd done when I was a child, waiting for the bad time to be over.

In the morning, when he was in the bathroom, I looked for my passport and the envelope with my money. I couldn't find them. When I asked if he'd seen them, he said no. There was no time to challenge him; we had an early teaching session.

When we were teaching together, we worked well as a couple, contrasting sharply with his sexual predation. I reverted to an old coping mechanism, becoming emotionally numb. I decided my only way to escape was to pretend everything was fine.

About two weeks after we'd left Vienna, we went to the train station, ready to go from Switzerland to France. He usually bought our tickets, but on this day he was distracted by pressing business. I casually offered to buy our tickets. He shrugged and handed me our passports and his wallet. Inside was the envelope with my money. I put it and my passport into my bag. I used his money to buy his ticket to France and stayed at the ticket booth until it was almost time for the train to leave.

He was already on the train, waving frantically. I boarded, handed him his wallet, ticket, and passport, waited a minute or so, then grabbed my suitcase and jumped off as the doors closed and the train began to move.

Stunned by the sudden turn of events, I sank down on a bench, watching the train slowly disappear. I was free. Free to wander around Europe for eight weeks. I celebrated by going to a café. The coffee was hot and comforting, the brioche delicious. Lots of choices to make, but for the moment, all was well.

How do you respond when you've made a choice that has dire consequences?

30

WORLD TALE

The Healing Water

NATIVE AMERICAN

A man travels to find a healing remedy. The stories, The Comfort of Wolves and Angels on Atalaya Mountain, describe different ways to heal.

• • •

THE VILLAGE WAS SUFFERING from a devastating plague. None of the people's prayers, rituals, or medicines were powerful enough to stop the disease. A young man, Nekumonta, having watched helplessly as loved ones died, now saw his wife struggle to breathe. He knew her only chance to survive lay in his finding the water that nourished the healing herbs the Great Manitou had planted.

He left on a cold morning, walking as fast as he could, taking no time to eat or drink. Whenever he encountered an animal, he asked, "Can you tell me where to find the water nourished by the healing herbs planted by the Great Manitou?"

Each animal reluctantly said no. Three days and nights passed. Too tired to go any further, he lay down on the frozen earth. While he slept, animals gathered around him, warming him with their breaths, remembering how kind he'd been to them. They begged the Great Manitou to help him.

As Nekumonta slept, he dreamed his wife was alive, singing a sweet song that sounded like water falling. When he woke, he continued to hear the sound and looked everywhere but could find no water. Suddenly he realized the sound was coming from beneath him. Digging frantically with a strong branch, he uncovered a spring. He jumped into the hole he'd dug. After bathing in the water, feeling refreshed and energized, he made a small jar out of clay and baked it in the fire until it was hard enough to hold the healing water.

Moving as fast as he could, without spilling any of the precious water, he arrived to find his wife barely breathing. Dipping his finger into the water, he wet her lips, then washed her face until she fell into a peaceful sleep. When she awoke, she had fully recovered.

Other members of Nekumonta's tribe followed in his footsteps, bringing back the healing water, eventually ridding the village of the plague. For the rest of his life, Nekumonta was known as Chief of the Healing Water.

❧ ❧ ❧

THE COMFORT OF WOLVES

At 92, Maria, my friend of many years, was ill, refusing to eat. She told her caregivers, "If Nancy comes to visit, I'll start eating." I arrived the next day. She told me she'd lived a long life and wanted to die but didn't feel she could do so peacefully. I asked if there was anything I might do to help her feel calm in this last stage of her life.

"I'd like to see the wolves once again," she said. I had no idea what she was talking about. I even wondered if she was hallucinating. "I know a woman who knows a woman who runs a wolf sanctuary. She's willing to bring two wolves to visit if the director will allow it. You need to talk with her. Please. You're a professor. You have a PhD. She'll listen to you." I didn't see what having a doctorate had to do with anything, but I promised I'd do what I could. "Go now," urged Maria.

I went downstairs and knocked on the administrator's door. She was a pleasant looking woman and greeted me warmly after I introduced myself. "You're Maria's friend," she said. "She talks a lot about you."

I couldn't imagine a director agreeing to have wolves in an assisted-living institution, but I promised Maria I'd ask. I told her Maria and I had been friends for more than forty years—we'd met when we were living in the same community. After a brief, friendly conversation, I told her why I'd come. "Maria would like permission for a woman who runs a wolf sanctuary to bring two wolves to see her."

I expected the woman to object, to dismiss such a foolish idea out of hand. Instead, she said, "Maria's friend called me. She told me the woman bringing the wolves would have them under control." She hesitated, then said, "I know how much seeing them would mean to Maria."

I tried to make a case for the wolves visiting. "Maybe the people living here"—I almost said inmates—"would like to see them as well? It would give them something exciting to talk about. I'd guess most of them have never seen a live wolf up close."

She looked surprised. "I never thought about that. I have the woman's contact information. I'll call and ask. How long will you be staying?"

"I don't know. It depends on how she's doing." I didn't tell her Maria wanted to see the wolves so she could die in peace.

Maria was asleep when I went back to her room. The caregivers said all she could talk about was seeing the wolves. None of us believed it could happen.

And yet, it happened. The director gave her approval. The residents, thrilled about seeing the wolves, agreed to wear dark clothing, no jewelry or perfume, and to stand against the walls of the entrance area as quietly and still as possible. The excitement in the building was palpable.

Two days later, I was in Maria's room, waiting with her. The woman with the wolves, two huge white Arctic wolves, entered. Maria's face lit up. She beamed happiness. The wolves went on each side of her and put their front paws on the bed. The wolf woman said something as one of them moved close to Maria's face, as if to lick her. The wolf backed off, but Maria leaned toward it, her hand resting gently on its back. The two of them looked intensely at each other. Then Maria turned to the other wolf and looked intensely at it. She put her arms out and the wolves rested their faces on her hands. Maria's joy was palpable.

When the wolf woman said it was time for her to take the wolves back to the van, Maria asked permission to kiss them. The woman said, "No kissing, but you can stroke their paws gently."

We watched the woman tell the wolves to come to her. She had them sit before she took them out. They had driven hundreds of miles to see Maria and needed to rest before the long drive back to the wolf sanctuary.

When the wolves had gone, Maria hugged me, thanking me over and over for helping her see the wolves. "Nancy, you're the best friend a person could have. Please tell the Angels [her name for the caregivers] that I'm going to stop eating, that you understand and approve."

Approve wasn't the word I would have chosen. I wanted Maria to live. She was a friend who'd seen me through many difficult situations. But it was what she wanted. If I could help her achieve a sense of comfort, it would help me let her go with ease in my heart. "It's your decision, Maria. I want what you want. I'll tell them."

Maria died peacefully a few days later.

How do you define healing?

❧ ❧ ❧

ANGELS ON ATALAYA MOUNTAIN

In August of 2006 I was still recuperating from a bout of leukemia—from being hospitalized, medicalized, and chemotized. Fatigue was my constant companion. Depression hovered, ready to overwhelm me at any moment. Doubts about my ability to recoup physically assailed me. Although I was increasing my stamina, strength, and fitness by walking up hills around where I live, it wasn't enough to lift my spirits. I decided I needed to climb Atalaya, 9200 ft, about seven miles round trip. It was one of the first mountain hikes I'd done after moving to Santa Fe in 2001 and remained a challenge even when I was well. I set a target date—the last Wednesday in August.

On a sunny summer morning, I packed my gear, shoved my doubts and can'ts into my mind's refuse bin, and set off. As I started toward the steepest part of the trail, I bent over and began chanting: "Don't worry about the steep part. Don't worry about the steep part." Totally engrossed in chanting, not looking where I was going, I bumped into two women, a mother and daughter, who had been watching with amusement, wondering if I'd really thump into them. Embarrassed, I showered them with apologies. The more I apologized, the harder they laughed.

I felt I owed them an explanation. I don't usually hike with my head down, not paying attention to where I'm going. They listened to what I'd been through and supported my effort to climb Atalaya. I told them, even though it was a lie, if I just got to the part where the steep and less steep trails meet, I'd feel okay. The daughter, a junior in high school, told me she and her mother hiked regularly and invited me to join them. I told her they'd better go ahead; I'd be too slow for them. They insisted I go with them and told me to set the pace.

When we got to the place where the two trails meet, I stopped to take a drink, not sure I had the energy to keep going. The daughter said, "You're not going to stop here, are you? I'm sure you can make it to the top." I wasn't at all sure, but her encouragement was manna to my soul. Without waiting to hear my worries, the mother started up, the daughter got behind me, and, before I could verbalize my fears, she was telling me about her life as we hiked up the steep incline. Listening to her stories distracted me from focusing on the steepness of the trail. They were both in very good shape, and I'm sure they didn't need the frequent rest stops and water breaks, but they did both with such seeming innocence and caring, all I felt was gratitude.

When we made it to the top of Atalaya, I could hardly believe I'd done it. The two of them were cheering and hugging me. People resting at the top wanted to know why we were hugging and laughing. Much to my embarrassment, the daughter told them about my having been so sick and my determination to hike to the top. The hikers responded with hugs and cheers and chocolate.

Fatigue and depression gave way to joy. I told the mother and daughter they were my mountain angels. I couldn't have made it to the top without their caring and support. The daughter laughed. "You can bump into us any time. We're always happy to help."

Have you experienced unexpected help in a time of healing? What was that like for you?

31

WORLD TALE

One Wish

IRISH

A woman is given one wish. The stories, Cat Tale, What I Wished, and Impossibly Possible, reveal ways to satisfy desires.

• • •

One morning, a woman gathering herbs saw an injured bird. She carefully picked it up and took it home. Her father made a box for the bird. Her blind mother tucked soft cloth into the box. Her husband brought food for the bird. The woman gave it water to drink.

In time, the bird gained strength, and its injury healed. There came a day when the woman opened the door and the bird flew out. She was happy to see the bird fly yet missed its cheerful chirping.

The next morning, when the woman walked outside, the bird perched on her shoulder and said, "Because you cared for me, I grant you one wish." The woman thanked the bird but wasn't sure what to ask for. "May I have a day to think about it?"

"I will come to you tomorrow. Be prepared to tell me what you wish for."

That evening, the woman told her mother, father, and husband about the gift of a wish from the bird. Her father said, "Wish for gold."

Her mother said, "Wish for my eyesight to be restored."

The husband said, "We have been yearning to have a child. Wish for a child."

In the morning, as the woman worked in her garden, the bird flew onto her shoulder and asked, "Have you decided what to wish for?"

"Yes," said the woman. "I wish for my mother to see her grandchild lying in a golden cradle."

The bird said, "So it shall be."

And so it was.

CAT TALE

In 1947, I was eleven, and had been wishing for a pet for a long time. I told my parents I'd settle for a dog or a cat. What I got was fish in a tank, not my idea of a pet. One day, alone in our apartment, the phone rang, startling me. It was rare for anyone to call during the day, and when they did, it meant trouble. I picked up the receiver, worried something bad had happened.

It was my six-year-old cousin, John. "Hi, Nancy, our cat had kittens and they're ready for adoption. Want one?"

"Sure," I said, enthusiastically, oblivious as to how I'd explain this to my mother, who hated animals and didn't much like me.

"If you do, you need to come today. Lots of people want one."

"I'll leave now. Don't let anyone take one before I get there."

I walked three blocks to the subway, put my nickel in the slot, and got on the next train. It took almost an hour to get to his Greenwich Village apartment, but during the ride, all I thought about was having a real pet. My cousin greeted me, holding a bunch of snuggled kittens. I was entranced. "Can I hold them?"

"Okay, but be careful; they don't know you." I took the kittens into my arms, enchanted by their soft, warm, cuddly bodies.

We both heard the mama cat yowl. "You better put them down," said my cousin. "I think she wants to feed them."

I stooped to let them go, but one of them stayed in my arms. "I think this kitten loves me," I said, full of hope and need.

"I think so too," he said. "You can have it."

"We need to hide it," I told him. "They don't allow animals on the trains." He found a carton and we made small holes on the top. Worried about the cat not having enough air, I made them bigger. Big mistake. As I happily walked to the subway, the kitten popped her head out of the box and purred.

Ignoring subway rules, I paid my nickel, walked through the turnstile, and waited for the train. When it came, I got on and found a seat. As the train started to move, the kitten popped her face up. I pushed it down. People around me looked on with surprise—some pleased, some not. Unfortunately, she popped her head up and meowed just as the conductor came by. "You can't bring animals on the train, little girl. You need to get off at the next stop."

People around me told him: "Don't be so mean." "It's only a kitten." "She's just a kid."

Nothing helped. He made sure I got off at the next stop. I got on the next train, was asked to leave, got on the next train after that, had to get off. It took a long time before I finally got to my stop. I walked home, suddenly feeling the trouble I was in. I kissed the kitten's face and said, "Don't worry. I won't let anyone hurt you." I pushed her face back into the box, walked up to the front door, up the stairs, and stood before the locked door to our apartment.

Trembling, I took out my key, wishing I had someplace safe to go. My mother often hit me for no reason. Now she'd have a whole lot of reason. I opened the door and heard my mother and sister in the kitchen. I rushed into the bedroom I shared with my sister and closed the door. I took the kitten out of the box and nuzzled my face in her silky fur. I didn't hear the door open.

My mother's wrath was swift and immediate. She knocked the kitten out of my arms and smacked me so hard I fell on the floor. My sister yelled, "It's running away!"

"Where did you get that thing?" she demanded to know. When I told her, she immediately called John's mother, full of rage.

I ran after the kitten, picked her up, and crooned, "Everything will be all right"—something I didn't believe. I poured milk into a dish I had covered with tin foil so my mother couldn't complain about my using our dishes, and took the kitten and dish into the bedroom. My sister came in and closed the door. "You're in big trouble." I shrugged. Nothing new.

"She's gonna make you give it back."

"No. She's mine. I love her."

"Mama's furious. She won't let you keep it."

We heard the front door open. My father was home from work. My sister and I heard our mother yelling about the cat. About me. I held the kitten, waiting for the worst to happen. My father came into the bedroom and closed the door. Hugging the kitten, I said, "I'm keeping her. I love her and she loves me." He told me all the reasons I couldn't keep the kitten. Nothing he said made a difference. "I'll go to the library. I'll get a book to teach me how to take care of a kitten. I'll pay for her food out of my babysitting money. I'll keep her in the bedroom when I'm at school. I'll clean up her messes."

My mother stormed into the room, rushing toward me. I was too worried about the kitten to care what she did to me. "I won't let you hurt my kitten." My father put his arm around my mother and whispered something to her.

There was a strained silence. I looked at my father, begging him to help. He finally spoke, quietly: "We'll be going to the country after school lets out in a few days." (Our parents rented a small bungalow every summer.) "It will be easy for Nancy to take care of it there." My mother shook free of my father and stomped out of the bedroom.

That night the kitten and I slept snuggled together. For the moment, all was well.

When you were a child, what did you wish for?

WHAT I WISHED

In 1985, I spent nineteen days in a twenty-eight-bed ward for critically ill women. When it was teatime, three of the women closest to my bed joined me at a small table to talk and drink our tea. They were poor women from towns outside of London. Despite the differences between them and me, we were all deathly ill. We'd been talking among ourselves for a few days when one of the women put down her cup and asked, "If you could wish for anything, what would you wish for?"

There was a long silence before one of the women said, "I wish I'd been to Paris."

The second woman, married with five children, sighed. "I wish I'd had a man tell me he loved me."

The third woman hesitated, then admitted, "I wish I had money to buy a home of my own."

They looked at me. I felt uncomfortable. I'd been to Paris. I owned my home. True, I never had a loving relationship with a man, but what I wished for was a PhD, a wish I couldn't share given how much I had compared to them. Fortunately, the discussion stopped when a sister (nurse) told us it was time for rest, to get back in bed.

It was a complicated two years—I was diagnosed with an anomalous form of a rare leukemia, participated in an experimental medical protocol, then had to find the energy to return to work and cope with the deaths of my son's father and my mother. My wish for a PhD faded. When I saw an advertisement for The Human Capacities Program, a three-year experience ending in a certificate for what would now be called a Life Coach, I signed up. Though the program had nothing to do with my work as a professor, I needed something to help me focus on more than figuring out how to manage each day's side effects from the experimental medication.

Over one hundred fifty people gathered together for the first session, in the winter of 1987, to explore a variety of exercises and readings about developing our capacities as human beings. In our two-week spring meeting, a man from Union University came to talk about its nationally accredited adult learners' programs. All those interested were encouraged to sign up for a five-to-ten-minute meeting. I deliberately signed up for the last slot so we might have more time to talk.

I met M., a well-dressed man who appeared to be in his mid-fifties, in the small living room of a cottage. He invited me to sit at a table piled with leaflets and asked why I'd signed up for the meeting. "I've always wished I had a PhD." I told him I'd looked at a lot of PhD programs, but none had seemed right for me. "I'm interested in stories. I want to understand why and how, in my teaching, they seem to unlock students' stories, which helps them discover more about who they are. I want to know and understand more about how this process works."

"The Union PhD program is multidisciplinary. What are your areas of interest?"

I didn't hesitate. "Literature, philosophy, and psychology."

We talked for a long time—him asking detailed questions, me having answers I didn't know I'd thought about. As the interview drew to a close, I told him about dealing with the leukemia as well as teaching full time. He was quiet for a minute or so, then said, "I know this is not an easy time for you, but I think you need to apply to our PhD program. Use my name as a primary reference. Don't wait."

I didn't. I quit the Human Capacity Program, applied to the Union Program, and was accepted. People I told were not encouraging. "You're already a full professor with an MA. Why bother with a PhD?" "It won't give you more money or prestige." "You're dealing with a catastrophic illness and teaching full time; why add more stress?" I stopped explaining why I wanted the PhD program, a way to explore my questions about the power of stories. I was too embarrassed to admit just how much I wanted a PhD after my name.

I designed my program focusing on what I wanted to learn, picked primary and secondary advisers, and selected my committee—a Jungian psychologist, a professor of English and Comparative Literature, and an adult learner studying the relationship of stories to his role as pastor. I wrote papers, attended week-long seminars arranged around my teaching schedule, did an internship, wrote a thesis—Beyond this Crossing Place: The Stories of a Year, The Stories of a Life—and a contextual piece detailing the research I'd done. It wasn't easy. I had to prove the research I wanted to do was valid. I had to overcome the prejudices of faculty who didn't understand or care about stories. And, I had to deal with the complexities of illness and problematic medication and depression. To quote whoever said it, "My eyes were on the prize." In 1990, age fifty-four, six years after being in a ward with critically ill women, my wish came true. I was now Nancy King, PhD.

Have you wished for something that made no sense to others? What happened?

❧ ❧ ❧

IMPOSSIBLY POSSIBLE

I'd been wanting to go to Machu Picchu for a long time, but none of the plans had worked out. When I saw the REI Peru trip advertised, I immediately signed up, but still had to be approved. A woman called to assess whether I was up to the degree of hiking difficulty. I told her I was eighty-three, in good shape, that I hiked regularly, sometimes up to fourteen miles. She signed me up, but, given my age, she said I could not do the hike that involved climbing two peaks of 14,700 ft in one day. I could do the alternative hike. I tried to change her mind by telling her I'd climbed Wheeler Peak in Taos, which is 13,100 ft, to no avail. She made it clear it wouldn't be possible.

Before visiting Machu Picchu, we were scheduled to hike in places tourists don't go. The hikes were challenging and invigorating, the vistas incredible. Most enjoyable was meeting children who regularly hiked down the mountain to go to school, and then up to go home, which filled me with admiration. We gave them oranges and apples and were rewarded with "Muchas gracias." I was able to engage with them, speaking basic Spanish, which made me happy.

The day of the two-peak hike, I managed to leave my bottle of electrolytes in the van. By the time we had hiked to the place where we split off into two groups, one doing the easier and the other, the harder hikes, I was feeling shaky. I told the head guide. He beckoned me to come with him. Much to my surprise, he mixed up a packet of electrolytes in a quart of water and told me to drink it. All of it. I'm accustomed to sipping, not gulping, but I could tell from the way he watched me, I'd better just do it.

As the groups divided, I walked toward those doing the easier hike. The head guide stopped me. "I heard you say you wished you could do the two-peak hike."

"I do, but the woman who vetted me said it wasn't possible. I was too old."

He shook his head. "You can do anything you want to do." I looked at him. Astonished. He pointed me toward the five people waiting to do the two-peak hike. "Go. I'll be right there."

More than a little dazed, I joined the group. Everyone knew I was in my eighties, at least twenty years older than anyone else. They didn't bother to hide their doubts. I kept the words of the guide in my head, took my place, and, with the others, started up.

It was hard going. Very hard going. But I remembered what a mountaineering friend told me. "When you're breathing hard, blow three hard breaths out to get rid of the carbon dioxide and help you breathe easier." I focused on my breath. I put one foot in front of the other. I kept up with the group. When we got to the top of the first 14,700 ft peak, I was ecstatic. I felt like superwoman.

When we started down toward the second peak, one of the hikers protested, "Why are we going down to go up?" The guide laughed. "You signed up for two peaks, not one. To get to the second you have to go down." And we did go down. Steeply down.

We started up toward the top of the second peak. The guide set a slower pace than he had when we went up the first peak. No one complained. I practiced the breathing. Like the little engine that could in the children's story, I kept telling myself, I think I can. I think I can. And then, there we were, at the top of the second 14,700 ft peak.

This time I stood off by myself, feeling as if I were in a holy place, filled with gratitude and a quiet sense of joy. I saw the guide looking at me. I grinned and bowed. He bowed back. I might be eighty-three. but I wasn't too old to fulfill a wish.

Have you fulfilled a wish that seemed impossible? If so, what was that like?

32

WORLD TALE

The Fig Tree

JAPAN

A couple chooses to act with future generations in mind. The stories, Winning and Losing, Taking a Chance, and Beginning with the Ending, explore choices that change lives.

• • •

THERE WAS ONCE AN old couple who spent much of their time growing food to eat and flowers for their beauty. Although they were poor and had little money or goods, working in their garden was a source of joy that made up for what they didn't have. One day, while planting vegetables, the woman said to her husband, "Look! This would be a lovely place to plant a fig tree."

He dug his fingers into the earth and said, "You are right. It is a good idea. Let us find a tree to plant."

Each time they asked people where to find a small fig tree, people laughed. "You're too old. Why plant a tree now? You'll never live long enough to eat any figs."

"That is true," said the old woman, "but our grandchildren are young. They will harvest figs for as long as they live."

"And," said the old man, "their children will enjoy figs as will their children."

They found a tree and planted it, enjoying every new sprout of green.

WINNING AND LOSING

I was eleven, playing a made-up kind of baseball with a group of kids, our last game before the end of summer. I was at bat when the pitcher accused me of cheating. I vehemently denied this and told him he was mad because I was a better pitcher than he was. He rushed at me, fists waving, calling me names. We started punching each other, I with my eyes closed, furiously banging away at him. Suddenly I heard him curse me as he stopped hitting. I opened my eyes. He was running away. I burst into tears. One of the boys asked why I was crying; I should be cheering. I'd won the fight. I didn't feel like a winner. I felt crappy.

That fall I started going to a Jewish school every Sunday morning. The teachers, all veterans who'd helped liberate Buchenwald, created the school so children could learn about Jewish history and culture. I had a lot of questions, and it felt safe to ask them in class. Although my classmates made fun of me, groaning each time I asked a question, my teacher—I'll call him Bernie—always responded respectfully. He often answered a question with a question. When I asked why he did this, he said his job was to help us learn to think for ourselves. The first time he didn't have an answer for my question, I asked what the point of asking questions was if there were no answers. He said, "The point of asking questions is to ask questions; some are so big there are no definite answers." I liked the idea of asking big questions.

I felt so comfortable with him that during a break I told him about the fight and asked him why I felt bad afterward. As always, he took time to consider his response. "I think that's a question only you can answer."

"But I won. Why did I feel bad about winning?"

"You tell me."

"It didn't feel good to hurt someone."

He grinned. "But you won, right?"

"Yeah, but what did I win? That's what I keep wondering."

"Keep wondering," he said. "It's the beginning of wisdom."

The next Sunday I asked Bernie, "Is it possible to win and lose at the same time?"

Not for the first time, he asked, "What do you think?"

"I think I won the fight and lost my self."

"What self did you lose?" he asked kindly, with obvious curiosity.

I'd spent the week thinking about the contradiction between winning and feeling bad. "I lost the self that thought she would never hurt anyone for any reason."

"If so," he asked, "how do you recover that self?" It didn't occur to me this was possible. I pretty much saw everything as black and white, good and bad. No gray.

"How can I recover something I lost? There's no do-over."

"No, but you can learn from the experience. The kid came at you, and you reacted. Afterward, you thought about what you did and how you felt. We all make mistakes. What matters is how we deal with them. This can only happen if you think about your actions."

"People say I think too much. I'm too intense. I'm too serious. I'm too sensitive."

He put his hands gently on each side of my face. "Nancy, whoever the people are, they don't get to decide who you are. Only you."

He reminded me life is complex and complicated. No single act defined me or anyone else. I could choose not to meet anger with anger. I could respond to unkindness with kindness. It was up to me to decide how I wanted to live, who I wanted to be.

What kind of person do you want to be? Are you who you want to be? How do you know?

TAKING A CHANCE

I read the student's note. He'd flunked out of the university but was sure he could pass the two courses needed for reinstatement if he could be in my production of *Peter and the Wolf.* I was a teaching assistant (TA) with no power, but I was moved by what he wrote and contacted him.

He was tall and skinny, visibly nervous as he walked into my small office. He told me how much he loved theatre and how, as a kid, he'd listened to the record of *Peter and the Wolf* so many times he'd practically memorized the words. He begged me to let him join the production. I told him I had no authority to cast him if he wasn't a registered student. He looked so miserable, I said I'd check with the Chair to see what could be done.

He read the student's note and said the decision could only be made by the Dean of the College of Arts and Sciences. He reminded me I was only a

TA. He told me it was not my concern. I had enough to do with teaching, writing the second half of the story of *Peter and the Wolf,* and directing the production. He added, "I know it's not my business, but you're also a single mother."

Still, the urgency of the student's plea stayed with me. I went to the dean. He was direct and clear. "You're only a TA. He needs to get help from a faculty member." He looked at me like I was a bothersome bug to be squashed.

"I'd like to help him. I'll take responsibility for his doing good work."

"You're a fool to bother," said the dean, "but if you're determined to do this, he has to get Cs in two courses in order to be reinstated as a full-time student." I thanked him, wondering why I was choosing to help when I'd been advised not to. Still, I felt sorry for him. I also felt he needed more incentive than two Cs to thrive in college.

I contacted the student, and we met in my office. I told him, "The Dean says you may be in my production, but"—and I lied—"you have to take two courses and get an A and a B in order to be reinstated as a full-time student in September."

He was so happy he danced out of my office. I questioned what I'd gotten myself into, but it was too late. The decision had been made.

Guess what?

He joined the cast. He got an A and a B. Graduated. Became an actor, playwright, and teacher. When he retired, students continued to contact him as he has continued to contact me.

What might make you take a chance when you're strongly advised not to do so?

❧ ❧ ❧

BEGINNING WITH THE ENDING

She reminded me of a porcupine, ready to shoot quills at a moment's notice. And yet, when I began each memoir class by telling a world tale, she, like the other eighth graders, listened attentively in the class sponsored by PEN, an international organization that supports freedom of expression for writers around the world.

One morning, after I told a tale about how Hummingbird faces her fear and helps Panther recover his eyesight, she told a student who'd come in late, "You missed a really good story." Fast forward to the end of class when we spent a few minutes reflecting on the session. She spoke up: "I hate the stories you tell. Why do we have to listen to such stupid stories?" I sighed, let the other students talk about their experience, then ended the session. She was one of the most difficult students I'd ever worked with. I felt as if her behavior changed faster than I could blink.

At the beginning of the next class, I asked students to paint a "telling" image—a visual abstraction of an important point in their lives—and then to write what came to mind. The class was busy writing when she walked up to me and said, "I made an image and wrote some, but it's too hard a story to tell. I can't write it."

"Okay. Is there another story you'd like to write? Remember, the only rule is, whatever you write has to be meaningful to you."

"I'll write about a camping trip with my uncle." I nodded and watched while she painted an image of what might be a sleeping bag with a bump in the middle, grass, trees, and a stick figure looming over it all. She wrote for a few minutes, then crumpled up the paper and said, "I don't want to write this story."

"Maybe you need to write the hard story. Sometimes when we write what's difficult, it helps us feel better."

"I did something awful. How can writing about it make me feel better?"

I knew her story. It was hard. Very hard. "After what happened, did anything or anyone help you feel a little better?"

She nodded. "My grandmother told me it wasn't my fault. She told everyone it wasn't my fault."

"Okay. Why not start by writing the ending, how someone you love told you it wasn't your fault. Then, remembering how the story ends, you can write the beginning. Every time the story seems too hard to write, you can look at your ending."

She shook her head. "It's too hard. I can't do it."

"Could you do it if your Language Arts teacher and I help you?"

"How you gonna help? You can't change what I did." I could feel the quills shooting out.

"You're right, we can't change what happened, but we'll help you every way we are able. I think you're very brave to be willing to write such a hard story."

It took a lot of doing, a lot of anxious moments when she tore up what she'd written, only to have us tape up the pages. A lot of encouragement by her teacher and me. Up until the last moment, I wasn't sure she'd finish it, but she did. We sent the class's stories to PEN. They printed the stories and made them into a book, with a cover designed by the class.

After the Author's Celebration, I handed each student a copy of their memoir book. She hung back, looking distressed, clearly waiting until the other students had gone. When she walked over to me, I waited for one of her verbal zingers. Instead, she said, looking at the floor, "I know we're only supposed to get one book, but could I have two books? I want to give one to my grandmother." I was so shocked, it took time for me to register what she was asking. She sighed, thinking I wasn't going to do it. Looking at me, she pleaded, "Please give me a book for my grandmother. I promise I won't tell the other kids."

No porcupine quills. Only a troubled kid who'd written a powerful memoir that took a lot of courage to write. "Of course, you can have two." I handed her the books. She took them, carefully put them in her backpack, started to leave, then returned, gave me a quick hug, and ran off.

How do you keep going when all you want to do is quit?

33

WORLD TALE

The Dancing Granny

AFRICAN

A woman discovers a way to solve a difficult problem. The stories, Not Too Old and Walking into a Story, explore situations that inspire creative responses.

• • •

THERE WAS ONCE AN old woman who loved to dance. People called her Dancing Granny. All day long, no matter what she was doing, she managed to sing out the beat and dance to the rhythm. She sang and danced as she planted her vegetable garden, as her seeds sprouted, as they grew into plants.

One day Spider Anansi came walking by and saw the luscious vegetables growing in the old woman's garden. He noticed how much she liked to sing and dance, so he started to sing. Once she was singing, she began to dance. Though she was old, she sang and danced like a young girl. Her pleasure in hopping and skipping led her out of her garden and into the village. Spider Anansi watched her leave. When he could no longer see her, he helped himself to all the corn he could carry. That evening his family had a fine meal.

When Granny returned and saw her corn was gone, she knew whose voice she had heard. "That Spider Anansi, he stole my corn. The next time he comes I won't listen to his music. I'll catch him and give him what he deserves."

But the next day, when Spider Anansi returned, she could not resist his singing, and soon she was dancing her way out of her garden and into the village. Spider Anansi took all the peas and beans he could carry and took them home. Once again his family had a delicious meal.

When Granny returned and saw all her peas and beans were gone, she sat on a stone and thought. “What am I going to do? I can't resist that thieving rascal's song. At this rate, I'll have no food for all my work.”

Granny was so upset, she picked all the remaining crops so there was nothing more for him to steal, yet she knew he would be back.

Sure enough, the next day, Spider Anansi returned, singing the song Granny couldn't resist. But this time, instead of dancing by herself, she grabbed Spider Anansi and began to dance. “Let go of me,” he cried. But Dancing Granny held on. She whirled and twirled with Spider Anansi holding on as best he could.

Soon, he couldn't resist Dancing Granny's joy. Together they whirled and twirled and hopped and skipped. Dancing Granny never had a better partner, and Spider Anansi never had more fun.

❧ ❧ ❧

NOT TOO OLD

I was twenty-one when I chose to stop performing as a dancer. Too many experiences of being told I was too short, too heavy, too slow, too difficult . . . To earn a salary, I taught dance and on occasion choreographed dance programs, but never felt fulfilled. I started a children's theatre company in a settlement house in a poor section of town. I earned an MA in theatre and began teaching movement and nonverbal communication for actors in a university theatre program, which I loved. I found a way to love moving that was not dancing.

More than twenty years later, I was using a Raven tale from the Indigenous Peoples of the Northwest as the basis for students to improvise. The story is full of action as Raven is called upon by the community to defeat Evil. I told them to let the story resonate within, to think about characters and energy and what motivated their movement. As they began, my students invited me to join them, which I sometimes did, to provide inspiration and challenge. It was utter chaos in the beginning with no specific instruction, just the story living inside each of us. We moved as we felt, sometimes interacting, sometimes bumping and falling over one another. As we moved, something shifted. Our movements became less chaotic. We started paying attention to one another. I called out some of the key words in the story. Students responded by echoing my words.

Unbeknownst to me, the dance teacher, checking on noise he heard in the dance studio, came in and watched. When we stopped moving, he applauded. "I want you to make what you just did into a piece for the dance concert," he said to me.

"That's up to the students. It's their class and their work," I responded.

"No," he said, "I want you to create the piece and dance it. I've been watching you move. You're mesmerizing. I couldn't take my eyes off you."

I laughed. "I'm forty-six. It's been more than twenty-five years since I last danced. I don't miss it."

Before I could say any more, my students joined in, like a Greek chorus. "Great idea. Let's do it."

Seeing my discombobulation, the dance teacher said, "If it makes you feel better, we'll call it a movement piece, and all of you *movers* rather than dancers." As he left the room, my students let me know they were ready to begin working on the piece.

At the start of our next class, one of the students brought his drum, another brought her flute. I suggested one person read the text and the rest of us move according to how we responded to the words and music. "We need to cast the story," said a student. "I think you should be Raven." I disagreed. The class agreed. I was Raven. They chose their characters; most wanted to be villagers. Two volunteered to be Evil. After a short discussion, the two students agreed to work together as one since Evil was so powerful.

I began rehearsals as we had the first time, with no instruction, just improvisation, to see what ideas would emerge since we had two months to work on the piece before the concert. At first there was the usual chaos. We knocked into each other. Students lifted me up to counter Evil, and I fell backward. Luckily two students saw and caught me. I felt awkward and uncomfortable about being the main character. When I suggested a student take my place, the class answered as one. "No! You need to be Raven." Oy!

The night of the first performance, I was so anxious one of my students laughed and said, "Professor King, you're making us nervous. Calm down." Laughter helps.

All too quickly it was our turn. The lights went out. We took our places. The beat of the drum set an ominous tone. The flute countered. The lights came on. The villagers surrounded me, in my role as Raven, and the students portraying Evil. I stepped out of the circle, shaking, unable to find my center. Wobbling when I tried to balance. Then, Evil pounced—two students in one costume.

Something shifted inside me. As memories of abuse, of feeling hopeless and alone began to overwhelm me, I could feel the villagers moving behind me, supporting me, urging me on. I was tired of feeling helpless, tired of not speaking out for myself. I suddenly felt a surge of energy, of power I didn't know I had. Moving with strength and balance and conviction, I countered Evil as the drumbeat echoed my movement, the flute encouraging me to keep going. We moved against and with each other, vying for victory. I felt the villagers' encouragement even though I couldn't see their movement. Finally, with a decisive thrust, using my whole body, I forced Evil to the floor and stood on top of the horizontal bodies. Evil lost all energy. Evil was defeated.

Without having decided to do so ahead of time, we formed a circle, bowed our heads, then turned to the audience and bowed. The flute stopped. The drumming stopped.

There was silence. No applause. I felt bad for my students. I knew I was too old to perform. I should have refused. Suddenly, to my astonishment, the audience stood up. Cheering. Clapping. Whistling. My students, including Evil (who had moved out of their joint costume) and the musicians, surrounded me, pushing me out in front of them to bow separately before bowing with the cast.

One of my students whispered, "See, we told you. You're not too old to dance or move or whatever you want to call it."

How old is old?

❧ ❧ ❧

WALKING INTO A STORY

In 1988, as part of my work for a PhD, I chose a seminar in Hawaii: Cross Cultural Community Cooperation. To feel rested before beginning the first session, I arrived a few days early. Even in my summer clothes I was too hot. I looked around at Hawaiian women, many of whom were wearing long, flowing, loosely fitting dresses in bright patterns. They looked a whole lot cooler than I felt. I was wondering where I might find a place selling dresses like theirs when I noticed an advertisement for a shop that made muumuus to order. I didn't know what a muumuu was, but when I saw the image of the dress, I realized it was exactly what I was looking for.

I found the store, nestled in the corner of a group of shops in a hotel. I walked in, taken aback by the numbers of women crowded into the space, some being measured, many looking at fabric, others trying on what I learned had been made for them.

I was ready to leave, discomforted by all the activity, when a woman came up to me and said, "If you're looking for your muumuu, we have it. It's ready to go."

Shocked, I told the woman, "It can't be mine. I've never been here before."

"Well, then," she said, grinning, "the universe knew you were coming and told us to get it ready for you." Too dumbfounded to say anything, I let her take me by the hand and lead me to a dress that was hanging where everyone could see it. "How do you like your muumuu?"

It was beautiful, a bit fancier than most, with two different fabrics for the sleeves and hem. "It's lovely, but . . . "

The woman, who looked to be in her late fifties, unfazed by my bewilderment, took the dress off the hanger, gave it to me, and said, "I'll show you the dressing room. I can't wait to see it on you."

I've never been in an alternate universe, but I felt like I'd walked into a weird world. When we got to the dressing room, she smiled when she saw it was empty. "There's been someone trying on dresses up until now. Your dress is waiting for you."

I took off my skirt and blouse and put on the dress. It was the right length, the right amount of fabric, and I felt degrees cooler in it. I didn't want to take it off. I walked out of the dressing room and the woman beamed. "You look lovely. It's perfect." Women close by murmured how pretty it was, how good I looked.

I was too unsettled to hide my feelings, so I told her how bizarre it felt to be wearing a dress that really seemed to be made for me, yet I'd never been in the shop.

She told me strange was normal there. I asked what that meant. She offered me a cool drink and sat us down in a corner. She told me that years ago, the woman who owned the shop, now in her eighties, had been walking along a deserted path and heard a mewling sound, which she thought was a kitten. When she walked to where she heard the sound, she found a padded box and inside was a baby, newly born. She took the baby home. Washed, clothed, and fed her, then notified the authorities she'd found a baby and intended to keep her. When they told her seventy was too old to adopt a newborn, she let them know she worked in a shop with women of all ages. She'd bring the baby to work, and every one of the women would help mother the child. She was so persuasive they allowed her to keep the baby.

"What happened to the child?" I couldn't imagine adopting a baby when I was seventy.

"She's growing up just fine. The little baby is now almost eleven, and everyone who works here helps mother her. Too bad you didn't come in sooner. You'd have met her."

"What about the woman who adopted her?"

"She's fine. Going strong."

I was fascinated by the story and was about to get up when the woman said, "We made your dress yesterday. The owner picked out the fabric, designed the dress, told us how much material to use and how long to make it. She told us you'd be here to pick it up tomorrow." The hair on my neck rose. I had goose bumps.

"How is this possible?" I asked.

The woman shook her head. "I don't know. We tell her she dances to a tune none of us can hear.

She laughs and tells us to stop talking and start dancing."

More than a little incredulous, wearing my dress, I danced out of the shop.

When was the last time you danced?

34

WORLD TALE

Mereaira and Kape Tautini

MAORI PEOPLE, NEW ZEALAND

The threat of violence is ended by a mother's plea for peace. The stories, Unseen Friends, Troubled Kids, and Incident in London, reveal how people respond to violence with caring.

• • •

The Ngāti Awa chief, Te Keepa Toihau, had a daughter, Mereaira. She married a young Whakatōhea chief, known as Kape Tautini, who came from the Ōhakana Island. Even though Kape Tautini's people were known to be enemies of the Ngāti Awa, the couple lived happily with her father in his house. In time, a child was born.

After a while, Kape Tautini became restless living among his wife's people. He longed to be with his own community. One night, without telling anyone, he made his way back to his Whakatōhea people.

Mereaira missed her husband. Each day she grew sadder and more unhappy. She worried. Questioning why he had gone. Fearful of what might happen.

Not long after he left, a fleet of Whakatōhea war canoes was seen approaching with Kape Tautini leading the way. Mereaira and her people were unprepared for an attack and grew more afraid as the warriors shouted their grievances of past insults and wounds.

Filled with love and dread, Mereaira was determined to do what she could to prevent a war. Before the warriors had a chance to begin their assault, she ran to the edge of the cliff and stood there, holding her baby above her head.

She cried out, "This child I hold is born of the marriage between our two peoples. Why create a child if the price is continuing bloodshed? Why not choose peace?" She held the baby out in front of her. "If this violence does not end, I will throw my child against the rocks. His life is in your hands. His death will haunt you forever."

Kape Tautini and his warriors stopped their attack, their hearts filled with shame and respect for Mereaira. They put away their war spears. Peace was made.

Kape Tautini walked to Mereaira. She moved toward him. They held their child between them.

❧ ❧ ❧

UNSEEN FRIENDS

When I was fifteen, I applied to be a junior counselor at a summer camp in upstate NY for "underprivileged" children. Part of the application process involved spending time during the winter and spring, before camp opened, volunteering at the Settlement House sponsoring the camp.

I took the train into Manhattan, then walked through unfamiliar neighborhoods strewn with garbage, smells of decay, broken stoops, dirty children playing in the streets while darting among cars that sped by. I felt as if I'd entered a foreign country. My parents had recently bought a modest three-bedroom, one-bathroom, two-story house in a quiet neighborhood of well-kept houses. There was no comparison.

When I entered the Settlement House, I was assaulted by noise and motion. Kids in groups, singing, playing games, running around. Adults vying for attention. I stood by the doorway, ready to leave, ready to admit I wasn't up to being a junior counselor if it meant being part of so much chaos. I'd be sixteen in the summer; maybe I could find another camp job.

A harried woman asked my name, checked a paper on her clipboard, and said, "You wrote you have experience with dance and drama, right?" I nodded. "We need you to do creative drama with a group of seven-year-olds." Without asking if I could do this, she strode off, with me following, wondering what I was going to do, given I'd had no training or time to plan.

She led me to a room filled with a group of kids waiting impatiently as they lounged against pillows. She introduced me. "This is Nancy. She'll be doing drama with you today," she said, and left. Fortunately, they were eager to participate and joyfully entered into the world of "what if" I created. The session went well. I was invited to return, same time, same day, next week.

When I walked outside, it was dark. I hoped I remembered the way to the subway. I wished there were more light. I tried to push away my fears, but the unknown sounds and smells upped my anxiety. I started walking as fast as I could, trying to avoid trash. Suddenly a hand grabbed my hair and pulled me back. A strong arm pinned my arms to a body. A deep male voice said, "Hey, sweetheart, let's you and I have a little fun." The grip on my hair was so tight and hurt so much I couldn't move. Fear paralyzed my voice. He reeked of cigarettes and liquor.

As he was dragging me, I heard male voices shouting, "Let her go!" Voices cursed. Unseen hands grabbed the hand on my hair. Unseen hands grabbed the arm from my body. Two guys came up to me and noticed I was shaking. One of them took off his jacket and put it around me. The second guy said, "It's okay, we'll make sure you stay safe."

The first guy said, "You're the one doing drama, right?" I nodded. "My sister said you were great, that it was the best time. She said you're coming back next week, right?" I nodded.

The second guy, soon joined by a few more, asked if I was okay. I nodded, still unable to speak. They told me it wasn't safe for me to walk by myself; they would go with me to the subway and make sure I got on to the train.

Surrounded by the guys, I slowly stopped shaking. They walked into the subway with me. I gave the jacket back and thanked him. He shrugged, looking embarrassed. When I put my coin in the slot and the turnstile opened, I headed toward my train. They snuck in under the turnstile, waited with me until the train came, then told me they'd meet me at the train next time.

I thanked them. They grinned. "See ya next week," I heard as I entered the train.

They never missed a day.

Have you experienced unexpected help in a dangerous situation? What was that like?

❧ ❧ ❧

TROUBLED KIDS

I'd been working at the mental hospital for about a week when I was told my supervisor wanted to see me. Immediately. Wondering what I'd done wrong, thinking I was going to be fired and have to find another summer job, I walked into her office ready to hear bad news.

said she'd heard I was a storyteller. When the psychiatrist in charge of the small group of hospitalized children heard this, he requested I tell them stories. I would be given time off from my work with the adult women. She told me when and where to go. I was not asked if I wanted to do this.

Before meeting the children, I met with their psychiatrist. He admitted they were difficult. "But," he said looking at me, "they're children. Children love stories. You're a storyteller. Tell them stories." He told me there were seven children between the ages of seven and eleven. I'd see them in their playroom.

As an attendant walked me to the children's room, she warned me, "They're like wild animals. They bite and scratch and kick for no reason. I told my boss, I'll quit before I have to work with them again. Don't know why you're here, but if I were you, I'd leave. They're dangerous. And, I'm not the only one who feels like this. No one wants to be with them."

Even through the locked door I could hear yelling, banging, crying, cursing . . . The attendant had experience; she was much older. Why would anyone think I could do what she and others couldn't? The attendant stopped outside the door. "If it were me, I wouldn't go in. You're a kid. Who knows what they'll do to you." Before I could think of a response, she unlocked the door, opened it, pushed me inside, and locked the door.

There were three steps leading down to the room that had padded walls and floor. I sat on the top step, terrified. Would they attack me? I'd never seen children so violent. I felt helpless, resting my head on my knees, wondering how I could get the attendant to let me out. I don't know how long I sat there, but after a while I realized the noise had stopped. I looked up. The kids were staring at me.

"Who are you?" asked a boy, his hair a mess of tangles, his voice full of anger.

"I guess I'm a storyteller."

"We don't want to hear stories," said a small girl with red messy pigtails.

"I want to hear a story," said a skinny boy, seemingly the youngest.

"What kind of stories do you like to hear?" I asked him, hoping the others might settle down if I told a story that interested them, which seemed like wishing for a miracle.

"No stories. We can tell our own," said the girl with messy pigtails.

"I'd like to hear your stories," I said, grateful the kids seemed less dangerous. "Would it be okay if we sit in a circle, and whoever wants to tell a story can tell a lot or a little. If someone wants to add to it, that's good too."

I walked down the steps and sat on the floor. Much to my surprise, they sat around me. The boy who'd asked who I was began. "My name is James, and no one likes me. That's my story."

The girl sitting next to him said, "My name is Elora, and no one likes me."

One by one they said their name and the phrase, "No one likes me." It didn't take long for it to be my turn. I couldn't help myself. Laughing, I said, "My name is Nancy and none of you likes me, and we all lived happily ever after."

What I said was ridiculous. Maybe that's why they laughed as hard as they'd been fighting. Laughter is contagious, and it took a while for everyone to stop.

Much to my astonishment, Elora asked, "You gonna come back?"

I didn't really have a choice, but I said, "I will if you want me to."

"Yeah," said James. "You tell good stories." They thought this was hysterical and started giggling.

I had no idea when the attendant would come to let me out. I had no idea what to do next. The small boy, Eric, looked around the group and then at me. "Could you tell us a story?"

James, seemingly the spokesman for the group, said, "We don't want to hear a 'happily ever story,' do we?"

The group shouted, "No!"

"Okay. No happily ever after. What about a story I make up?" This seemed acceptable. Having no story in my head, I stalled for time by beginning: "Once upon a time, long ago, in a place far away, there lived a group of children." As I started to describe the characters in the story, how they lived, what they wanted, the children drew closer to me. I spoke slowly, having to image the story in my mind's eye.

When the attendant opened the door, she found us in a small circle, nestled like puppies, the kids listening to me tell the story I was making up as I went along. I told them I had to go, but I'd be back to finish the story. I felt like Scheherazade.

Have you walked into a terrifying situation? If so, what did you do?

INCIDENT IN LONDON

My boyfriend and I were walking down a dark street toward an underpass in a not-great section of London. By myself, I wouldn't have gone, but he was six feet three and well built. I figured no one would bother us. As we entered the underpass, I saw a big, heavy-set man, dressed in filthy clothes, his hair a matted tangle, drinking from a large liquor bottle. In between sips he yelled and cursed. Suddenly he aimed his bottle at the heads of a young couple who had entered the underpass from the other direction. They ran, shouting for the police.

The man whirled around and came toward us, lurching and screaming. My boyfriend shrugged off my hand, yelling at him to calm down, fists out, ready to stop him. Terrified, I pleaded, "Let's go. He's crazy."

"He's gonna hurt someone if no one stops him."

"Please, let's go. He could hurt you." He moved toward the man. I tried to stop him. I begged him to stop. When he wouldn't listen to me, I told him I was leaving. I headed toward the entrance. My boyfriend trailed behind, still wanting to stop him, but when the man threatened to kill us, we hurried toward the entrance.

Suddenly the police arrived in the person of a small uniformed woman We stopped to see what would happen. She walked to the man, moving past us with a smile on her face. In a calm, soft voice, she said to the man, "It's okay, sir. I'm here to help you."

He screamed he didn't need no help. He told her to get away from him. She paid no attention to his words or his yelling, moving gently toward him, crooning compassionately spoken words. He threatened to smash the bottle over her head.

We watched from a safe distance, mesmerized by the woman's lack of fear.

What happened next seemed unbelievable. She held out her hand, speaking quietly the whole time, always looking at him kindly. When she was close enough, she took the bottle from him. He actually let her take it, then collapsed against her, crying, telling her how terrible his life was. Small as she was, big as he was, she held him, stroking his back, comforting him, telling him he would get help.

Several policemen came. The policewoman walked the man toward them, continuing with the mesmerizing words of caring. We watched, stunned, as he allowed the policemen to help him into the waiting police car.

The policewoman threw the bottle into a nearby trash can. As she left, she said to us, "It's all in a night's work."

She was small, calm, and unarmed. He was big and angry, waving the bottle like a weapon. She saw past his violence. Talked to his pain and suffering. Her softly spoken words disarmed him. Human to human.

Have you experienced a time when compassion stopped violence? If so, what was that like?

35

WORLD TALE

Who's in Rabbit's House?

AFRICAN

A challenging situation ends with a surprise. The stories, Where There's a Cookie, Barefoot on the Table, and Black Blob, all start with difficulties resolved in unexpected ways.

• • •

One day, when Rabbit returned home, he noticed strange tracks in front of the door to where he lived. He shouted, "Who's in my house?"

A loud voice roared back, "I am all powerful. I eat elephants for breakfast. I turn rhinoceroses into dust. I am invincible." Terrified, Rabbit ran away. What could a small animal do against one who was so powerful?

As he ran, he saw Jackal, who agreed to go to Rabbit's house to help him get rid of the mighty creature. Jackal called out, "Who's in Rabbit's House?"

The loud voice roared back. "I am all powerful. I eat elephants for breakfast. I turn rhinoceroses into dust. I am invincible." Jackal turned and left, saying he could do nothing against one so formidable.

Rabbit continued asking bigger, stronger animals to help. But after hearing the fearsome words of the powerful stranger, Leopard said he had a toothache. Tiger said he had a prior appointment. Lion said he was too busy. Privately, they all admitted that whoever was in Rabbit's house was too fierce for them.

Discouraged, Rabbit met Frog and told him of his troubles. Frog agreed to see what he could do. When they reached Rabbit's house, Frog shouted, "Who is here in Rabbit's house?"

The voice roared, "I am all powerful. I eat elephants for breakfast. I turn rhinoceroses into dust. I am invincible."

Frog gulped. Took a deep breath. Shouted back, "I am the strongest of all living creatures. I leap over mountains. I fly over rivers. I fear no one. Whosoever arouses my wrath will live to regret it."

Suddenly, out crawled Caterpillar. "Please, don't hurt me. I'm only a tiny caterpillar."

When Frog and Rabbit saw Caterpillar shaking with fear, they all had a good laugh at the trick Caterpillar had played.

❧ ❧ ❧

WHERE THERE'S A COOKIE

It was early afternoon on Christmas Eve, our first in the new apartment, our two-and-a-half-year-old son healthy after more than six months of illness. I celebrate Chanukah—lighting candles on the menorah and making latkes (potato pancakes). My husband's Christmas celebrations had always included a fancily decorated tree. I didn't mind having a Christmas tree. What I minded were the baubles, tinsel, and glitter. I understood his wanting a Christmas tree, but we had no money to buy one. We could barely pay our bills. Still, Christmas without a tree was not Christmas for him. After pacing up and down the living room, increasingly unhappy, he stopped and said, "I'm leaving. I'm going to get a tree." I asked how he intended to pay for it. Ignoring my question, he stormed out.

Our son, feeling the tension, started to cry. "Let's make cookies," I said. Leading him into the kitchen, I made dough for sugar cookies. He formed little mounds of dough and flattened them, making interesting shapes as he put them on the baking sheet. The air smelled sweet. While we decorated the cookies with different colored icings, I worried about my husband. He'd been gone for hours.

When I heard banging on our apartment door, I froze. My husband had a key. Who could it be? Controlling my anxiety so as not to frighten my son, I went to see what was causing the noise. The front door to the house was open. My husband was standing in the hallway. "I need your help. Come with me." I followed him outside. There, on top of our beat-up station wagon, was the biggest tree I'd ever seen. I stared at him. More than a little defensive, he said, "It was in a lot, leaning up against a wall. No one wanted it."

"I can see why. How'd you get it on top of the car?"

"A guy came by and offered to help. Can we stop talking and get the tree into the house?" I put on a jacket and told our son to watch through the French-door windows. Struggling with its size and weight, we managed to drag it onto the porch. I opened the French doors, and he pushed as I pulled until we got the tree into the house.

The tree was so large, despite the fourteen-foot ceilings in our living room, he had to cut about eight inches off the top. "How are we going to keep it upright?" I asked, dismayed by its size.

"I found boards on the lot. I'll nail them to the bottom of the tree." Easier said than done.

When we finally got the tree up, my husband did not look happy. "We gotta decorate it. How we gonna do it?" We didn't have any traditional tree decorations, had no tree decorations, but even if we had money, by now all stores were closed.

"We could hang cookies on the tree with the red shoestring licorice I bought." He looked doubtful. This was not his idea of a decorated Christmas tree. "I'll make holes in the cookies. You get the ladder."

My husband stood on the top rung. He bent down so our son could give him the largest cookie to hang on the top. We'd made so many cookies, there were enough to hang on most of the branches. Using red thread, I made chains of cranberry and popcorn.

My husband looked a bit less unhappy.

I brought in a tray with cups of hot cocoa and cookies.

Our son looked at the tree with such joy, he began to laugh and sing. "It's not a Christmas tree, it's a Cookiemas tree." He was so delighted with himself, he started dancing in front of the tree singing, "Cookiemas. Cookiemas. Come and eat the Cookiemas tree . . ."

Our son's reaction was contagious. We drank our cocoa and munched on cookies. All of us, especially my husband, feeling a lot happier than we'd been a few hours earlier. Cookiemas became our family tradition.

If you have a tradition or ritual, how did it begin?

❧ ❧ ❧

BAREFOOT ON THE TABLE

In 1990, I was in Budapest, Hungary, where I'd been invited to give a talk and workshop at an international conference on innovative teaching methods. As people milled around, registering, speaking in a variety of languages along with heavily accented English, I felt lost among the crowd—mostly men in dark suits with fancy briefcases. I was wearing a long pastel-colored skirt and a white blouse with dangling earrings, carrying an embroidered cloth bag. While waiting in line, I picked up a conference program and searched for information about my presentation, legitimizing my presence.

I overheard a group of men talking about the presenters, not paying much attention until I heard my name and then the title of my paper and workshop, "Imagemaking and Storymaking: Techniques to Develop Imagination, Creativity, and Communication," with such disdain I felt like letting them know they were talking about me. I pretended I hadn't heard.

After registering, I looked at them—middle-aged males, making fun of anything that differed from their way of teaching, even though this was a conference about innovation. I was sure they wouldn't sign up for either my talk or workshop. I hoped some people would.

I went to check out the room I'd been assigned and discovered it was much larger than I'd anticipated. There was no podium, no speaker system, and no way to see most of the people who'd be sitting in chairs on a flat floor. I left the room, looking for the conference coordinator.

No matter who I asked, no matter where I looked, I couldn't find him, or anyone who might be able to help. There was nothing I could do to change the room. Nothing I could do about the poor visibility and acoustics.

When it was time for my talk, I went to the room, hoping something had miraculously changed. It hadn't. I watched people walk in, talking in a mixture of languages, holding briefcases and the conference agenda, occasionally looking at me, but more interested in finding seats with friends. Much to my astonishment, the men I'd heard dismissing my work entered the room and found seats in the front. These were the faces I'd see most easily. Why had they come?

I'm always nervous before a talk. Giving one in a foreign country, speaking in what would be a foreign language for most, in a room not set up for a talk, made me so anxious I dropped my paper, pages streaming down on the floor.

Two of the men helped me gather up the pages. If they remembered talking about me, they gave no sign. I thanked them, grateful for their help, hoping their presence meant they'd at least be willing to hear what I had to say without disparagement.

I started my talk by welcoming everyone but was soon greeted with shouts of, "We can't hear you." "We can't see you." No way could I continue, but how could I change the situation?

I looked around. In the corner was a large desk. I started pulling it into the middle of the front, but it was heavy. The two men who'd helped me gather the pages once more came to my rescue. As they pushed, I pulled and guided. The three of us moved it to where a podium ought to have been.

The desk was made of polished wood. No way could I stand on it in my shoes. There was nothing to be done but to take off my shoes, and, since the surface was glossy, I took off my stockings so I wouldn't slip. Any thoughts of dignity disappeared. I comforted myself—the conference was about innovation, and I was innovating. Sort of.

As soon as I climbed up onto the top of the desk, papers in hand, shoeless and stockingless, ready to begin, laughter greeted me. Waves of laughter. The situation was ridiculous, but what else could I do?

When the laughter died down, I asked if they could see me. "Yes." Could they hear me. "Yes."

A man close to the front stood up and yelled, "All hail the barefoot professor." The group stood up and echoed his words. I grinned, suddenly at ease with myself and what I had come to share.

I gave my talk, ending with a story. People clapped. Even the men in front had smiles on their faces. A happy ending to a difficult beginning.

Was there a time when you had to make do? What was that like?

❧ ❧ ❧

BLACK BLOB

The university honors students walked into my classroom looking as stressed and anxious as if they were going to a funeral. None of their usual talking and wisecracking. I watched as they sat in the circle of chairs, wondering what was wrong. When everyone was seated, I told them, "Take out your paints and paint an image of 'myself at this moment.' Then write a few words that come to mind."

When everyone finished, I asked the class to hold up their papers so they could see each others' images. There was a collective gasp. In every person's painting there was a black blob, some larger than others—all prominent.

They'd written words like: stress, fear, nervous, anxious, failure, hopeless, no use . . .

"Anyone want to talk about the black blobs?" I asked.

Obviously upset, a student explained: "We have organic chem after this class, and Dr. B.'s tests are really difficult. We're all afraid of failing." There were nods of agreement, many offering stories about how hard they'd studied, how worried they were. The tension in the class was palpable.

I scrapped the plans I'd made for the session, realizing they needed an activity that would help them relax, and perhaps take their minds off the upcoming exam. I told them the story, "Who's in Rabbit's House?" They listened intently and smiled at the ending, but their misery was evident.

"Okay," I said. "I want you to pair up. One person will be Rabbit who comes upon a character. You decide who you want to be. Rabbit tells the listener what happened without worrying about facts. Exaggerate. Make the story as large as possible. Become the brave warrior. When Rabbit is finished, change places. The listener becomes Rabbit, Rabbit, the listener. When you're finished, sit, so I'll know when everyone is ready to share."

It took a few minutes for the group to get going, but soon the room was buzzing. Characters were telling stories with gestures, sounds of animals roaring, worrying, making excuses, laughing. The tension was dissolving.

The first pair up involved a Rabbit who not only ate elephants as snacks, but nibbled on boa constrictors, wrestled with tigers, and stridently went into her house, found a huge snail, and quickly tossed it out. "That's how powerful I am," she said, grinning. Her partner, as Rabbit, told the story of how Tiger, Lion, and Jackal offered to help but she, Rabbit, told them she didn't need any of their help—she was so strong and fearsome, all she had to do was outyell the creature, stride in, and kick it out.

The tales got more and more outrageous as each pair tried to outdo those who came before them. By the time the last pair finished, the students could not stop laughing.

I told them to paint an image of 'myself at this moment' and to write words that came to mind. After they finished, I asked them to hold up their images. In some, the black blob had gone; in others, it was much smaller. No one's second blob was as big as the first. Everyone had used brighter colors. Some of their words were: fun, laughter, silly, ridiculous . . .

They left class in a far different state of mind. Once again I was reminded: never underestimate the power of story. It can even dissolve black blobs.

What do you do to release tension?

36

WORLD TALE

Maui Muri and the Sun

SOUTH SEA ISLANDS

Time is moving too fast for people to live and work. In the stories, Black Ice, Bond Paper, and Missing Student, time seems to slow down or speed up.

• • •

Maui Muri noticed that no matter how hard people worked, they never had enough daylight to finish their tasks. The Sun-God, Ra, moved too quickly across the sky. Maui Muri decided toe decided find a way to make Ra move more slowly.

After Maui Muri and his brothers made a tough rope out of coconut fibers, Maui Muri lay in wait for Ra. When he saw Ra, he threw the rope around him, but the rope broke. Ra flew across the sky as quickly as ever.

Maui Muri made a second, stronger cord out of coconut husks, which he braided into an even stronger rope, but for the second time, Ra escaped.

After much thought, Maui Muri asked his sister Hina to give him some of her hair. He cut off long strands and braided them into a strong rope. When Ra appeared, Maui Muri threw the noose around Ra's neck and held tight.

When Ra realized there could be no escape, he asked Maui Muri what he wanted.

"You must move more slowly across the sky, so we have enough time to do our work. Promise me this and I will let you go."

Ra agreed, but just to make sure he kept his word, Maui Muri left a few strands of Hina's hair hanging from the sun.

You can still see them when the sun is going down and the last rays of light fill the sky.

Maui Muri is a trickster figure commonly found in Polynesian mythology.

❧ ❧ ❧

BLACK ICE

Winter break ended. I was returning to the University of Wisconsin where I was a graduate student. I'd bought a used Oldsmobile from a friend of my parents and was accompanied by a guy who needed a ride to the university and was willing to share driving and the cost of gas.

We'd started from my parents' home in New York City and were now on the border between Illinois and Wisconsin. We'd been driving for hours and were tired, but neither of us wanted to spend money to rent a hotel room. It was pitch black. No moon. My turn to get behind the wheel.

I took a sip of coffee from a thermos and began driving. Just as I crossed into Wisconsin, I hit a patch of black ice. The car swerved into the oncoming lane. Time seemed to slow down, as if I'd entered another time zone. How I did it, I don't know, but I managed to maneuver around the approaching cars without hitting any. The traffic was heavy, and I couldn't steer the car back into my lane. It was like being in a shooting gallery, with objects coming at me with no way to stop them.

Then, just as suddenly as I'd swerved into the left lane, still avoiding oncoming traffic, the car swerved back into the right lane with such force it spun 360 degrees, landing on a grassy spot next to the highway, turning over on its side.

"Are you okay?" I asked my passenger when the car stopped.

"I will be if you turn off the ignition and take your goddammed guitar off of me." I did.

The only way out was the door on my side. It was so heavy it took both of us to push it open. I was shaking uncontrollably and couldn't figure out where the ground was. He climbed over me, carefully let himself down and then helped me get out. The ice was so slick we both fell. Hard. No blood from the accident, only from falling. A tow truck righted the car, and, unbelievably, I was able to drive it to Madison, jaw clenched all the way.

Have you experienced time slowing down? If so, what was that like?

BOND PAPER

In 1968, masters' theses had to be typed on a typewriter with carbons to make copies. To correct mistakes, one had to use white-out, then type in the correction and hope it looked like there'd been no error—a tedious process at best. I wasn't a good enough typist to type my thesis, so I hired one. I picked up the copies, signed my name, and drove to the University of Delaware Graduate School Office a few hours before the noon deadline.

I waited in line to hand in the copies of my thesis and have it checked by an administrator. When it was my turn, I expected her to look it over, have me sign the acceptance document, and leave. Instead, she looked at what I'd handed her and said, "This isn't acceptable. It has to be on bond paper, not typing paper. If you want to graduate with your class, you'll have to hand in the appropriate copies before noon."

I was so shocked, I stood there, trying to make sense of what she'd said. "Couldn't you approve this, and I'll take a copy and—"

She interrupted me. "The rules are clear. All theses must be submitted on bond paper before twelve o'clock today. Surely you read the requirements."

I couldn't remember what I'd read. I couldn't think. My boyfriend, who worked for a large corporation, had asked me to call him when my thesis had been submitted so he could congratulate me. Instead, I called him, too distraught to clearly explain what had happened.

He was quick to respond. "Come to my building. I'll empty out a copier and we can make however many copies you need on bond paper." I was grateful for his help but scared I didn't have enough time. His place of work was half an hour from the university.

"I'll be there as quick as I can." He gave me a code to give to the guard for valet service. It's a wonder I didn't get stopped by the police as I zoomed way above the speed limit into Wilmington, yet felt I wasn't going fast enough. I gave the guard the code and rushed into the building.

Time was moving too fast. Everything was taking too long. I felt speeded up and slowed down. He met me at the elevator and grabbed my thesis. A bunch of his colleagues standing by the copier, pages in hand, looked aggrieved. I told him how many copies I needed. While he was busy with the copier, I apologized to the men watching. To assuage their annoyance, I told them my sad tale of woe.

I kept looking at my watch. When I had the collated copies in hand, I muttered thanks and ran. It took forever for the guard to bring me my car.

I drove back to the university like a crazy woman, going through red lights, speeding in slow zones. Time was not on my side.

I parked in a no-parking zone with my blinkers on and rushed to the Graduate School Office. According to the clock on the wall, it was one minute after twelve. The administrator was closing the door. I pushed it open and handed her my thesis on bond paper.

"It's after twelve," she said.

"Only a minute or so. Please!" I begged. With no energy left, even to stand, I crumpled to the floor.

I waited, not daring to breathe. "All right," she said, reluctantly, "I'll make an exception, but don't count on it happening again. As far as anyone knows, you arrived before noon."

I graduated on time, with an MA in Theatre.

Have you experienced a time constraint with serious consequences if you didn't meet the deadline? If so, what was that like?

MISSING STUDENT

In 1987, I was the lead faculty member of a first-year honors course titled Interdisciplinary Arts. We used Othello as the subject, studied the play by Shakespeare, the opera by Verdi, "The Moor's Pavane," a dance created by José Limón, and various paintings based on the story. The capstone event was a trip to New York City.

As part of the pre-trip planning, students were asked to sign an agreement to stay together. If they needed to leave the group for any reason, they would let a faculty member know.

One student complained we were treating the class as if they were children; they were adults and should be treated as such. I ignored her comments. Since none of them had been to New York City, I explained the necessity for the request. "It's a big city. Easy to get lost. Since we're responsible for your safety and well-being, we need everyone to stay together." The student continued to complain. I lost patience. "If you don't agree to the terms, you're welcome to stay home. Your choice." She signed the agreement so reluctantly I almost told her she was not welcome to join us.

After the students left class, I told the other faculty I didn't trust her. They pooh-poohed my concerns, but I still felt uneasy. I suggested we ask students to choose a buddy as a precaution. Once again, they dismissed my worries. We had two classes left before the trip. The student avoided me, tersely answering questions, participating as little as possible. My qualms increased.

The day of the trip, she arrived just as we were boarding the van. Unlike the others, who were dressed casually, with little or no makeup, she was dressed in a tailored suit, high heels, carefully made up. My stomach clenched. I vowed to keep my eyes on her no matter what.

Each student had a copy of our itinerary and where and when we'd be boarding our train back to Delaware. En route to the city, I went over the itinerary, where we'd have lunch, and stressed the importance of staying together.

The first part of our visit went according to plan. After lunch, we arrived at the Metropolitan Museum of Art, and I went to contact our guide. When I returned, the student was not there. y fear, I asked where she was. Silence. Shrugs. No one noticed her absence. We checked the bathrooms and cafeteria. No student.

I told the faculty to continue with our plan. I would look for her and, if necessary, meet them at the train station when it was time to board. I walked out of the museum wondering how in hell I could possibly find her in the two hours left before our scheduled departure.

It's difficult to explain what happened next. I felt guided, as if I knew where to turn, which stores to look in, which restaurants to check. Time slowed down as I crossed busy avenues and walked down small side streets, constantly looking in windows, trying not to panic.

I came to a street with a lot of restaurant marquees. What possessed me to look carefully in the windows of each of them, I don't know. What possessed me to walk into the one I did, I don't know. There she was. Comfortably sitting at a low table in the bar area, with two well-dressed men in their forties, drinking what looked like cocktails, munching on appetizers, smiling at the men, having a wonderful time.

I was furious and relieved. For a moment I stood, watching them laugh and flirt, trying to calm myself. When I felt ready, I walked over to them and said to the men, "She's a seventeen year old student on a school trip." They looked horrified and muttered something about how they thought she was much older.

She glared at me and stood up, ready to run. I grabbed her arm and said, "Let's go. We need to hurry. The train won't wait, and I'm not willing to spend a night in New York with you."

She was taller and heavier, but my anger gave me strength she couldn't counter. I decided it would be better to walk to the train station since the traffic was so heavy. She struggled, but to no avail. My fury was greater than her resistance. I was not about to miss the train because she chose to flirt with men old enough to be her father. Despite her struggling to get away, I marched her down to the train station where we met the others who had just arrived.

She tried to pull away, but I told her, "You will stay with me until we're on the train and it's moving." When she complained I was hurting her, I said, "Then stop fighting me." I ignored the looks of the other students and faculty members. My entire focus was putting her on the train with no chance of getting off.

She sat by herself during the ride home. When we left the train, and she was about to get on the university van, she turned to me and snarled, "So, are you going to fail me?"

"I'm one of four faculty members. It's a group decision."

Have you had an experience when time was not on your side? What did you do?

37

WORLD TALE

The Little Parrot

TIBET

Little Parrot needs help. The stories, Chinny Chin Chin, Gang Action, and Help Troubles, explore complexities involved in asking for help.

• • •

LITTLE PARROT LOVED THE jungle. Every morning she flew over the greenery, looked at what lay below, and counted herself fortunate to live in such a beautiful place. Only when she was sure all was well did she fly back to earth and eat her breakfast.

One morning, while flying overhead, she saw nothing but thick, dark smoke. The jungle was on fire! Little Parrot flew to the river as fast as her small wings permitted, took a big gulp of water, flew back to the fire, and spit out the water, trying to quench the massive flames. Back and forth she went, from the river to the fire, from the fire to the river, trying to put out the blaze. She soon became exhausted but kept on going. Her beloved jungle was at risk.

As she was flying to the river for the umpteenth time, worried the jungle would burn before she could put out the fire, she heard a loud laugh, then a cackling voice say, "You're a silly parrot. You're too little to put out such a big fire."

Little Parrot looked up and saw Eagle, the largest bird in the jungle. "I don't need advice," she said, "I need help," and continued flying to the river. The next thing Little Parrot knew, a huge stream of water poured from the skies dousing part of the fire. Little Parrot did not stop to see who was helping her, she just kept flying to the river and back, hoping that with help the fire would soon be out.

When there were no more flames, Little Parrot looked around to see if she could find the source of the help for which she was so grateful. Surprised, she saw Eagle. Though she was utterly depleted, she flew up to Eagle and said, "Thank you. Were it not for you, the fire would still be burning."

"No," said Eagle, "it is I who must thank you."

❧ ❧ ❧

CHINNY CHIN CHIN

Seventy-eight years later I can still see him. Feel his gentle hands on my face. His caring.

My parents, sister, and I had taken a ski train from New York City to Catamount Mountain in upstate New York. When we got off the train, with our boots, skis, poles, and suitcases, to get on a shuttle to the ski area, the cold was biting. The wind made me shiver even though I was wearing warm pants, a thick sweater, hat, heavy coat, and mittens. Still, despite the frigid weather, I was looking forward to skiing.

The ski lodge felt cozy with skiers chatting, eating, and drinking, dancing flames in the fireplaces adding warmth. I had just finished eating a hamburger with sweet pickles and ketchup, the bun lightly toasted, when my parents started teasing me.

"Are you going to sit and eat hamburgers all day?"

"I thought you came to ski, not eat."

I remembered how cold I felt walking to the lodge, but I said, "Okay. You want me to ski, I'll ski." I was ten years old. Old enough, they told me, to lace up my leather boots without help and dress warmly.

Leaving my family inside the lodge, I walked outside and noticed the thermometer. Nine degrees below zero. I pulled my wool hat over my ears and walked to the T-bar, the lift that would take me to the top of the mountain. Hardly anyone was skiing. At least I didn't have to wait in line.

I managed two runs before I was so cold I couldn't stop shivering. When I walked into the lodge, my chin burned as if it were on fire. Terrified by the pain, I stood among the crowds of people, unable to move. Tears pouring down my face.

A man came up to me. "I'm a doctor," he said. "Your chin is bone white. May I look at it?" I nodded, comforted by his caring manner. He gently held my head in his hands and said, "You have frostbite. Is it very painful?" I nodded.

"I'll help you. Come with me." Using a soft cloth, he soaked my chin in warm water and then put some cream on it. He asked who I was with. "My parents and sister," I told him. He offered to come with me to talk with them. I told him I'd be fine; he didn't need to come. I thanked him for his kindness and caring.

I was in too much pain to tell my parents why I let a stranger help instead of coming right to them. I didn't want him blamed for helping me.

If you received unexpected help, what was that like for you?

❧ ❧ ❧

GANG ACTION

In 1965, I started Magic Circle Theatre, situated in a poor neighborhood of Wilmington, Delaware. From the beginning, I recruited urban, suburban, Black, white, young, and older people to participate in any way they chose. I wrote and directed plays for children. Volunteers helped design sets and costumes. Our "ticket" was an ice-cream-cup top with details of the performance printed on it. Twenty-five cents for adults, ten cents for kids. At the entrance, the ticket taker would twist off the little tag and direct the person down to the performance space in the basement.

When the actors asked who would watch their belongings during the shows, I thought about a group of older boys who'd been hanging around. When I invited them to watch rehearsals and give me feedback, one of them expressed surprise. "We're usually kicked out, not invited in." I shrugged and said they were welcome. About five or six, sometimes more, came and sat, watching as the play evolved from improvisation and my writing. Initially they hesitated before making comments, but when they saw I took their suggestions seriously, they freely voiced their opinions.

At the end of our first dress rehearsal, I asked the group if they'd be willing to watch the actors' belongings as well as help people down the narrow staircase leading to the performance area. Their astonished looks seemed odd. They'd been helpful and respectful. What was the problem? I didn't ask. They talked among themselves and agreed to help anyway they could.

The afternoon of the first show, the boys arrived about an hour before the performance. A few volunteered to escort people needing help down the stairs to whatever seats were available. The leader of the group and two others offered to watch the room with the performers' valuables and clothing. Three others placed themselves around the performing area in case anyone needed help. I invited them to join the cast party after the second performance.

All went well. No one fell down the stairs. Nothing went missing from the room they guarded.

After the cast party, after the cleanup, after everyone had left but the Director of the Settlement House and me, he said, "I think you should know that the boys you asked to help are part of a notorious gang."

I shrugged.

How do you decide who to ask for help?

~ ~ ~

HELP TROUBLES

After being accepted as a participant in the Hairy Cell Leukemia (HCL) protocol in May of 1985, I had to figure out how to get to the National Cancer Institute (NCI) facility in Frederick, MD. In the beginning, I needed to go once a week for blood tests and medication (interferon). After a few weeks, it was every two weeks, and eventually, once a month, always on a weekday. It took about two hours to get there from my house in Delaware, and I didn't have the energy to drive myself. I needed help.

As I child, if I asked for help from my parents, I usually got a sarcastic response like, "What? A smart girl like you needs help?" "You can't figure out a little thing like that?" Or my father's stock reply: "You're strong. You can manage." It might not have been so hard to ask for help getting to NCI if I needed a ride once or twice, but the continuing need for rides left me feeling embarrassed, anxious, tense, and full of shame. I shouldn't need so much help.

Desperate to find another way to get to NCI, I discovered there was a flight leaving from Wilmington, ending in Washington, D.C. I booked the flight knowing someone from NCI would pick me up. All went according to plan. I was relieved. I could now make the trip by myself.

At the clinic, I was scheduled to have a bone marrow biopsy, but it took five tries on each side of my sacrum before the doctor could get enough material to test. A hurricane was forecast. Blood was oozing from where the needles had gone in. Nurses told me I had to stay the night. I just wanted to go home. Stubbornness kicked in. I was beyond reason, unable to listen to the sensible and caring advice of the medical staff. They gave up and arranged my ride to the airport.

As I waited for the hurricane to blow over, I felt wet on the back of my clothing. I went to the bathroom and saw blood seeping from the biopsy areas. I used paper towels to clean myself up and stuck them in my clothing to stop the leakage.

Hours late, a plane arrived, but it was not going to Wilmington, where I'd left my car. It had been rerouted to the Philadelphia Airport. I could get a shuttle from the airport to my house, so I boarded. When it was possible to stand up, a flight attendant noticed blood on the back of my seat. My dress was a bloody mess. She got me a towel to wrap around my body and suggested they call for an ambulance when we arrived. "I'm strong. I can manage," I said. Words from my childhood reverberating, shutting out any possibility of asking for help.

When we landed, a friend who tended to worry about me tracked my landing in Philadelphia instead of Wilmington and met my plane. He put newspapers on the seat so I wouldn't bloody the upholstery. When we got to my house, he offered to stay. I told him to leave. "I can manage." I told him. I did. Sort of. Weak from loss of blood, I had to crawl to the bathroom where I lay on the floor on towels to stop the bleeding. It took a hurricane, loss of blood, and exhaustion to make me realize asking for help did not mean I was weak or stupid or needy, nor was it a crime or cause for shame.

How and when do you ask for help?

38

WORLD TALE

The Golden Eagle

VENEZUELA

The relationship between two friends saves a life. The stories, Gino, What the Psychic Promised, and Caring, reveal the surprising power and significance of friendship.

• • •

FOR AS LONG AS anyone could remember, the tribe cherished the statue of Golden Eagle, given to them by god Ches for their goodness and wisdom. They were told to guard it well for it had magical powers, but there would come a time when they would have to give it back. For generations, the god's gift brought victory and good fortune to the tribe.

Then a ruler died, leaving no sons; but, according to their law, a daughter could reign. The young woman was wise and kind, and accepted by the tribe, who loved her gentle ways. She had not ruled for many moons when she became ill, so ill nothing the tribe and healers did—making medicines, creating brews, doing sacrifices, painting their bodies, or performing special dances—cured the princess.

One morning, she woke early and spoke to her dearest friend and companion. "Mistafa, god Ches appeared in my sleep. He asks us to return Golden Eagle to his temple on the mountain peak. Only then will I be well." Mistafa told the princess it was only a dream, but the princess was clear. "I am too weak to travel. You must go in my place."

Mistafa was besieged with doubts and fears. "Who am I to approach a temple only chieftains visit? How will I find the way? What if I am not strong enough to carry Golden Eagle all the way?"

The princess told her, "Do not be afraid. God Ches will support and protect you. He will show you the way. When you reach the peak of the mountain, bury Golden Eagle at the side of the temple. Call out to god Ches three times. He will hear you. Listen well to what he says."

Mistafa wrapped Golden Eagle in a soft cloth and began her journey. Her arms ached from carrying the sacred sculpture. Her feet ached from the miles she walked. Seeing the mountain peak gave her new strength and energy.

Using a sharp rock, she dug a hole deep enough to bury Golden Eagle, then cried out to god Ches three times. All was quiet. She fell asleep nestled in the cloth in which she had carried the sacred golden statue.

When she woke the next morning, she saw what she had not seen before. Where she had buried Golden Eagle there was now a lovely bush covered with green leaves and purple blossoms. A voice commanded, "Gather leaves in the cloth. Bring them to the healers. Tell them to brew a strong tea and serve it to the princess."

Mistafa did as she was told, then made her way back without stopping to eat or drink or rest. She brought the leaves to the healers who prepared the tea. With each sip of the strong brew the princess regained her strength and ruled wisely for many years.

GINO

I was five years old. The elementary school where I attended kindergarten was fourteen blocks away. I always worried about crossing one wide busy street before the light changed. One morning, I closed the door to the apartment and walked down the outside steps to the sidewalk. A boy I'd seen playing stickball with a bunch of kids was standing at the bottom, looking at me. He was eight or nine, big for his age. I stopped. Some of the kids on the block had yelled out a word I didn't understand when they saw me. I had asked my father what the word meant. "Some people don't like Jewish people, so they call them bad names. Ignore them."

I didn't know that boy. I worried he'd call me that ugly word, but he didn't look angry like the kids who called me names. He smiled and said,

"Hi Nancy, I'm Gino. I think you're too little to walk such a long way to school by yourself. I'll walk with you. Okay?"

"Sure." I liked the idea of having someone to talk to as I walked to school. He told me not to worry about being too slow. He took my hand, which felt comforting. When we came to the big street, he didn't rush. The light didn't change until we were safely across.

Each day from then on he waited for me at the foot of the steps. When I asked him to come in, he shook his head. "My parents wouldn't understand. It's okay. I'll wait for you here."

A few days after he'd started walking me to school, I noticed he had bruises on his face. His right hand was bandaged. "What happened?" I asked, worried. He didn't answer. The next day he had worse bruises. I begged him to tell me how he got them, but he said they didn't matter.

I told my father about Gino's injuries. He knew a lot about first aid. Maybe he could help Gino. My father sighed. "Some kids on the block don't want him walking you to school, so they think they can stop him by beating him up."

"Why do they care if he walks me to school?"

"Because he's Catholic and you're Jewish."

"What difference does that make?"

"It makes a difference to them."

The next time I saw Gino, I said, "I don't want you getting hurt because of me. I can walk to school by myself."

Gino shook his head. "I'm not about to let a bunch of stupids tell me what to do." He took my hand, and we started walking to school.

Have you experienced an unexpected friendship? What was that like?

WHAT THE PSYCHIC PROMISED

In November 1985, after seven months of dealing with a rare form of leukemia, a friend, seeing my distress, paid for me to see a psychic. "Maybe he'll tell you about your illness." She was so determined to help me feel better, I agreed to go.

The man's office was pleasant, decorated with Oriental rugs and flowering plants. He greeted me warmly, showed me where to sit at a table, and looked at me intently. "I think I'll use the cards," he said. I knew nothing about cards, but I nodded as if I'd made a choice.

As he turned them over, he told me what they were and what they might mean. Nothing he said provided information about my illness. Then his face lit up, his voice full of excitement. "You're going to meet a woman. She's a New Yorker, like you, and the two of you have a lot in common." He talked at length about how amazing she was and what great friends we'd be.

His enthusiasm was contagious. "When will I meet her?"

"I can't tell you," he said, "but I promise, the two of you will have a deep and lasting friendship." I left, looking forward to meeting this astonishing person, wondering how and when she would appear. Days passed. Weeks passed. Months passed. I stopped thinking about her.

In 1991, I received a complimentary letter from a woman who'd enjoyed reading my books and liked my work with stories and literacy. I noticed, from the return address, she lived about forty minutes from me, so I wrote back, inviting her to visit. We arranged a meeting at my house.

She walked in the door, uncertain, nervous. I looked at her and felt I knew her. The more we talked, the more we realized we had in common, the deeper our conversation. When she left, it suddenly hit me. She was the woman the psychic promised I'd meet. I laughed, excited and pleased to have a friend with whom I could share my work and life. At the same time, I wondered: *what took you so long?*

The psychic was right. He'd described her perfectly. From our first meeting we felt close in ways that cannot be explained by reason. Since then, despite geographical distance, there is no emotional distance; our friendship deepens with every conversation, every email, every visit.

Have you met someone for the first time, instantly feeling as if you knew them. Are you still friends?

❧ ❧ ❧

CARING

We met in 1991. I was her college professor and thesis advisor. As we got to know each other, we discovered our fathers and paternal grandfathers had the same names and came from a similar shtetl in what was then called Russia. We discovered we shared a passion for stories and making art, always searching for ways to make life meaningful. After she graduated, we became friends, staying in touch through visits, phone calls, and letters. The thirty-five-year age difference between us didn't matter.

In 2001, I moved to Santa Fe. Since she lived on the East Coast, our primary contact was by email and phone. I felt grateful she continued to want me to be a presence in her life. I appreciated her willingness to talk about difficult situations—personal and professional—with candor and trust. My life, by comparison, was quiet: teaching short seminars, writing, weaving, enjoying the outdoor life. She always asked how I was doing.

In 2004, illness and family troubles exacerbated the depression with which I live. During a phone conversation, she asked how I was doing. I knew she was going through a challenging period, so I said, "Fine." She heard the insincerity and asked, "How are you really doing?" Touched by her response, I told her about the emotional issues between me and family members, the difficulties of dealing with a chronic illness, the hovering depression.

"I'm coming to see you," she said.

I was stunned, feeling a mixture of shame for talking about my troubles, yet grateful for her caring. I assured her I'd be okay. She ignored me. "I'll call you back when I've booked the plane ticket." I kept thanking her. She kept telling me to stop thanking her.

She arrived a few days later, traveling two thousand miles to lift my sagging spirits.

Her hug was spiritual medicine, somehow diffusing the weight of my family problems. Depression lightened. We stayed up too late talking. Spurred by her interest in ceramics, we went to a variety of galleries and museums. She convinced me to eat in restaurants I had not tried. It was a magical week.

When she was leaving, she reminded me. "You may live alone, but you're not alone in your life."

What part do friends play in your life?

39

WORLD TALE

The Maiden with the Wooden Bowl

JAPAN

A wooden bowl becomes a form of protection. In the stories, Nothing is Forever, Deputy Security Guard, and Hawaii, appearance may not be what it seems.

• • •

THERE ONCE LIVED AN old couple with their young daughter. After her husband died, the widow worried about what might become of their lovely daughter when she was no longer able to take care of her. The mother told her, "The world can be a cruel place to a fair and kind young woman. To protect you, I am placing a wooden bowl on your head. Wear it when you go outside. When I am no longer in this world, always wear it. The bowl will keep you safe from harm."

After her mother died, the maiden put the bowl on her head and went to work in the rice fields. Many laughed at the sight of a woman with a bowl on her head; some jeered and made nasty remarks. She remembered her mother's words and ignored the comments. Some men even tried, with no success, to take the bowl off of her head.

A neighboring farmer noticed the diligence with which she worked, paying no attention to those who spoke and acted harshly. He invited her to work in his rice fields where she would be safe from those who chose to harm her. In time, he and his wife grew fond of the young woman and treated her like a daughter.

One day, their eldest son returned from the city, tired of the life he'd been living. When he saw the maiden with the bowl on her head, he asked his father who she was. "She is a kind young woman who works hard." The son labored alongside her, and the two became friends. He grew to love her and asked her to marry him. Although she loved him, she refused. She was a servant. A woman with a bowl on her head.

That night she dreamed her mother visited her, encouraging her to follow her heart, and if she did, all would be well. The next morning, the son asked her again. This time the maiden said yes.

On the day of the wedding, she tried to take the bowl off of her head, but it stayed fast. The son tried, but he could not remove it, nor could anyone else. The maiden asked if he would like to change his mind about marrying her, a woman with a bowl on her head. He smiled and said, "I love you as you are. Let the wedding proceed."

After the wedding feast, as the maiden took a sip of the ceremonial wine, the bowl fell off her head and crashed to the floor. She heard her mother's voice, saying, "Yes!"

NOTHING IS FOREVER

I was fourteen, at a summer camp where counselors came in many sizes and colors. My favorites were a married couple, a Black man and a white woman, who liked to sit on the steps of their tent before dinner, always encouraging me to talk with them. One afternoon, I was feeling particularly bad about myself. Since their tent was close to the one where I lived with seven other girls, I knew, if they saw me, they'd want to talk. I wasn't in the mood to speak to anyone, so I quickly walked on a path away from their tent, looking for a place to hide.

For the two weeks I'd been in camp, the girls in my bunk kept talking about periods and cramps and bras and breasts and being touched and touching. It was clear to them, and me—from the waist up, I looked like a boy. One girl wondered out loud if I was a boy in girl's clothing. I began to wish I were a boy. They got to do what they wanted no matter how they looked.

I was tired of being teased about my body. Tired of not understanding half of the girls' conversations. Tired of being called midget and shorty and weirdo and clueless by my bunkmates. Tired of them making fun of me for not caring about makeup and nail polish and fashion. Tired of boys refusing to let me play ball with them because I was a girl, despite being as good as many of them. Most of all, I was tired of feeling like a freak.

I walked away from my tent wanting to stop hurting, intent on finding a hiding place. I didn't pay attention to the man who called out to me. I kept walking even when his wife called out to me. What would I say to them? I was an undeveloped fourteen-year-old? No friends? A total misfit? No place to be me? No. Best to keep walking.

The two of them caught up with me. She asked what was wrong. "Nothing," I said. "I'm fine." They didn't believe me and shepherded me back to their tent.

When we were cozily ensconced, sitting on pillows, he asked, "What's wrong?" I did my usual shrug, feeling embarrassed to be talking about my difficulties. I knew the two of them dealt with big problems, like people calling them names and attacking them just because the colors of their skin didn't match.

"Out with it," she said. "We can't bear to see you looking as if you carry the weight of the world on your shoulders." I didn't realize they'd been watching me.

They sat quietly, waiting for me to speak. Finally, too tired to lie, I told them everything—the name calling, feeling like a weirdo, even the embarrassing bits about no boobs, no period, no way of knowing I was a girl, except for my long hair. They listened without interruption.

When I finished, she gave me a hug and said, "Nancy, nothing stays terrible forever. I promise, by the time you graduate from high school, you'll be a fine young woman."

He patted my shoulder and told me, "Boys take more time to mature. Don't give up on them."

They were right.

Was there a time when you felt you had no place in your life? What was that like?

❧ ❧ ❧

DEPUTY SECURITY GUARD

In the late sixties, most of the few Black students at the University of Delaware were football players. Some of us faculty members had written letters to the Board and President urging them to admit more Black students, but the university continued to send Black student applications to Delaware State College in Dover.

At the end of one spring semester, an outdoor honors ceremony was planned. A stage and roof covering were built and plans made for students, faculty, and alumni to attend. I don't know how word of a possible protest by Black students reached the president, but some faculty, I among them, were chosen to become deputy security guards to make sure order was kept and safety provided.

My partner was a chemistry professor, originally from Argentina, who'd seen a lot of political violence. He found it ironic that the two of us, both pacifists who agreed with the protesters, had been chosen to stand closest to the stage to protect attendees from violence. He was tall and slight. I was short and not particularly muscular. As we watched the administrators and others walk to the podium, we teased each other as to who would protect whom from what.

When everyone on stage was seated, the president got up to speak. Suddenly four Black students wearing their football uniforms walked up to the stage, climbed the two steps, and stood with their backs to the audience, hands clasped behind their backs. Silent. Imposing.

The president said something off mic I couldn't hear. The four students did not react, standing like statues, continuing to face the people on the stage. There was a long, uneasy pause. Clearly something was happening between the officials and the students, but nothing was audible.

Then the announcement came over the loudspeakers: "The program for today is cancelled. Please leave quickly." The tension among attendees was palpable. People scurried away.

With that, two of the Black students turned, walked slowly down the two steps, with administrators following closely behind. I heard one of them ask the students, "What do you want?" I guffawed. What they wanted was abundantly clear. More Black students admitted.

The other two Black students heard me and walked over, looking grim. "What's so funny?" one of them asked me. My partner stood watching, letting me know this was my problem. No help.

"I heard one of the officials ask the two students who walked away what they wanted," I said. I looked at them. "They want what they should have. Admission with no racist barriers."

One of them said, "I figured because you're a DE-PU-TY, you'd agree with the administration."

I pretended to be insulted. "I might be a DE-PU-TY, but I thought I was here to protect you."

We all laughed at the absurdity of this. I took off my black deputy armband and gave it to one of them. "Here, you might need this." He rolled his eyes. My partner gave his to the other. As the four of us walked away from the stage, I couldn't help teasing them: "You know, looks can be deceiving."

Have you experienced someone thinking they knew you based on their assumptions? What was that like?

❧ ❧ ❧

HAWAII

In 1988, I was in Hawaii attending a PhD seminar: Cross Cultural Community Cooperation. The heart of the seminar involved meeting with a group of veterans who had blockaded an area they maintained was a sacred site, wanting the government to recognize their native Hawaiian ownership. They created an encampment where they'd made a huge garden, established a community kitchen, and developed programs to treat vets' alcohol and drug addictions.

Our group was invited to spend a day in their compound helping in various ways—cooking, working in the garden, serving food—and listening to their stories, how they were cleaning up and rehabilitating the area belonging to their people.

After a lunch break, the leader of the project, who'd been a drug addict after serving in Vietnam, and I walked to a nearby beach. I asked how he came to lead the program. He told me he'd been in prison, in solitary confinement, when he was "visited" by his grandmother. She rebuked him for forgetting his heritage and the stories she'd told him. She let him know she was extremely disappointed in him and his choices. He laughed when he told me how she'd kept at him until he promised to change his ways, to help his buddies change their ways, and to remember and tell the stories she'd told him. From this encounter had come the encampment and programs.

At dinner, he related one of the stories he'd learned from his grandmother, which was followed by a few of the men telling old stories they'd learned from ancestors. The silence after the last story was companionable, as if we were connected despite the differences in our lives.

I was reflecting on the lovely end to a full and thought-provoking day when one of the seminar members suddenly said, "Nancy is a storyteller. She even knows Hawaiian stories."

I was so embarrassed all I could do was shake my head and murmur, "No." How could someone suggest I tell a Hawaiian story to native Hawaiians after hearing how sacred their stories were to them? I hoped saying no would be the end of the matter, but other members agreed, saying I was a good storyteller and knew Hawaiian stories.

When the leader of the project asked me to tell a story, I couldn't think of a polite, viable way to refuse. Everyone's eyes were on me. Waiting. I chose to tell one of my favorite stories, about the goddess Pele. Before I began, I stopped looking at the group and focused on the landscape, the huge boulders standing watch over the ocean as it crashed against the rocky cliffs. In my mind's eye, I could feel the power of Pele's actions as my words found their telling. When I finished, I bent my head, a kind of thank you to the audience, afraid to look at anyone.

This silence felt different from the silence after the men's stories. This one seemed filled with a jumble of thoughts and feelings. The people in the seminar remained as quiet as the men. All I could think was, I had transgressed; as a white woman from the mainland, I had no business telling a Hawaiian story to Hawaiians. I was prepared to be reprimanded, told never to tell other people's stories.

The leader of the group stared at me until I looked away, dreading what he'd say. When he spoke, his voice was gentle and kind: "Thank you for telling our story with such care and reverence. We have never heard a stranger tell our stories. You are no longer a stranger. You are a friend of our hearts."

I tried not to show my relief as I thanked them for their stories, for the memorable day, for their willingness to share their lives and struggles. The seminar ended with all of us in a circle, the Hawaiians teaching us PhD students a prayer of gratitude and blessings. The chanting felt healing, creating one community.

As we were leaving to get into our van, the leader took me aside. "Nancy, don't stop telling stories. What you look like is of no consequence. What matters are the stories you tell and the way you tell them." I was grateful for his kindness, but I would never willingly put myself into this situation.

Was there a time you felt like an outsider and then welcomed? What was that like?

40

WORLD TALE

The Basket

SAN PEOPLE/AFRICAN

Two people see differently. The stories, Show and Tell, Believing/Seeing, and Vision, reveal how belief can affect what we see and how we act.

• • •

ONCE UPON A TIME there lived a man with a large head of well-cared-for cattle he regularly grazed in fine pastures and milked twice a day. One morning, when he went to milk them, he found they'd already been milked. He thought this very curious. He took even better care of them, but when he tried to milk them, their udders were wrinkled and dry. That night, he sat in his barn to see if he could discover the cause.

About midnight, he saw a cord come down from the stars. Climbing down were a group of people. When he ran toward them, they ran for the cord, but a young woman with a calabash and basket remained. She so filled him with light, he asked her to marry him. She agreed but said, "There is one thing I ask of you. Never look into this basket without my permission." He promised.

For a time, all was well. They lived happily together, sharing the work. She cultivated the fields. He looked after the cattle. One day, when he returned to have a drink of water, he saw the basket and looked into it. He saw nothing.

In the evening, his wife came home and, after one look at him, knew he'd opened her basket. "You looked in my basket, didn't you? Even though you promised you would not do so."

"Yes, I have," he admitted, "and I don't understand why you made such a fuss. The basket is empty. There's nothing in it."

"You saw nothing in the basket?"

"No. Nothing."

With great sadness she said, "If you see nothing in my basket I cannot stay." She turned away from him and vanished, back to the stars from whence she'd come.

❧ ❧ ❧

SHOW AND TELL

In 1965, I had a grant from the Delaware Mental Health Association to help improve the self-esteem of inner-city children in low-income neighborhoods. To stimulate the children's imagination and creativity, I used a combination of drama, storytelling, puppetry, painting, sculpting, and props, always encouraging children to feel good about what they made and to tell their stories with confidence.

At the end of a meeting with first graders, I asked them to bring in something they wanted to share with the group and to tell us why they brought it. I assured them whatever they brought would be fine. They peppered me with questions: "Is this all right?" "How big?" "How small?" I told them there was no right or wrong choice—to bring whatever mattered to them.

At the beginning of the show and tell session, children gathered in a circle holding their possessions, looking at what each had brought. Lots of stuffed animals. Some artwork. A few dolls.

One by one, some shy, some too excited to speak clearly, others almost rehearsed, they shared their treasures. One child remained silent, holding something covered in a rumpled cloth close to her chest, attentive to what was said, but never offering to participate.

When all the other children had gone, everyone looked at her. Several of them said, "Your turn." She remained as quiet as she'd been all morning. Usually she eagerly participated, full of energy, quick to respond, often smiling as she talked and sang and danced, depending on the activity. Now, given the change in her behavior, I wondered if I should let her pass.

The other children did not share my wonder. They began chanting, "Your turn. Your turn." She looked at me.

"It's your choice," I told her. "It's okay if you don't want to share what you brought."

"We want to see it," a number of children hollered. Six-year-olds are not always kind or sensitive.

She bit her lip, then said, "Okay. If you want to see what I brought, I'll show you." She carefully took the worn fabric off the doll she was holding. It had threadbare fabric arms and legs and head, tangled braids, with faded painted eyes, nose, and mouth. It was dressed in ineptly patched clothing. "This is my beautiful doll. My gramma made it for me."

Before she could explain why she'd brought it, a boy sneered, "It's not beautiful."

"It's ugly," said a girl. Others chimed in, making fun of the face, the hair, the clothing . . .

I was about to intervene when the child spoke up.

Unfazed, she said, "That's because you don't see it with my eyes."

What does beautiful mean to you?

❧ ❧ ❧

BELIEVING/SEEING

I was home after spending nineteen days in a London hospital, saved from dying from an undiagnosed illness by seven different antibiotics and more blood transfusions than my body could tolerate. Sent home so doctors in the US could diagnose an underlying undiagnosed illness.

I was home, alone, after being taken care of by a neighbor for a week, exhausted from family phone calls—relatives wanting me to visit my mother who was ill, not believing I was ill.

I had just woken up from a nap when the phone rang. A colleague from the university, also an ordained minister, heard about my illness—could he please come visit. He had attended a storymaking workshop for faculty I'd led and had taken an interest in the stories I told, often complaining I left out important connections. I told him this was so listeners could fill in the blanks, an explanation he found unsatisfying. Still, we'd developed a kind of friendship, so when he asked to come see me, I agreed. Ungraciously. "Okay, but no platitudes, please."

We were sitting on the deck on a sunny day in early March. He asked how I was. "When I look inside me, all I see are dead trees, barren ground, and darkness. There's no life left inside me." When he started to object, I interrupted and said, "No sermons, please. I see what I see. I feel what I feel."

He knew better than to argue with me. Instead, he took my soft cold hands into his big warm calloused hands. "Look at your hands. What do you see?" he asked.

"Cold bluish hands."

He gently held my hands until they were warm. "Now what do you see?" he asked.

"Warm pinkish hands."

"That's life," he said. "If you can't see it, you have to believe that under the dark, seemingly barren landscape, new life is forming."

"I can't see what's not there to see."

"You might be looking, but you're not seeing."

"There's nothing to see. I'm dying and I'm too tired to care."

"I care," he said, hesitating only for a second before he added, "your students care."

"They'll find other teachers."

"Not like you. You're the only professor who's a storyteller. You know better than anyone the stories we tell ourselves shape what and how we see."

"You need to go. I'm exhausted."

"Okay," he said, "but promise me you'll believe what I see in you until you can see it yourself."

I agreed, more to end the visit than from any faith he was right.

That was forty years ago.

Has someone seen something in you that you couldn't see or feel?

VISION

In the spring of 1992, I was invited to teach English as a foreign language at a university in Hungary. After the first session, I realized I was facing cultural, political, and pedagogical issues I'd never experienced in the US. When the Russians were in charge, teachers dictated; students wrote what had been said, repeating words they didn't understand. Papers were marked for accuracy. Essay topics ranged from electrical transmission lines to dog licenses, but nothing about people or feelings or dreams. Although the Russians had left two years earlier, authoritarian teaching was still the rule.

In order to get to know people in my class, I would always begin by having students say something about their lives. But now, when nobody offered to speak, I asked what I thought were casual questions—if they had brothers or sisters, did they have a pet . . . Their response was to tell me some version of: "Your question is too personal." According to my students, my way of teaching was not only strange, it transgressed permissible classroom topics. They let me know my job was to teach them to read and write English; their personal lives didn't matter. As if conversation wasn't part of learning a language?

Initially, when I asked them to paint and sculpt responses to the world tales I told, and then to share what they'd made, they complained. They were not children. This was not kindergarten. They were grownups, many of them working parents returning to school to get a professional teaching degree. I finally resorted to the pedagogy they were used to—authoritarianism. "This is how I teach, and this is what you will do." They understood this language and did as they were told, even though they disliked the activity.

As Easter break approached, the provost announced the last class before vacation would be on Thursday. A few days later, he amended the schedule; spring break would begin on Wednesday.

All classes were canceled on Wednesday. Our last class before students left for vacation was at 1:00 p.m. on Tuesday. As part of their language development that day, I asked them how they'd spend their time off. When the session ended, I wished them a good holiday and said I'd see them when classes resumed in ten days.

The next morning, I woke up feeling weird. I couldn't figure out what was wrong, or why I kept seeing the classroom in my mind's eye. The vision wouldn't go away. Increasingly irritated, I asked myself: what was wrong with me. The provost had clearly announced vacation started today. The students had been excited about their plans, more than ready to leave. I tried to ignore the image of the classroom, but it wouldn't budge. I cleaned the apartment. Shopped. I washed clothes by hand since I couldn't read the Hungarian instructions on the washing machine. Nothing dissolved the image.

Feeling stupid, exasperated, and cross, cursing the part of me unable to quit imaging the classroom, I walked to the university and entered the now-empty halls. Climbing up the stairs, hearing no sounds, I almost turned around, but I'd come this far, so I decided to go to the classroom and pick up books I'd left.

I opened the door. Stared. Disbelieving. Grinning faces welcomed me. "What are you doing here?" I asked. "It's spring break." All but one of my students were sitting in the circle of chairs we'd formed from the rows of seats.

"We're here," said Ivan. "You're here. Let's have class." He laughed. "Petra's going to be furious. She left early so we couldn't tell her we'd be here."

After Tuesday's session, they'd decided among themselves to come on Wednesday, even though class had been canceled, sure I would be there. Why they were so certain, no one could say. Why I had such a strong image of the classroom I felt forced to go to class remains a mystery.

Have you had a vision that made no sense, but compelled you to act? If so, what was that like?

41

WORLD TALE

A Story Not Told. A Song Not Sung

INDIA

A woman's stories and songs go unheard. The stories, Camp Counselor, Which Way, and No Logic, reveal what can happen when no one wants to listen.

• • •

THERE WAS ONCE A woman who kept her songs and stories to herself because no one was willing to listen. Her memories and longings remained buried deep within. After a time, her stories and songs grew restless—they wanted to be heard. They struggled to come out, but the woman could not share them. Finally, they made their way into her dreams. While she slept, she tossed and turned as the dreams roiled around inside her. She woke up, confused.

"What's the matter?" asked her husband.

"I don't know," she replied.

One morning after her husband left for work, she was so tired she lay down on the kitchen floor and fell asleep. Her mouth opened and she began to snore. The stories and songs escaped into the air, hovered above her, watching her sleep.

"We cannot leave her like this," they said. "What will she do without us?" The stories turned themselves into a robe and hung it on a peg by the bedroom door. The songs became slippers and rested underneath. When her husband returned from work, he became suspicious.

"Who was here while I was gone?"

"No one."

"Who do those slippers and robe belong to?"

"I don't know," she said.

They argued. When night fell, they were still arguing. I this village, when a couple disagrees and can't settle their disputes by the end of the day, it is customary for the husband to spend the night in the Temple of the Monkey King.

The husband stormed out of the house and went to the temple. He lay down to sleep in one of its darkened rooms. The wife sat at the kitchen table trying to make sense of what had happened. Finally, she blew out the candle, put her head down on the table, and fell asleep.

Each night, in this village, when people put out the candles, the flames go to the Temple of the Monkey King to chatter and discuss the day's events. As the husband lay on the floor, one by one, the candle flames danced into the darkened room where he slept. They chatted, waiting for all the tongues of flames to arrive. After a while it was clear one flame was late. "Where is it?" a flame sputtered.

Finally, the last flame showed up. "Where have you been?" they wanted to know.

"My couple had an argument. The husband came home and found a strange robe and slippers by the bedroom door."

"Oh, he must have been angry!" the others exclaimed.

"Yes, he was, but it isn't what he thinks. The woman has stories to tell and songs to sing, but no one listens. All her life she has kept them locked inside her. This morning while she slept, they found a way to turn the stories into a robe and the songs into slippers."

The husband, wakened by the flames, heard what had happened. He immediately left the Temple of the Monkey King and ran back home. In the moonlight, he could see his wife slumped over the kitchen table. He awakened her gently, putting the robe around her shoulders and the slippers on her feet. Then he sat down beside her. "Tell me your stories. Sing me your songs. I am here. I will listen."

CAMP COUNSELOR

I was eighteen, hired to teach swimming at a posh summer camp where more than a few maids unpacked campers' trunks. The girls were used to having everything done for them. When I told them they were responsible for keeping the bunk clean, they looked at me in disbelief. "I don't clean at home," said one. "Why should I clean here?"

"We'll do it together," I said, more cheerfully than I felt. "We can make it fun." They were expert eye rollers. I quickly learned my assumptions—they were here to make new friends and have new experiences—were wrong. Most of them came because they were sent by their parents. Their only choice was which camp, and that decision was made on the basis of where their friends were going. Even after the first week, maids continued to bring some campers requested items. I had no experience living in their world.

Shortly before the middle of the summer, talking with my campers, I suggested we go on a canoe camping adventure. They were excited by the idea. The director permitted the three-day trip; parents were notified and gave their approval. I told the campers, their parents, and the director we would canoe to a wilderness area, set up tents, dig latrines, cook our food, and do short hikes. They all said they liked the plan.

We started our trip on a gorgeous sunny morning. The girls enjoyed canoeing, and we made it to the camping area in good spirits. I showed them how to set up the tents, and then I said, "Now we have to dig our latrines."

They stared at me. Incredulous. No way were they going to poop into a hole. Where were the toilets? When I reminded them I'd said we would dig latrines, one of them muttered she didn't know what a latrine was. "Well," I said, "there are no toilets here. We'll take turns digging the holes. Four should be enough. If we dig them deep enough, we can cover the poop with dirt so there'll be no smell." I showed them how to use the latrine and what to do with the toilet paper.

The good mood from canoeing evaporated. Sullenly, they took turns digging holes in a place that gave some privacy. I took them on a hike, ending with a lovely view of the area, and handed out chocolate bars. Silence. After a bit I led them back to the campsite and asked for their help gathering wood for the fire. They refused to move. I was tempted to make a small fire and cook my meal, but I knew this would make things worse. I gathered wood, started the fire, and invited them to cook. One girl joined me. They ate their meal in silence.

Making s'mores for dessert helped a little. One of them started singing; some joined her. By the time they were in their sleeping bags, two of them thanked me for a lovely day. Shortly after we returned to camp, I was called to the director's office and told I was fired. So shocked I could barely ask why. "Our campers do not dig latrines," he told me. I tried to explain I had told him, their parents, and the campers what we would do, but he wouldn't listen. He told me to go. I left the office in shock.

Word spread fast. By the time I returned to my bunk and started packing my suitcase, the girls were crying. Apologizing. They told me they didn't mean for me to be fired. All of them went to the director's office to beg him to let me stay. I was the best counselor they'd ever had. They'd had a great time on the trip . . . The director was unmoved. I was given a ride to the nearest bus station.

Have you been fired? If so, what happened?

❧ ❧ ❧

WHICH WAY

In 1959, before traveling to Europe, I joined an organization called SERVAS. People with rooms to spare offered them at no cost to travelers for two nights. The aim of the program was to encourage peace and understanding through travel and hosting. Since I'd be traveling on a tight budget, any help with the cost of lodging meant a lot, but I especially looked forward to meeting local people and having a chance to visit and share experiences.

I was in Florence, Italy, the first time I decided to ask a host for housing. I checked my suitcase at the train station, taking only a small bag with what I needed for the two nights. To save money, I hitched a ride. The man was pleasant and spoke pretty good English. I told him where I wanted to be let out. All too soon I realized he was driving in the wrong direction. When I questioned him, he grabbed my thigh, then put his hand on my crotch, and told me there was a price to be paid for the ride. I shoved his hand away and told him to let me out. He drove even faster. When we came to a red light, he didn't stop, but when he slowed down, I opened the car door and fell out, scrambling to run off the road. I had no idea where I was. I took care of my scrapes and bruises as best I could.

Through a combination of mime, a few Italian words I knew, and my Italian/English phrase book, I discovered the house I wanted to stay in was about four or five miles from where I was. I walked to the pensione, arriving about 4:00 p.m., exhausted, hungry, and thirsty. I checked to make sure I had the correct address and rang the bell.

A gaunt woman, dressed in black, who looked to be in her sixties, opened he door, spewing Italian that did not sound friendly. I finally understood I had transgressed local custom. I should have known it was siesta time. Anyone with a modicum of respect would never ring the bell before 5:30.

I apologized, trying to say I didn't know, but she refused to listen, told me to return at 5:30, and slammed the door. I stared at the closed door, not sure what to do. I walked to a small park near the house, drank from the fountain, ate a few nuts I discovered in my bag, found a somewhat secluded place, lay down, and fell asleep. When I got up, I washed my face, and, more than a bit afraid of how I'd be received, walked back to the house.

This time I was greeted by the host, a woman in her seventies who spoke pretty good English. Once again, I apologized. She looked at my SERVAS book, reminded me never to appear at a host's house before 5:30, and showed me to my room. I lay down on the bed, and when I woke up it was dark. I had to use the bathroom. After washing my hands, I went to turn off the faucets, but couldn't tell which way was off. No water appeared no matter how I turned them. I twisted them in the direction I guessed was off and went back to my room.

In the morning I was woken by an irate host who told me I'd ruined the water system. Because of me there was no water in the house, and didn't I know which way to turn off a faucet? Stunned, I tried to tell her what had happened, but she was too angry to listen. She told me to leave. I didn't know if she meant for the day or not to return, but I packed my bag and left. No way could I go back.

Have you tried to communicate in a language you don't speak? How did you manage?

NO LOGIC

After being diagnosed with a rare, anomalous, and fatal form of leukemia, I was able to join a protocol sponsored by the National Institute of Cancer (NCI). Since the protocol was research-based, I saw different doctors each time I went for blood tests, physical exams, and the medicine—three units of interferon, injected into subcutaneous tissue, every day for seven months, after which time we would be cured. Except we weren't. As soon as the medication was stopped, remission ended. What it did was keep the disease at bay.

When I learned every participant, no matter their size, weight, or gender, was given the same dosage, three mgs, I complained. "It makes no sense," I told every doctor I saw. "Logically, the amount we take should depend on height, weight, and gender." Doctors hadn't considered gender; all the research had been done on men. Their defense—75 percent of those diagnosed were men over sixty. I was a forty-eight-year-old woman. Doctors ignored me. Some suggested the side effects I experienced from the medication were due to neurosis or hysteria. Even after I told them about a cousin who did a search of the literature, which showed women had more severe symptoms than men—because, it was theorized, women have proportionally more fat cells in their bodies than men, and fatty tissue holds medication longer than lean tissue. Doctors still dismissed my experience.

The side effects increased exponentially: painful muscle spasms, fatigue, diarrhea, depression, flu-like symptoms. Even after the frequency of dosage was changed from daily injections to three times a week, the symptoms worsened. I begged doctors to consider height, weight, and gender in deciding how much interferon participants needed. They told me this was the protocol; I could take it or leave it.

After seven years of increasingly severe effects from the medication, I decided to leave it. I talked to the doctor I'd been seeing most recently and said, "I'm done. I can't take it anymore. I'm leaving the protocol."

He told me he was going to be promoted to Director of Research soon—could I take it for just another few weeks? "No," I said. "I'm done. Finished. Through. Kaput!" He reminded me that stopping the interferon meant the return of the leukemia, which, untreated, was fatal. "I know," I said, "but the life I'm living is not worth the miseries, which are just getting worse. I'm tired of pretending I'm fine when I'm not. The last seven years have been hell. No more." Nothing he said changed my mind.

I stopped taking the interferon. The nausea abated. Flu-like symptoms disappeared. Depression lightened. Diarrhea ended. Muscle spasms happened less frequently, then stopped. No more black and blue marks on my thighs from injections. People noticed the change. Students and friends commented I seemed lighter, happier, with more energy. No one knew I had chosen death. The improved quality of my life, even if temporary, was a huge relief.

A few weeks later, the doctor I'd spoken to called me. He was now Director of Hairy Cell Research. "Nancy, you have every right to say I told you so, but you were correct. We've been looking at research from Italy, which shows, absolutely, the most effective dosage is height and weight specific." I was silent for a moment, taking in the enormity of what he'd just said. "According to your height and weight, you should be taking one mg, not three." He didn't mention gender. I didn't think to ask.

For seven years, I'd been taking two-thirds more medication than my body could handle. For seven years doctors had been ignoring my protests, my body's reactions to the medication, suggesting I was irrational, hysterical. For seven years I'd been living with nausea, muscle spasms, depression, diarrhea, low energy, and flu-like symptoms. No more. I was done.

"Please, Nancy," pleaded the doctor. "Please take the new dosage. I promise you; your life will be a lot easier."

"I have to think about it," I told him. I hung up, not at all sure I wanted to go back on the interferon, even with reduced dosage. I'd been close to dying several times, and each episode had been peaceful. Death was better than the life I'd been living.

A few days later, my son called. I told him about the conversation with the doctor. "Please, Mom, please go back on the medication. I need you in my life."

His plea was impossible to ignore. I decided to continue in the protocol, taking the lower dosage. I still had symptoms, but they were milder, easier to live with. No doctor could give me back the seven years of unnecessary misery.

Have you ever decided to listen to yourself rather than experts? What did you do?

42

WORLD TALE

How People Came to the Land That Was Home

TEWA

A couple decides to find the place that is home. In the stories, What it Takes and Unexpected Arrival, home has different meanings.

• • •

THE PEOPLE WERE BUMPING around in the dark and the cold. Someone asked, "Is this all there is? Will there never be anything more?" No one could answer. It was the only world they knew.

They continued to live in their cold, dark world until one day a strange animal appeared. They asked it, "Is this the only world there is?"

The strange creature answered, "I do not know, but sometimes I go to a place that feels different."

"How is it different?" someone asked.

"I cannot tell you for I am blind. All I can say is that it feels different."

One brave person made a request. "Will you take us to the place that feels different?"

"Yes," answered the creature, whose name was Mole. "I can take you to that place, but when I travel, I dig out the earth in front of me and put it behind me. If you come with me you will never be able to return to where you came from."

The people talked among themselves. Some were frightened to leave the only place they knew. Others were willing to try anything to live a better life. And so it was that Mole burrowed his way to the place that felt different, digging out the earth in front of him, passing the earth back to the people who put it behind them. It was a long, difficult journey. People complained. They were tired and cold. It was still dark. Some longed to be where they had been. At least there they could stand up. Then, without warning, Mole said, "This is the place that feels different. This is where I must leave you."No one knew what to do. Although it was dark, it did feel different: it was not as cold. People began to walk around. A few ventured out into a place that hurt their eyes so badly they retreated into the dark, crying and moaning in pain. Now there were many who wished they had never left the place where they lived for so long.

In the dark, nursing their eyes, they heard a small kind voice. "Hush, my children, do not cry. Listen to me."

"Who are you?" they asked.

"I am your Grandmother Spider. I am here to help you. If you do as I say, all will be well. Your eyes hurt because they are not used to light. The sun is bright. Give your eyes time to learn to see light. When you walk outside, keep your eyes shut and your fingers closed against your face. Slowly, open your fingers. Take a few breaths, then open your eyes. Never look at the sun, for it will hurt your eyes. Do as I tell you. Your eyes will thank you."

People followed Grandmother Spider's advice, and it was as she promised. Their eyes learned to see. But all too soon the light began to disappear. Not knowing what to do, people huddled together in the dark, wondering and waiting, too frightened to leave.

Once again Grandmother Spider spoke to them. "Hush, my children, do not despair. All shall be well if you listen to me. The light will return. When it does, you will see four mountains. To the north is White Mountain. Do not go there for you will find ice and snow. You will freeze to death. To the east is Red Mountain. Do not go there for you will encounter fierce creatures. You will bleed to death. To the west is Black Mountain. Do not go there for your crops will not grow. You will starve to death. To the south is Green Mountain. It is the furthest and the path is uncertain, but if you keep your eyes on Green Mountain, you will find your way. And, when you see a creature that reminds you of Grandmother Spider, but is not Grandmother Spider, and a creature that reminds you of Mole, but is not Mole, you will know you have arrived. You have found your home."

Just as Grandmother foretold, the light returned. Some people looked at White Mountain and said, "White Mountain is not far, and we are not afraid of cold. We will tell you what we find when we return." They never came back.

Soon, a few people became restless and said, "Black Mountain is quite close. We know how to manage darkness. We will tell you what we find when we come back." But they too did not return.

"We are not afraid of fierce creatures," agreed all but two of the people. "Why walk a long distance when there is Red Mountain, a place we can see. We will fight whoever attacks us and win. We will tell you what we find." None of them were seen again.

One man and one woman remained. Even in the bright sun, they could barely see Green Mountain. The woman said, "We must listen to Grandmother Spider. We must walk to Green Mountain if we wish to survive." The man agreed. They began walking toward the south. It was a long journey. Walking in the hot sun was exhausting. The memory of those who had not returned kept them from giving up. They walked and walked and walked toward the mountain that seemed to keep its distance. It was all they knew to do.

One morning, as they stopped to rest, the woman saw a strange creature. Cautiously, she moved closer to it. The man said, "Be careful, it might be dangerous." The woman kept looking.

The man joined her, and they crept close enough to see the markings on the creature's back. "Look," said the woman, "it reminds me of Grandmother Spider."

When the creature heard the woman's words, it pulled in its head. "Oh," said the man. "It cannot see where it is going. It reminds me of Mole."

The man and woman remembered the words of Grandmother Spider. They had arrived at Green Mountain. They had come to the place that was home.

❧ ❧ ❧

WHAT IT TAKES

Before he was my cat, he'd been hanging around Exit 7 of the New Jersey Turnpike for weeks. No one knew anything about him. A woman picked him up, gave him a cuddle, then went into a restaurant. When she left the restaurant and walked toward her car, the cat leapt onto her shoulder. She gave him another cuddle and put him down. When she opened the car door and sat down, he jumped in and settled on her lap. A cat lover, she took him to her vet. The cat was a pedigreed Bombay, emaciated, mangled, neutered, with no front claws, but otherwise healthy. When she took him home, he attacked her two cats mercilessly. She put him in the basement where he howled for two weeks. Desperate to find him a home, she called everyone she knew. I was last on the list; we'd met once at a practitioner's office where we'd exchanged contact information.

When she called to ask if I'd like to have a beautiful cat, I told her, "I'm not about to take a cat I've never met." I hadn't thought about adopting a cat.

"I'll be right over," she said. She brought the cat, a litter box and tools, food, food dishes, and a brush. Within fifteen minutes, the cat, who I later named Funus Pushkin Bernhardt, otherwise known as Funi, had eaten, pooped, and was sleeping against my legs.

"He's home," she grinned, and left before I could change my mind.

Thirteen years later, I bought a house soon after I saw it and prepared to move to Santa Fe. After eating a poisoned mouse a few years before, Funi, who'd always been healthy, became a "throw-up cat." I came to learn which cleaning products were most effective after too much experience dealing with his messes. Since I had to leave the house while the packers packed and the movers moved, friends invited me and my cat to stay at their house. They had fine furniture and rugs. I brought extra cleaning supplies hoping there would be no permanent stains. Amazingly enough, he didn't throw up.

A friend offered to drive the two thousand miles to Santa Fe with me. The back seat of the small SUV was taken up by my cat's litter box, food tray, and carry case, which he sat on top of, looking out, when he wasn't snuggled in the lap of whoever wasn't driving, not that he didn't try to nestle in the driver's lap. I smuggled him into motels, unwilling to pay the extra fee for animals, carrying my cleaning equipment along with my luggage. Territorial as he was, he was an equal-opportunity lover, spending half the night with me, half with my friend. He didn't throw up.

Given the heat, I smuggled him into restaurants with air conditioning. He didn't throw up.

We arrived in Santa Fe, and for three days, while awaiting the furniture's arrival, we stayed with a couple I'd known in Delaware. For three days I worried about their furnishings. I gave them a lot of cleaning materials when I left to go to the new house to unpack and put things away. For the whole time he was at their house, he didn't throw up.

When I finally emptied all the boxes, created order from the chaos, and stashed whatever I didn't want to keep in the garage, I brought Funi to my house. Immediately, he threw up in every room, used the litter box, then fell asleep on my lap. He was home.

What does home mean to you?

❧ ❧ ❧

UNEXPECTED ARRIVAL

I moved from a community of people living in mostly small cottages, nestled among large trees with green leaves and flowering bushes, amid grass and perennials, to a triangle house set apart from nearby houses by juniper and piñon trees. No landscaping to speak of. Muted tones of brown. No neighbors offering me welcome. No neighborhood. No job. I was sixty-five, living by myself. The last time I'd moved, I was twenty-eight with a husband and son. Although I loved the house I'd bought so spontaneously, I did not feel at home.

Despite living less than a mile and a half from the Plaza, I had to ask three people where it was before I found it. I'm not good with maps, so figuring out where different neighborhoods were meant a lot of walking, exploring, and getting turned around, if not lost. I was used to living in a small community where I knew and was known by many people. Now I knew hardly anyone. Here the air was dry, the landscape earth tones, none of the humidity and greenery I was used to. By moving to New Mexico, I stopped being a professor. Who was I now? Did I need an answer? Why couldn't I just be? See what opportunities I could create or find?

A few weeks later, my son called. "You need a new business card. Tell me what you want to put on it and I'll make you one."

My thoughts were focused on the house—the repairs needing to be done, finding doctors and dentists, a landscaper, contractors, a vet . . . I hadn't had time to decide what kind of life I'd make for myself. Without thinking, I answered quickly, "Storymaker," then laughed. So much for my identity crisis. One problem solved.

I had a house I loved. A new identity. I was writing each day, working to finish two novels and a nonfiction book I'd begun while still a professor. I was enjoying finishing the weaving that had been on the loom when I moved. I happily visited the many museums so close to where I lived. Still, I felt like a visitor.

I found local hiking trails, and, after acclimatizing to altitude, dryness, and steep ups and downs, I began hiking regularly by myself because I didn't know any hikers. I joined a local tennis club to find people with whom to play, quickly realizing players were there to play tennis, not to make friends.

I felt good about my new life, free of the constraints imposed by people who'd known me for thirty-seven years. I could be who I was, rather than who I'd been. And yet, something undefinable was missing. I didn't regret leaving the university, the community where I lived, or moving. With everything going so well, what could possibly be missing?

I like walking. Santa Fe is a good town to walk in. Occasionally people nodded to me as I passed, some smiled; a few times there were words of welcome when we exchanged hellos. All this felt good, but I continued to feel like the stranger I was.

One day, while walking in the railyard area, I saw a sign: El Museo Cultural. Curious, I walked in. A woman came toward me, holding out her arms. Smiling. She gently held my hands and said, "You have come home."

Magically. Mystically. The missing piece dissolved. I was home.

What do you need to feel you are home?

43

WORLD TALE

Return of the Flowers

ABORIGINES/AUSTRALIA

Elders find a way to restore life to barren earth. The stories, Creating a World and Water, Windows, and Books, explore what can emerge after a disaster.

• • •

WHEN THE CREATOR BAIAME no longer walked the earth, the flowers and trees all died except for three trees he marked as his own. Only here could bees make honey. Only here could parents show their children how the earth used to look when flowers and trees graced the earth. They wished to taste the honey yet dared not.

After seeing their longing, the All-seeing spirit told Baiame how people appreciated his trees, yearning to taste the honey. As a reward for their respect, Baiame sent them *goonbeams* and manna, though the drought continued. The earth remained bare. The children were delighted with the newfound food, but older people mourned the absence of life as it had been.

One day, a group of elders decided to journey to Baiame to plead with him to restore the earth, to return the flowers and trees. Just before dawn, they traveled to the foot of the great mountain, searching for the path of stone steps, cut by the spirit of Baiame.

They climbed for four days and four nights, unwilling to rest before reaching the summit. At the top, too exhausted to go any further, they drank from a spring of fresh water, which quenched their thirst and revived their spirits.

In the distance, they saw stones piled in the shape of a circle. No longer tired, they made their way to the center of the circle. Here they heard the voice of Baiame's spirit messenger, who asked why they had come. They told the spirit how all but the three trees of Baiame had died when he no longer walked the earth, how the bees had disappeared. They asked how the flowers and trees and bees could be restored, the earth fragrant and fertile.

The spirit messenger told the attendant spirits to lift the elders to the place of Baiame, where flowers and trees bloomed eternally. Through their tears, the elders gasped with awe at the sight of so much beauty. They listened carefully as Baiame told them how to return fertility to the earth.

Following his teachings, the elders gathered as many different trees and flowers as they could hold. The spirits then carried the elders down into the stone circle where they learned how to cradle the tiny plants and carry them to safety.

The people of the earth welcomed the elders, looking with awe and astonishment at the brilliant colors, smelling the sweet fragrances, welcoming the bees gathering nectar. Once more trees and flowers graced the earth, filling the hearts of the people with hope and joy.

As the spirits foretold, there are still times of drought, when the *goonbeams* and manna take the place of honey, but the trees and flowers thrive, sheltering the bees who return with the new rains.

CREATING A WORLD

As a child, I had no friends, so I developed ways to play by myself. I liked being outdoors, roller skating, riding my bike, walking to a large park less than a mile from my house. Sometimes, the kids on my block played games and let me play with them because they needed people. During bad weather, I created play from my imagination.

When I was nine, I spent months playing what I called *school.* I constructed an imagined world—classroom, teacher, principal, parents—using various kinds of paper I took from my real classroom. As the teacher, I wrote short bios for the ten children in my class, took attendance, created tests, wrote behavior reports that were sent to parents on the same yellow paper my teacher used. I imagined parent/teacher conferences, and sent notes to and from the principal arising from various classroom experiences. I marked files parents, students, and principal, and kept them in separate folders stored on my desk.

The material describing each child began with the usual information—name, birthdate, sex, family members—but when I added new information, such as absenteeism, behavior, grades, etc., the file on every child grew thick, especially as I included teacher, parental, and principal responses. I made up achievement reports including the strengths and weaknesses of each child, and how they progressed during the year.

I was so fully engrossed in my imaginative play, hours would go by, so absorbed I wouldn't hear my sister and her friends playing, or my mother calling me to do chores. Occasionally she would storm into the room and ask if I was deaf. It was always startling to be interrupted, as if I were dreaming and suddenly a noise stopped the dream.

I found books in the library about innovative teaching methods and read them with great interest, using what I learned to create new kinds of teaching, where children had a say in what they learned and how they were taught. The contrast between the school I created and the school I attended made me wonder why school had to be what it was, often boring, sometimes painful, rarely interesting. I hated when teachers belittled classmates, made fun of someone who didn't know the answer, or chastised me for asking too many questions or raising my hand so much.

In the school I created, the notes that got sent home were not about students being "bad." Instead, as the teacher, I focused on how well a student was doing. This was a marked contrast to the real notes my real teacher sent home about me. Since the notes required parental comment and signature, I'd respond with my father's impossible-to-read handwriting, saying I'd do better, then would sign his name, accurately copied from his real signature on a letter I'd found in a wastepaper basket.

As months passed, I spent a lot of time writing about the lives of the children in my class, both in and out of school, creating worlds of families with the child as the focus.

One day, when I came home from a piano lesson, much to my shock and horror, I discovered my three-year-old sister tearing up the last of the papers of my school creation. My desk and the floor around it were covered with scraps of paper of every size and color. Each piece of paper and folder was torn to bits. I stared at the devastation, at what my sister had done, unable to take in what I was seeing.

When I yelled her name, she ran out of the room. I followed, ready to kill her, but she took refuge behind our mother. When I told her what my sister had done, she said, "It's just paper. You can make it again."

No. I couldn't.

It was as if something inside me had died. At home, I'd sit at my desk, now empty, mourning the loss of what I'd worked so hard and intently to create.

A few months later, when I was in a stationery store with my mother and sister, I saw a notebook—not big and difficult to hide. No. The one I saw would fit into a large pocket. I bought it but kept it hidden, not yet able to write in it. One day, when I was feeling lonely, I remembered the notebook and took it out of the pocket. I started writing stories I never showed to anyone. More often, I wrote stories in my head. No one could find these. No one could destroy them.

Has anyone destroyed what you created? What happened?

❧ ❧ ❧

WATER, WINDOWS, AND BOOKS

My house is an equilateral triangle. No rooms have four walls or right angles. My study has five walls, four of which have ten floor-to-ceiling bookcases, all filled with books: world tales, fiction, nonfiction, essays, poetry, spiritual exploration, and healing. I also have material from former students; copies of books, novels, and papers I've written; as well as journals and lots of children's literature.

Above my desk is a fixed window that fills most of the upper wall, allowing me to look out at the mountains and the sky. A couch fills the space underneath a window on a side wall. The wall-to-wall carpeting is a soft surface on which to stretch and exercise. The room is a pleasant place to write and read.

One evening, I was on the phone, talking with a friend, when suddenly water started pouring in through the fixed window above my desk and the window above the couch. I ended the call and ran outside. It wasn't raining. I called P., the man who's done all my house renovations, and told him what was happening. "I'm on my way," he said. I rushed out to the utility room to turn off the main water faucet, but the threading was stripped. I couldn't turn it off.

P. arrived, found a way to turn off the faucet, then raced upstairs and discovered a valve in the bathroom toilet had burst. While he was doing what he could to shut it off and stop the water flow, I was covering my computer and desk with plastic sheeting. Too many past water emergencies resulted in my having a large roll of plastic sheeting on hand.

The devastation was immediate and complete. Water flowed through windows and the ceiling onto the plastic sheeting covering my desk and computer, flooding the floor, drenching the couch, and pooling on the tops of bookcases. P. helped me hang plastic sheeting over the bookcases and showed me how to poke holes in the bulging areas of the ceiling to release water into pots. By the time we placed all the pots to contain the water, mopped up the tops of the bookcases, the plastic sheeting covering my desk, and the wet floor upstairs to stop further flooding, it was almost eleven.

Just before he left, P. said, "My men will be here at eight tomorrow morning. We'll have to gut the room—remove the books, strip the carpeting, take out the walls and ceiling." I nodded, too exhausted and shocked to take in the totality of the wreckage and what it would take to remediate the damage.

The next morning, as promised, the crew arrived. The first thing they did was to put all my books in cartons, labeling them according to my description. By the time all the cartons were stored in the garage, other members of the crew were busy moving bookcases into the guest room, wiping down any remaining wet surfaces. At the end of the day, my study was an empty shell—wallboard, ceiling, floor, and rug removed. All that remained were studs, subfloor, and a dehumidifier. Before they left, the crew helped me set up a makeshift office in the guest room.

It took months before the walls, ceiling, floor, rug, and bookcases were installed. My books had been sitting in the garage all this time, unprotected from temperature and mice. Although the cartons had been carefully packed and labeled as to which bookcase and shelf the books belonged, I was worried. Had I labeled the cartons correctly? Had the books been damaged by their time in the garage? Would the crew be able to shelve them in the right order . . .

I came home just as the crew was putting the last of the books back on the shelves. I walked into my study and gasped, seeing a mix-up of books. The crew's looks of pride changed to disappointment. Seeing how upset they were, I quickly realized what an incredible job they'd done. The new arrangement was different, but more than good enough. When they offered to rearrange whatever needed to be changed, I assured them everything was fine, more than fine. I apologized for my initial reaction, congratulated them on the amazing job they'd done, profusely thanking them for their hard work restoring my study and managing to put the books on the shelves in good order. They looked relieved. I felt terrible. They'd done such an unbelievable job, better than I could have imagined, and all I could see were books I'd put on a top shelf now stored on a bottom shelf. I did what

I could to remedy my thoughtless initial reaction, thanking them over and over, telling them how pleased and grateful I was for their astounding work.

After they left, I sat in my newly restored study, surrounded by my books, most of which had survived the flood and the garage, overwhelmed with gratitude.

Have you survived a disaster? How did you respond?

44

WORLD TALE

A Way of Seeing

CHINA

There was once a King and Queen who yearned to have a child; the King worried he would die without an heir. In time, a baby was born, and there was great rejoicing throughout the land. Although the infant was healthy and grew like any other, the King's counselors noticed the child often stumbled and suggested the King's physician examine the child. The King's joy turned to grief when he learned his child was blind. How could a blind person rule a kingdom? In a fit of rage, the King ordered his servants to take the child to the far-off mountains to be devoured by the wild beasts.

• • •

IN THE FAR-OFF MOUNTAINS, Tiger was first to see the child. He roared and said, "I will eat you," but the child had never heard a creature roar and could not see the beast. Tiger was astonished to see this small child stand so still, utterly unafraid. Such a brave child, laughing with delight at my sounds, thought Tiger. Impressed, he called to all the animals, "Come see this child who feels no fear. Let us help this child survive." Mama Tiger fed the child with her milk. Fox used part of his fur to make the child a warm coat. Peacock made the child a hat of beautiful feathers. Each bird and animal in the forest helped and taught the child to live and grow.

In the morning, birds sang to the child, "Wake up, wake up." The child tried to answer the birds' songs, but could not make sounds as beautiful as the birds. The child asked for help. One animal brought strong bamboo, for that was what she knew to bring. Another brought thick hairs. Still another brought thin hairs. The child played with the animals' gifts, attaching the hairs to the stick, tightening them until they made sounds. The thin hairs went "Pi," and the thick hairs went "Ba." Now the child could sing to the birds, answering their songs with the sounds of the PiBa. In the evening, when the animals gathered around the fire and told the child stories of their lives, the child listened and felt something stirring inside.

Years passed. One day, the child heard the animals talking about blue sky and asked them, "What is blue? What is sky?"

Tiger said, "These words describe the world above the earth."

The child said, "I do not understand."

Tiger answered, "This is because your eyes do not talk to you the way ours do. You are blind."

"Can you make my eyes talk to me?" asked the child.

"No," said Tiger. "I do not have the power. But these mountains are not the whole world. In other places there are people, like you. Perhaps they will know how to help your eyes speak to you."

"Oh," said the child, "I want to go and find these people."Tiger said, "Before you go, there is something you must know."

"What is that?" asked the child.

"Every creature born has a special name, but when you came, you did not know your name. When you go among the people, they will ask you for your name."

"Oh," said the child. "What shall I do?"

Tiger said, "I will call the animals together. We will have a conference to discuss the matter. Naming takes time and thought." Tiger convened the meeting and presented the problem. "Our friend is leaving and must have a name." All the animals suggested names. Many names.

Totally confused, Peacock protested. "My head is spinning. Please, let Tiger, who is known to be wise, have the honor of suggesting the name." The animals agreed.

Tiger stared into the fire and thought. "Over the years we have told you about our lives. You have taken what we told you and turned it into stories we can tell our children and grandchildren. This is indeed a gift. To honor you and your gift, we call you Storyteller, for you take what you hear and add something of your own.

Although the animals were sad that Storyteller wanted to leave them, they understood. Each animal gave Storyteller a present. Tiger said, "As my farewell gift to you, I will tell you words that humans use so you can talk to them. Their ways are different from ours."

When it was Mouse's turn, she put her arms around Storyteller's foot. "All I have to give you is this small hug. Perhaps it will keep you from being lonely." With the presents of the animals, Storyteller left the far-off mountains to walk among people in places of heat and cold and rain and snow and dust and wind.

While traveling, Storyteller played the PiBa and asked many questions of people. It came to matter less and less that Storyteller's eyes did not speak, for Storyteller's fingers created many sounds for people to hear, and Storyteller's mouth created pictures everyone could see. Just as many streams flow together to make a river, many stories come to one who listens. Stories give birth to stories, and soon, Storyteller had many stories to tell.

One day, as Storyteller was telling stories in the marketplace, a merchant grabbed Storyteller's left arm and said, "Don't be stupid. Why give away for free what they will pay for?"

A second merchant grabbed Storyteller's right arm and yelled, "Come with me. I will make us rich." The two merchants, arguing over who owned Storyteller, created such pandemonium the King's guards arrested them and brought them to the King.

"What is going on?" growled the King. Once again, the two merchants began to fight about Storyteller, making such a commotion the King's ears hurt. "Guards, take these two away." When all was peaceful, the King asked Storyteller, "Why were they fighting over you?"

"I do not know. I was telling stories in the marketplace, and suddenly the two men grabbed my arms and began pulling and shouting."

"Tell me a story," ordered the King. Storyteller struck the PiBa's strings and began. The King listened. Sometimes he felt so sad he cried. Other times he laughed with delight. As he listened, he grew thoughtful; there was more wisdom in Storyteller's stories than in all the words he had heard from his many advisors.

The King asked, "Who taught you to speak as you do?"

"I grew up among the beasts in the far-off mountains. I have learned from them."

The King recognized Storyteller, the child he had sent to the far-off mountains to be devoured by wild beasts. "I have been given a second chance, and this time I am wiser. Though you are blind, you have your own way of seeing. I can die peacefully knowing you will take my place as ruler of our kingdom."

"No," said Storyteller, "I cannot. Stories are like the river. Just as the river needs streams to keep it flowing, I must have stories to keep me seeing. If I stay here I will lose my vision."

Storyteller left the King's palace and traveled throughout the world, playing the PiBa, hearing and telling stories. Thus did Storyteller give the gift of storytelling to the world.

What stories do you have to tell?

Author's Biography

Nancy King, author of essays, plays, books on creativity and imagination, novels, and a memoir, Breaking the Silence, writes monthly stories based on world tales. She teaches in a variety of settings with people of all ages, using her experience of trauma and the power of stories to heal and transform, creating a safe space for people to tell their stories. King lives, writes, weaves, and hikes in Santa Fe, New Mexico, with her once-feral cat, Lira. To learn more about her work, please visit: www.nancykingstories.com. For questions or comments, please email her at nanking1224@earthlink.net

Acknowledgments

Storytellers need audiences. From the time they were little, Eliora and Hadara Ancowitz listened to my stories with rapt attention, each time responding, "More stories, please." Now they have a book of stories.

I thank Marlene Simon, who responds to every story, each month, letting me know how much my stories mean to her—that they matter. I'm grateful to Rachel Grier-Reynolds, Phil Eagleton, Carole Owens, Nancy Shiffrin, Rachel White, Lola Wilson, Diana Wolff, and others who take the time to read my monthly stories, email comments or leave them on the Weebly site.

Gill Hague and Claudia Reder are part of my life—readers, writers, colleagues, and friends. I depend on them for their honest, caring thoughts and questions, which deepen and nourish my writing and life.

Issa Nyaphaga and I share a love of making art. He's a friend of my soul, and reader of my stories.

Leslie Marmon Silko's novel *Ceremony* helped me realize the power of stories, how stories are medicine, and the importance of telling one's story.

I thank Mari Angelo who first suggested turning the monthly stories into a book.

Janet Angelo has generously and wisely guided my writing of the monthly stories on my website for many years. She offers insightful questions, thought-provoking comments, and remembers if I've told the story before. Our Zoom conversations are a delight.

Working with Judyth Hill and Mary Meade, publishers of Wild Rising Press, has been a challenging, collaborative, creative experience. I am grateful for their knowledge, support, and caring. The *Cracked Pot's Gift: Stories to Challenge and Comfort* is testament to their foresight and wisdom. Their vision guided me to become a better writer, and supported me throughout the process of creating this book.

The richness of places, times, cultures, reflected in the insightful choice of fonts, mirrors both the fertile and vibrant range of the wsorld tales and the intimacy of the personal reflections. Body text is Adobe Garamond Pro, a contemporary typeface family created by type designer Robert Slimbach, based on the original 1540 Roman types of Claude Garamond and the italic types of Robert Granjon. This font is an enduring masterwork, and a cherished piece of printing history. Garamond evokes the hand; its beautifully balanced, artisanal letters and warm, humanistic character echo the warm voice of the storyteller threading through the book.

Chapter titles are set in Kefa. This modern serif font blends old-world elegance with distinctive, contemporary look, uniting serif and sans serif fonts for delicious visual consonance. Designed by Jérémie Hornus to support Ethiopic script, showcasing its global appeal, Kefa combines clarity with a subtle futuristic twist, ideal for a collection of tales that bridges diverse cultures and eras, and matches the narrative's vibrant depth and breadth.

All other fonts are in weights of the modern sans-serif font Muli, designed by Vernon Adams. Muli Light is understated, with clean, simple lines, providing a gentle contrast and contemporary complement to the traditional serif of the body. Muli Semi Bold, used for country names, reengages its' simplicity but with strength that emphasizes the diversity and individuality of each tale.

The combination of serif and sans serif fonts, like the silken flow between the world tales and personal story, invites the reader into the immersive magic of story, and bridges the old and the new, the near and the far...and reflects the luminous spirit of connection this book embodies.

www.ingramcontent.com/pod-product-compliance
Lightning Source LLC
Chambersburg PA
CBHW071232210726
48293CB00002B/681

* 9 7 8 1 9 5 7 4 6 8 5 1 8 *